THE SEQUEL TO CERBERUS

TERRA STATION

JOHN FILCHER

ISBN: 978-1-955622-98-1

Published by

Fideli Publishing, Inc.
119 W. Morgan St.
Martinsville, IN 46151

www.FideliPublishing.com

TERRA STATION

CHARACTERS

Capt. Dan Ronin — Captain of *Cerberus*

Cmdr. Diane Mueller — Commanding Officer of *Cerberus*

Lt. Cmdr. Elvis Lazarus — Chief engineer, *Cerberus*

Lt. Pierre Delacroix — Sensors, *Cerberus*

Lt. Kristoff Alphonso — Fabrication, *Cerberus*

Lt. Matt LeCroy — Tactical, *Cerberus*

Lt. Marcy Anzio — Weapons, *Cerberus*

Lt. Maria Delgado — Communications, *Cerberus*

Lt. Hirohito Taketa, Chief Medical Officer — Medical, *Cerberus*

Chrizanne "Anne" Abara, Nurse — Medical, *Cerberus*

Lt. Antonio Perez — Helm, *Cerberus*

Lt. Kelvin Sunderland — Commander Air Group (CAG), *Cerberus*

Adam Taylor, Deck Chief — *Cerberus*

Erin Johnson, Pilot Officer — *Bulldog 1* pilot

Hal Patterson, Chief — *Bulldog 1* rearseater

Antonio Russo, Pilot Officer — *Bulldog 3* pilot

Michael Jonsey, Chief — *Bulldog 3* rearseater

Lt. Adolph Gustav — Marine team commander

Brett Mackey — Marine Bravo team

Ed Wilson — Marine Bravo team

Carlos Guthrey — Marine Bravo team

Terry Allison — Marine Bravo team

Steve Cupper — Marine Bravo team

Ty Jeffries — Marine Bravo team

Toshi Kanagawa — Marine Echo team

Adrian Longman — Marine Echo team

Rhee Lee — Marine Echo team

Han Pak — Marine Echo team

David Danfries — Marine Echo team

Julio Gonzales — Marine Echo team

Nancy Dos — Marine Echo team

Brett Blackwater — Marine Gamma team

Jefferson Langley — Marine Gamma team

Louis Caron — Marine Gamma team

Victor Berger — Marine Gamma team

David Addington — Marine Gamma team

Juan Diaz — Marine Gamma team

Aldo Pena — Marine Gamma team

Ambassador Prisha Gadre — Protocol Officer, *Cerberus*

Dr. Winston Wright — Protocol Officer, *Cerberus*

Ryan Kutsler — Crew Class descendant

Louise Abernathy — Cargo Class descendant

Adm. Wallace Seaver — Officer Class descendant

Esmeralda Centon — Crew Class descendant

Air Sergeant Jeremiah Baker — Pilot of *Eagle Two*

Air Sergeant David Hoffman — Pilot of *Eagle One*

Tobias Wilson — Officer Class descendant

Secretary Stanton Ellis — Officer Class descendant

Speaker Dennis Hayward — Officer Class descendant

Erick the Lieutenant, aka Loki three niner — Cargo Class descendant

Lt. Grant Richardson — Officer Class descendant

Cmdr. James Hunt — Cargo Class descendant

Lt. Buckingham — Cargo Class descendant

Maj. Percy Cartwright — Officer Class descendant

Lt. Evan Peugot — Officer Class descendant

Sgt. Adams Timson — Cargo Class descendant

Private Dunhill — Cargo Class descendant

Private Melchoir — Cargo Class descendant

Captain Lawrence Devaney — Officer Class descendant

Sgt. Drew McNully — Cargo Class descendant

Pvt. David Bradshaw— Cargo Class descendant

Capt. Reggy Smith — Argo Station

Adm. Jessup Rodding — Wayside Station

Col. Hobson — Fleet Intelligence

CHAPTER 1

THE HINTERLANDS

As Dan Ronin made his way to the back of the cozy little pub, he could feel their eyes on him. He could hear them whispering.

"There he is, the Captain."

"He's the man who nuked our cities to win the war."

"The Herald of Death."

"Look, it's the Reaper."

He'd never become used to the whispers. Always noted the shock of recognition in someone's face: it's the guy whose terrible deeds stopped another Fall. The guy who made the hard decisions that ended the lives of millions, in a terrible bargain to save billions.

There had been no way to avoid it. Dan Ronin had made the tough calls, because no one else could have.

Dan mostly managed to avoid making eye contact with the civilians in The Hinterlands as he circled around the square, wooden bar and made his way to a dimly lit back area surrounded by dark, wood-paneled walls. He found his father, Robert, sitting at a small table.

Robert was in his early sixties, with dark hair and graying sides. He had grown accustomed to being the father of the most famous, or infamous, man in modern times — unfortunately, it depended upon a person's point of view. At least here in The Hinterlands, the fedora he wore, working in concert with the dim lighting, hid his visage and Robert could avoid the scrutiny of civilians as he nursed a dark beer with a creamy head. No such luck for his son.

As Dan sat down, Robert's wizened, gray eyes looked up at his son. "Tough day at the office?" he asked.

After noting no one sat within twenty feet of them in the sparsely populated bar, Dan snorted softly in reply, "I've had worse."

I know you have, thought Robert, as he sipped his beer. "I wish the government could have delayed the reports about nuking those cities until after *Cerberus* departs for her next mission."

Dan nodded in response, not saying anything. A young waitress, who seemed blissfully unaware of who her customer was, brought his beer to the table.

"Here you go, sir. Enjoy," she said.

Father and son watched her go, both thinking she obviously never watched the news. Robert fixed his gaze upon his son. "How much longer?" he asked.

Dan semi-shrugged, tilting his head to the left and raising an eyebrow at the same time. "A few weeks. The new power plant is testing out well. Our weapons system upgrades went well. Same for the sensors. Engines still seem to handle the new power source without complaint."

Robert knew that was a gross oversimplification of the ship's transition to being powered by dark matter, but he figured harping on the hiccups they'd experienced wouldn't be productive. For the Confederation, it was new technology, even though it actually came from before The Fall. Obviously there would be plenty of technical challenges.

Robert looked at his son, who remained pensive as he quietly regarded his beer. The two had always been close, and he clearly sensed his son's feelings better than Dan himself did. "Still gloomy from the onslaught of media coverage?" Robert asked, hoping to bring Dan out of his shell a bit.

Dan's eyebrows shot up again as he tilted his head up to look at his father. "Dad. I hate this. Everything. I can't go anywhere without the stares and whispers. The rumors. I can't turn on the television because they don't seem to talk about anything but *Cerberus* and the Battle of Earth. I can't get away from it!" Dan said, clearly exasperated. The bags of worry and exhaustion under his eyes were only magnified in the dim light as he looked at his father with tired, sad eyes.

Robert was both proud of his son and highly concerned for his well-being. Dan had been under a great deal of stress for years in battling the Collective, and he had always been able to go home to relax and recharge in the North Woods of Wisconsin. Until now. Thanks to The Battle of Earth, Dan couldn't show his face anywhere on the planet without attracting a huge amount of unwanted attention.

"It's only a few weeks, and then it'll all be left behind. Far behind," Robert replied.

Dan sighed and nodded. His father was right, of course, but that didn't make hearing it any better. Dan just wanted to escape to deep space and forget about the past. As he took another sip of his beer, Dan glanced around the bar. Only a few furtive glances in his direction, with eyes rapidly averting as they noticed Dan's gaze falling upon them.

Yes, Dan definitely couldn't wait to depart. This leave and many months of upgrading his ship had already lasted too long. There was just no place for him to find peace here.

CHAPTER 2

ARGO I

"**S**ystem checks are complete. *Cerberus* is the first ship to run on dark matter."

Ronin glanced over at Reggy Smith, Captain of the Argo I, and nodded silently. They both turned their gazes back to the spectacular view of *Cerberus* ensconced in one of the Argo's construction wings. Smith, an engineer by training and a former tactical officer on a frigate, certainly knew his business and what it takes to build ships to withstand the demands of combat.

"Every simulation checks out. The crew has been training for weeks. They're ready," Ronin finally commented. "Just need to load out the ship and be on our way."

It was Smith's turn to nod silently. "I hear you're making a supply run out to Ninebase on your way out of town," he replied.

"That's affirm. *Cerberus* is hauling their mail, and dropping off a few candy bars and extra personnel for them. We're the baddest delivery truck in the business."

Smith snorted a soft laugh. Ronin's witty response was fairly typical of naval officers. He decided to change the subject somewhat.

"The new diamond black metal skin for *Cerberus* was completed ahead of schedule. I sent the specs to your inbox. It might help out there in the dark," Smith stated bluntly.

Ronin turned to look at Smith. "You're serious? I thought they were going to lay off with that due to all the problems and just use black hull paint instead. And why didn't anyone keep me up to date?"

Smith raised his eyebrows as he looked back at Ronin over his glasses. The two were at least twenty-five years apart in age. "Dan, sometimes the yard just moves ahead when they solve a problem. I don't guarantee much, but this I do guarantee. *Cerberus* will be better for having this skin. She'll be quite difficult to detect as it will block the ship's emissions, and the matte black doesn't reflect light or energy. It will also be more difficult to damage if you encounter energy weapons."

Ronin nodded somewhat tiredly, thinking that energy weapons were the stuff of childhood fantasies. "Nobody has energy weapons, Reggy. They just don't have the range to do anything before they become too diffuse."

Smith nodded, taking his time before responding. "Yes, based upon OUR tech. No promises for what you might encounter out there, though."

That reminder sent chills down Ronin's spine. Smith was potentially correct.

"Being nearly invisible at all times instead of needing to use the jump drive to do it will be handy because it's difficult to hit a ship you can't see," Ronin noted approvingly.

Smith nodded. "Yep. You might be able to hide in plain sight now while retaining the ability to jump at the same time. That can be handy when you want to quietly take a look around."

"Any other upgrades we're still wrapping up?" Ronin asked after a few more moments of gazing at *Cerberus*.

"Just the usual stuff. More powerful rail guns. Much more powerful gravity wave sub-light engines instead of fusion propulsion, which is a huge plus for the ship's stealth. You won't need to light up the skies with a fusion burn that anyone can see. Better gravity compensators to withstand the higher acceleration and deceleration Gs from the more powerful engines. More powerful sensor arrays. Oh, and far more robust mining and fabrication facilities, which you'll need on that long road trip you've got planned," said Smith, grinning at Ronin's reaction.

"This will be the first mission where a ship has more than rudimentary fabrication capabilities because we won't be able to just stock up on supplies at the corner store when we run low. Given enough time, we could replicate an entire ship if need be. Instead of being a sub-function of another department under Lieutenant Alphonso, it's now a full-fledged department for the first time and he'll be focused on fabrication full time," Ronin said. "I'm pretty excited to see what Alphonso and his mad scientists can do with it."

Another few moments of silence passed as they watched the final preparations. Smith turned to face Ronin and held out his hand. "Best of luck to you out there, Dan. I hope you find what you're looking for." As they shook hands, Ronin's commlink node on his collar chimed with an incoming message.

"Ronin here," Dan stated as he answered the call.

"Captain, the ship will be ready to depart soon. When can we expect you to board?" Mueller said, with a slightly teasing tone of voice. Ronin's eyebrows shot up in surprise at being ribbed by his executive officer.

"Just wrapping up with Captain Smith and I'll be on my way in a few minutes," he responded. "And just admiring the view, for a few more moments."

Ronin knew that last comment would make Mueller jealous. Everyone loved admiring *Cerberus*, but few were fortunate enough to be able to see the ship with their own eyes instead of being filtered through cameras.

"You just don't play fair!" replied Mueller in an exaggerated tone of having been hurt. This caused the corner of Ronin's mouth to curl upwards. *All too easy*, he thought.

"Nope. Ronin out," he simply stated. Ronin paused to take in the spectacular view of his ship for a few more moments. It was time to go to work.

CHAPTER 3

DELIVERY TRUCK

"**A**rgo Control reports their board is green, and *Cerberus* is ready to depart, Captain," noted Lt. Antonio Perez from the Helm station.

Ronin simply nodded, as the only real surprise to the bridge crew would have been not departing for some reason. "Acknowledged. Advise Argo that *Cerberus* is ready and ask them to open the cage."

Lt. Maria Delgado passed that request from her communications station back to Argo.

Soon, a wing of the superstructure of Argo, which Ronin had called the "cage," began to open up. It took about twenty minutes because of the sheer size. At last, Delgado said to Ronin, "Argo reports the cage is fully open and wishes *Cerberus* Godspeed on our trip. They also reminded us not to forget to drop off the mail at Ninebase on our way out of town."

Ronin responded, "Lieutenant Perez, take us out. Lieutenant Delgado, thank Argo and tell them we'll try to bring back some nice souvenirs."

Delgado smiled, although her voice didn't sound any less professional as she communicated her captain's reply. She smiled even broader when Argo's captain, Reggy Smith unexpectedly replied instead of Delgado's counterpart in a very tongue-in-cheek manner. Everyone on the bridge heard him.

"Lieutenant, please remind your captain we took the liberty of padding his budget so he can bring us back the fine wines and pricy bourbons that befit the luxury lifestyle we're entitled to."

The bridge crew burst out in laughter at the quip. It's not often that Ronin gets bested by a quick-witted officer on the commlinks.

It didn't take long for *Cerberus* to clear the station. From Smith's vantage point aboard Argo, *Cerberus* was silhouetted by the red brightness of Mars behind it. Smith quietly wondered to himself as he watched the ship departing on a very uncertain mission, *Will I ever see* Cerberus *again?*

"Lieutenant Perez, prepare to jump us to Ninebase," Ronin ordered after they were safely away from Argo. "Aye, aye, Captain. Coordinates have been laid in, ready to jump."

Mueller then gave the order to execute. "Jump the ship."

With a much smaller jump flare than before the upgrades, the newly all black *Cerberus* disappeared from Martian orbit.

CHAPTER 4

NINEBASE

As *Cerberus* appeared at the now established jump coordinates for Ninebase, Ronin found himself thinking back to his first trip here several years earlier. *Hard to believe that much could possibly have happened in such a short period of time. Yet here we are again.*

Delgado then interrupted his thoughts. "Captain, incoming message from the Ninebase controllers. They say, 'welcome back' and will insert *Cerberus* into the local traffic pattern momentarily."

Mueller glanced at Ronin with a surprised look. "Traffic pattern? There's a traffic pattern way out here?" she asked.

Ronin shrugged. "Maybe it's the new galactic garden spot? Come on out, see the sights, enjoy the spa. Who knows?"

Delgado interrupted them with another incoming message. "Captain, the commander of Ninebase is requesting to meet with you and Commander Mueller to discuss some new information they have found. He said you can come down to the base, or he can come up to *Cerberus*. Your choice."

Ronin didn't have too much trouble deciding where. "Invite him to *Cerberus* in four hours, please. I'd prefer to have our AI and officers nearby if they're needed based on the information he's bringing." He looked over at Mueller before finishing his thought. "And our Bulldogs will be occupied delivering the supplies and personnel we brought, so it's easier if he comes to us."

The corner of Mueller's mouth quirked up slightly. *That's an understatement,* she thought.

"Captain, scans show 27 other ships in the traffic pattern!" said Lieutenant Delacroix, anticipating Ronin's idle curiosity about the other ships in the area.

"Really? That's rather impressive," commented Mueller in surprise before turning to go to the landing bay. She had work to do before the Ninebase commander arrived.

Four hours later, Ronin and Mueller were down on the starboard landing bay to greet the incoming commanding officer of Ninebase and his aide, Cmdr. Oliver Umberland and Lt. Cmdr. Logan Fergus. Both were Scots who hailed from the Shetland Islands northeast of the Scottish mainland, between the Faroe Islands and old Norway. Untouched by the plague during The Fall, the once sparsely populated islands had since become the thriving capital of Scotland. In the centuries since The Fall, Shetlander descendants reverse colonized the empty cities of Scotland after the plague ran out of possible victims.

"Permission to come aboard, Captain?" said Umberland, his bushy red handlebar mustache and blue eyes accenting his brogue.

Ronin smiled broadly as he responded, looking up at the hulking base commander who stood six feet, six inches tall. "Granted. And welcome aboard! Sorry we couldn't provide more of an arrival ceremony."

Umberland simply tilted his head towards the frenzy of activity on the landing bay before replying. "We're not ones to stand on ceremony here, Captain. It just gets in the way when there's work to be done."

Ronin and Mueller couldn't agree more.

They talked as they made their way to the main conference room on *Cerberus.* "Aye, tis a beautiful ship, Captain. Lines like a sleek predator. I see she's 'ad a bit of a paint job since last you were here."

Ronin smiled, liking Umberland enormously. "I understand we have your people to thank for that, Commander."

Umberland nodded, still walking. "There seems to be a treasure trove of discoveries to be found down there. I wish there was a catalogue for us to peruse, but for now we take them as we find them."

As he said that, they arrived at their destination and entered. Once they settled in and coffee was served, Umberland leaned forward and spoke. "Captain, we have been instructed not to transmit this information, either by wireless or laser. It is authorized for in-person communication only, and it was sent to Fleet Intelligence pursuant to the Hades Ordinance."

At the mere mention of the Hades Ordinance, Ronin and Mueller likewise leaned forward slightly. The Hades Ordinance is a secret subsystem hardwired into the Confederate fleet AI's that secretly gathers discovered information from before The Fall. The ordinance requires AIs to secretly encode and burst-transmit the information directly to Fleet Intelligence without retaining any record of the transmission.

Umberland continued. "The information we found is fragmentary. The first scrap contains references to something once called, "The Big Dipper." The blank looks on the faces of Ronin and Mueller told Umberland all he needed to know.

"Never heard of it," Ronin finally responded.

"What is it?" Mueller added.

With a nod to Lieutenant Fergus, who pressed a screen button to light up the holo unit on the table. A section of the sky as seen from Earth was highlighted, first by a red outline in a rectangular shape, then zooming in while simultaneously highlighting seven of the brighter stars in the Ursa Major constellation.

"This, Captain and Commander, is the Big Dipper."

Highlighted this way, it actually DOES look like a dipper, thought Ronin.

"Ursa Major has been a *constellation* since before recorded history, but at one time the Big Dipper was more easily recognizable in certain parts of the planet. The Fall changed that. We forgot about the Big Dipper, but somehow retained the ancient knowledge of Ursa Major."

As Umberland softly cleared his throat, Ronin and Mueller politely waited for him to continue so he could connect the dots for them.

"Now the information you obtained from *USS Constitution* previously speaks about the Baidam constellation, which translates into

Shark constellation. Information uncovered here at Ninebase has linked Baidam constellation to the Big Dipper."

Ronin's eyebrows shot up when Umberland said that. "Linked? How so? Like some sort of celestial navigational beacon?" he quickly asked.

Umberland shook his head. "Even better than that, Captain. Lieutenant, if you would, please?" he said with a nod to Fergus.

On the holo, the Big Dipper was rotated upside down, while the stars of all three constellations were highlighted in colors corresponding to each constellation. "This is as seen from the southern hemisphere of Earth now. Our AI has concluded, and we agree, that the Big Dipper is also the Baidam constellation, or at least most of it. We lack sufficient data to be sure if they're entirely the same or just mostly the same."

Ronin and Mueller both scrutinized the holo for several long moments.

"You're saying based upon available information, this is your best guess where the lost colonial neighborhood might be?" Ronin finally said.

Umberland nodded. "Yes, it is. The nearest of those stars is Megrez, which is about eighty-one light years away and located in the middle of the constellation."

As Umberland spoke, Fergus highlighted the star on the holo. The star at the point connecting the handle to the scoop lit up.

"We're recommending *Cerberus* begin its search here, and follow your instincts from there," Umberland concluded.

Ronin nodded. "I agree. Speaking for both of us, we'd like something more substantive to go on, but it's more than we had before."

Mueller nodded in agreement. "Agreed. In the absence of a compelling reason to start elsewhere, it's as good a place as any," she added.

"Sorry we couldn't offer you more, but this is what we have. I presume you'll be on your way when the supplies and personnel transfer concludes?" Umberland stated.

"Yes, a few more hours are all we'll need to ferry everyone and everything to the surface. The birds are all out of the hangar bay, and you saw how busy the landing bays are with returning Bulldogs. Adam Taylor, our deck chief, has a lot on his plate at the moment," Mueller responded for Ronin and herself.

Umberland stood and extended his hand while Fergus shut off the holo and handed Mueller a printed folder of material. "I really wish I could be going with you two," Umberland said with an infectious grin and he shook hands with them both.

"You might have the better pick of duties, Commander," Ronin responded with a broad smile. "Might be nothing but boredom out there. Rocks and dust. At least we know you'll be making all sorts of discoveries down on Ninebase."

Umberland laughed. "Still, exploration is what we've all dreamed of since we were children. Now you both get to actually do some!"

* * *

"Captain, all Bulldogs have returned to *Cerberus*, and all sections report ready for departure," announced Delgado over Ronin's commlink. He was sitting in his ready room reviewing the status updates as he quietly enjoyed a hot cup of coffee.

"Acknowledged. I'll be on the bridge in a few minutes," he responded, as he sat with his feet on his table while reading the rest of the status reports. *Game time*, he thought to himself when he was done. With a last sip of the wonderfully hot beverage, he dropped his feet to the floor and was about to stand when his commlink node chimed again.

"Captain Ronin, this is Dr. Winston Wright. Might you have time for a discussion about the inadequate facilities assigned to our diplomatic corps?" Winston Wright was the ship's new Protocol Officer and head of its civilian diplomatic corps.

Frowning to himself, Ronin opened the commlink. "This is the Captain. What seems to be the problem, doctor?"

"Well, six of us are crammed into a small, former utility closet with a single two sided desk. These are unacceptable working conditions for highly trained diplomatic protocol officers. We can't all be in that tiny little room at the same time," Wright complained.

Despite it being an audio commlink only, Ronin's face screwed into a look of incredulity and disbelief at what Wright was saying. Although they were referred to as protocol officers, the members of the diplomatic corps were civilian politicians who had been assigned to *Cerberus* at the last minute in case *Cerberus* managed to find a lost colony.

"Doctor, has it occurred to you the two-person size of your workspace matches a six-man department when factored into the three shifts in a standard workday on *Cerberus*?" Ronin responded, somewhat perplexed this civilian hadn't figured that out yet.

There was a moment or two of silence before Wright responded. "I wasn't aware we were expected to work in shifts, Captain. Isn't there a larger space available?"

"Mr. Wright," Ronin started to respond when Wright interrupted him.

"It's Doctor, Captain. I've earned the title," Wright insisted smugly.

"Your file says it's just an academic degree and title. You're not a physician," Ronin said sharply, annoyed at the rude interruption over banalities like academic titles. "DOCTOR Wright," Ronin said, overemphasizing the title a bit now, "your civilians were added to this mission as an afterthought. *Cerberus* is a warship on a deep space mission, not a diplomatic vessel. Workspace is at a premium, and priority goes to essential ship functions. Now, if you'll excuse me, I am needed on the bridge." Ronin ended the commlink as curtly as he ended the discussion.

Still standing, Ronin walked to the bridge. As he walked, he did his best to forget about Wright's ridiculous complaint.

"Captain on the bridge," announced Lt. Pierre Delacroix as Ronin strode into the command center for *Cerberus*. Mueller stood up as he approached the command chair she had been occupying.

"Time to get this show on the road?" Mueller said quietly with a huge smile, standing next to the command chair while he sat down.

"Indeed it is," he replied. There was no hiding his anticipation about leaving.

"Lieutenant Delgado, open a ship wide commlink," Ronin ordered.

Delgado quickly responded, "Channel open, Captain."

Ronin wasted no time and got right to it. "This is the Captain. When all of you signed up knowing we were headed out into the dark, you did so with a spirit of adventure and duty. At the time, none of us knew where were going, just that it was out there somewhere. While we are in deep space, we're also supposed to take a good look around. Survey our surroundings, and find out what is out there. If we're lucky, we might stumble across the mythical Lost Colonies of Earth. We've been given reason to look at a particular constellation in the sky. So that's just we're going to do. We are headed towards the star Megrez, which is eighty-one light years from Earth. All hands, prepare for jump." Ronin then closed the commlink.

He looked at the helmsman, Lieutenant Perez, who was sitting askew in his seat so he could watch Ronin make the announcement. "Lieutenant Perez, execute jump."

Perez grinned hugely, also doing nothing to try to hide his excitement at leaving the solar system. "Aye, aye, Captain!" he replied as he turned to his board.

CHAPTER 5

CARGO AND CREW

"Louise, when are you going down to watch the Landing Day festivities?" Ryan Kutsler asked quietly so no one else in the control room would overhear. Louise Abernathy, a vivacious redhead from the Cargo community, was a young civilian orbital traffic controller who got the job on merit due to her hard work. For a penniless Cargo girl, merit was one of the few paths available to escape the grinding poverty and lack of education that typified the Cargo Class folk. Her father had made sure Louise studied hard, instead of making her work the mean streets of First City where she grew up.

Abernathy flashed a huge smile to her boyfriend, Ryan, who was sitting in the next seat. Kutsler was a highly privileged Crew Class, and unlike Cargo, was actually descended from the crew who manned the sub-light colony ship, which had arrived at Terra Station centuries ago. Although Kutsler had been given his job because he was privileged and could slack off without repercussion, he had surprisingly turned out to be a hard and talented worker.

The mere fact Kutsler even deigned to speak to Abernathy was somewhat controversial. That controversy paled in comparison to scandal of a Crew actually dating a Cargo. Kutsler's well-known disdain for the pretentiousness and pompousness prevalent in the Crew, and his flouting the societal class separation by dating Louise, had made him a near outcast among the Crew. Abernathy knew Kutsler didn't care and could see he was destined for something more.

"Ryan, you know us Cargo types don't commemorate Landing Day like the Dreamers do. There just isn't as much to celebrate for us." When alone with Kutsler, Abernathy often forgot her manners and called the Crew by the more derisive slang, Dreamers. Kutsler never took offense because he didn't consider himself a Crew even though he enjoyed their privileges.

Kutsler sighed softly. Looking around at the other stations in the control room briefly before returning his blue-eyed gaze to Abernathy. "Yeah, I know. I just thought you might enjoy the music and fireworks part of the celebration. Nothing wrong with relaxing and watching those parts of the festivities."

Abernathy's smile again lit up the room. Kutsler was right. She did enjoy those. "You drive a hard bargain, Mr. Kutsler. How about we go right after our shift?"

Now it was Kutsler's turn to light up the room with a huge smile. "You're on! Let's see and be seen by the matriarchs. Ruffle their feathers by having fun together."

Abernathy just smiled and shook her head at the same time. The man's energy and enthusiasm were as infectious as always. It was one of the things that attracted her to him.

Hours later, the two found themselves on a darkened hill in Downers Park in the center of First City. The skyscrapers surrounding the park were likewise darkened for the occasion. It was midsummer, and the temperatures hovered just above 70 degrees Fahrenheit. An absolutely beautiful evening to be outside.

"I'm glad it's after sundown," Abernathy whispered to Kutsler as they sat on a blanket to await the firework show.

Kutsler nodded sleepily. Earlier they had stuffed themselves to the rafters on the food offerings at the fairground at the park's entrance and found a good band to enjoy while they ate. Even though neither had acknowledged the disgusted stares from the almost exclusively crowd of Crew in Downers Park that day, both were aware of the attention. It always happened. Dreamers strongly disliked it when some lowlife Cargo girl had the temerity to be present, and they weren't shy about making their feelings known.

"Mmm. Me, too. Now no one can give us the Stare of Death because they can't see us," Kutsler responded.

Abernathy laughed softly. "Yeah. Now we're just shadowy figures on a hill, waiting for the finale. Which occurs in ... three minutes," she said, after checking her watch.

Those minutes passed quickly. When thirty seconds remained, they looked to the east along with the rest of the people in the park. Soon they could see a huge star rising from the eastern horizon. It was far brighter than every other light in the sky. All around them a low crescendo of music rose along with it.

"Almost there," murmured Kutsler as they watched its light quickly cross the sky. It had followed the same orbit every night for the past 352 years.

When the huge orbiting spacecraft they called the Ark intersected with the light from the star for Earth, the musical crescendo peaked and the fireworks show began. It was choreographed with moving music. Despite her Cargo-born antipathy, Abernathy couldn't help but feel a thrill of excitement.

"Why do you think we've never heard from Earth?" Abernathy asked Kutsler.

He smiled, even though it was dark. It was the same question everyone asked from time to time. There were no answers. "If we knew the answer to that, we're grossly underpaid."

Kutsler was right.

CHAPTER 6

OFFICER CLASS

Wallace Seaver woke early, as was his custom. After a judicious stretch, he sat up in his king-size bed and looked toward the wall of windows facing to the east. The sun was just beginning to peek over the horizon, which irresistibly drew Wallace over to the windows.

As he stood and took in the incredible view from the 75th floor of the First City skyscraper he called home, his Cargo-born servant quietly brought his morning coffee and breakfast. Ignoring her, Wallace continued to gaze at the pink, orange and purple display coming over the horizon. It was supposed to be a clear, sunny day today.

The servant, Maureen, was relieved he didn't drag her into his bed again. Maureen's husband hated the uber-privileged Officer Class that perched atop Terra Station society, but they needed the income to survive. If he ever found out about Seaver's liberties with Maureen, he would die trying to breach the defense network of the officers in a futile attempt to kill Seaver.

Seaver was only able to enjoy the view for a few more moments before the first call of the day arrived, which he answered while holding his cup of coffee. "Admiral Seaver here."

The caller was his aide de camp, Chief Esmeralda Centon.

Damn that Crew woman, doesn't she ever sleep? thought Seaver for a moment, before he focused on her words. Seaver didn't dislike Centon, but at times her productivity and efficiency contrasted wildly with an otherwise enjoyable moment. Rising to watch a beautiful sunrise from his luxurious suite atop a skyscraper and enjoying the quiet and solitude without being interrupted by work was one such moment.

"Admiral, the morning situation report has been sent to your box. Do you have any orders to start the day?"

"Let me guess. Repairs to The Ark continue. Celestial mining operations continue producing the rare metals. And unrest continues amongst the Cargo out in the Borderlands?" he responded.

None of that was surprising to anyone who paid attention. The Ark required constant repairs due to its sheer age. Mining was, well, it was mining. Most of it was performed by machines out on the asteroid belt, so there were few complaints over the long hours.

The Borderlands continued to be a source of irritation to the Officers and Crew Classes. The Borderlands were slums infesting the outskirts of First City and the other major metropolitan areas. After the planet was terraformed, these slums sprang up beyond the boundaries of the settlement's original habitats because the Officers and Crew pushed the Cargo Class out of the comfortable cities. At the time, it was easier to insulate and protect the privileged elite from the Cargo when the elite were clustered together in the center of the cities rather than the other way around. Seaver wasn't so sure, and tended to believe the Cargo should be contained in the city centers instead.

"Affirmative, Admiral. It's the usual litany of Cargo grievances and complaints. Those people just don't know their place. Local law enforcement is tasked to assist the military's Special Forces and Armored Cavalry units for the next few days to quell some riots they suspect might occur."

Seaver snorted softly to himself at the need to call in the heavy hitters to quell rioting. Again. Not for the first time, he mused whether Cargo Class might view the military as an occupation force because the military's officer core came solely from society's Officer Class, while the lower ranks exclusively came from the Crew Class. No ranks in the military or law enforcement were allowed to come from the Cargo Class because the Cargo were deemed unfit to enjoy the privileges associated with those services. *Shutting the Cargo out from all good employment means it's 'us versus them'. Cargo Class simply has no interest in enforcing society's current status quo.*

"Thank you, Chief Centon. I don't have any new orders to issue at this time. I'll be coming into the command center today and not working remotely due to the heightened unrest. The Special Forces and Armored Cav like to have orbital units on standby if they go into action. Better to be in the control center if that happens." Seaver stood as the comm line closed. *Time to do my duty*, he thought as he stepped into the shower.

Thirty minutes later, Seaver was on the roof of the building where he lived, stepping into the air car that was waiting for him. As he settled in, the pilot received clearance from the Officer's air defense system and lifted off. Seaver occupied his time by reading the brief on his tablet for the short, fifteen-minute flight. The pilot took note of the fixed and mobile weapon systems that kept the Cargo and Crew out of the area.

Soon after his pilot delivered him to their destination, Seaver strode into the Terra Station Command Center. "Good morning, Admiral," said Chief Centon with a salute. As usual, she was dressed in her sharply creased, dark navy uniform, and she stood as she greeted Seaver.

"Good morning, Chief. Has our timetable moved up since we last spoke?" asked Seaver in response as he returned the salute.

"No, sir. Go Time is still at 10 a.m. There will be a heavy military presence moving into the Borderlands."

Seaver nodded as they walked to his office overlooking the rest of the space control center.

"Good, good. The morning report suggested they intend to hit much harder than in the past to try to purge those Cargo leading the unrest. The military units will bring their own air cover, but let's preposition our own orbital assets. Task a couple of observation satellites and a bombardment satellite."

Chief Centon nodded, her tightly pulled back black hair highlighting her pale, angular face and dark brown eyes. "Very good, sir. I'll issue the orders."

Seaver sat down at his desk and poured a cup of hot coffee from the thermos on the cabinet behind the desk that the Chief had put there before he arrived. As he sipped, Seaver's eyes drifted over to the glass wall on his left. From there Seaver idly watched Chief Centon first speak to Ryan Kutsler at the Orbital Weapons desk, and then to that civilian, red-headed Cargo girl seated next to Ryan at the Orbital Optics desk. Seaver didn't recall what her name was.

Cargo Class has no business working amongst more respectable members of the Crew, or even anywhere near an Officer, Seaver thought before he turned his attention to the work queue on his screen.

CHAPTER 7

FOXTROT STATION

As *Cerberus* drifted along in interstellar space about eighteen light years from their target star of Megrez, the placid, dark exterior of the ship belied the pace of activity occurring inside the hull.

"Lieutenant Delacroix, don't forget the next wave of Bulldogs carrying sensor packages is about to launch," said Commander Mueller as she hovered over Delacroix's shoulder.

"Yes, ma'am. We'll get a solid picture of our extended surroundings from their disbursal pattern. I anticipate their return with the data they gather about three hours after they jump away." Delacroix was busy coordinating the extended sensor scans of this jump point so they could build more precise navigational charts for future reference.

While Delacroix and Mueller were keeping busy with the huge volume of sensor activity, Ronin didn't have much reason to stay on the bridge as his presence just wasn't needed. While a worthwhile endeavor, making short jumps and detailed navigational charts wasn't terribly exciting work.

"Lieutenant Gustav, this is the Captain. Is today's boarding exercise about to start?" Ronin called to the lieutenant who was now in command of the ship's Marine units.

Although he was born and raised in a central European area once called Germany, Lt. Adolph Gustav spoke with a slight Wisconsin accent. He had attended college in Green Bay before enlisting in the Marines.

"Aye, sir. If you still would like to watch, Go Time is in ten minutes," came the swift response.

"I would, indeed. See you in a few," Ronin replied. He rose, exited the ready room and made his way down to Marine country. *This ought to be interesting*, he thought as he walked to the landing bay.

With the Bulldogs gone for a few hours and the Tomcats over in the hangar bays, it was the perfect time for Marines to practice their craft in the empty area of the landing bay. As he walked in, Lt. Gustav motioned from where he was standing to acknowledge Ronin's presence and pointed to a spot where Ronin could best see how the exercise progressed.

As he sat, the exercise began with the simulated blare of an alarm and loudspeaker warning to repel boarders in the landing bay. Gustav's pre-mission brief had designated Bravo team to be the boarding party, while Echo and Gamma teams would seek to evict them from the ship.

As the attack progressed, the ship's chief medical doctor, Hirohito Taketa, joined Ronin for a few minutes. "I heard Echo and Gamma teams were going to release the hounds on Bravo team today," Ronin whispered to Taketa when he arrived.

"Hounds? Figuratively or literally?" Taketa responded with a raised eyebrow.

Surprised, Ronin looked at him for a moment before connecting the dots. "Ah. You probably weren't informed of the newest addition to our Marine teams. It's literally. The Marine teams onboard now have designated K9 handlers, and some impressively trained war dogs. The Fleet added them to our Marine teams since we were hoping to explore some planets. We didn't have canines aboard *Cerberus* until this mission," Ronin explained.

Taketa, himself a dog lover, nodded approvingly. "Ah. K9 units are really quite something. Takes a lot of training for the canines as well as the Marines to work effectively together but once that has been done, they can do a lot."

As Taketa was responding to Ronin, their eyes followed the streaking blur of Echo team's war dog as it went after a hidden Bravo team Marine who had positioned himself behind some crates he could peek between. It was that Marine's attempt to find a good hide to cover Bravo team's advance. Moments later, Pvt. Terry Allison's unpleasantly surprised yell brought evil grins to both Ronin and Taketa's faces. Bravo team just discovered the hounds of hell were hunting with Echo and Gamma today.

Ronin and Taketa watched the exercise for about an hour before it wrapped up. As Lieutenant Gustav gathered in all three of his teams to relay initial impressions and critiques before breaking to run it again, Ronin's collar node commlink chimed with an incoming message.

"Captain, this is Lieutenant Delacroix. Can you come to the bridge, immediately? We've found something you should see."

Ronin's eyebrows shot up in surprise. "Acknowledged. I'm on my way," he said as he quickly strode to the hangar exit while Dr. Taketa headed back to his sickbay.

Soon after, Dan walked onto the bridge and over to where Delacroix and Mueller were standing at the sensor station. They looked up as he approached. Ronin had a standing order that his entrance onto the bridge not be announced while they were on mission, as he just found it distracting for both himself and the crew.

"What did you find?" Ronin asked as they glanced at him. With a nod from Mueller to begin, Delacroix responded first.

"Captain, *Bulldog 3* returned already from their forward observation post. They're headed to the main conference room now. The sensor net and the drones they deployed are picking up the faintest of radio waves. They're intermittent, but the ship's AI tagged them as artificial in origin with high probability."

When Delacroix finished, Ronin's surprised face spoke volumes. "Let's get down to the main conference room and hear what the flight team has to report there," he said as the three of them quickly moved to the exit.

Having anticipated Ronin's reaction, Delacroix had already called up his backup who immediately replaced him at the station. By the time the three of them arrived in the main conference room, the *Bulldog 3* team of Pilot Officer Antonio Russo and his rearseater Chief Michael Jonsey had already pulled up the navigational chart and plotted their flight data on it.

"Lieutenant, Chief. Report," Ronin said as he walked in. He was all business now.

Jonsey took the lead, as he was the drone and sensor operator for the assault shuttle. "Captain, the AI was analyzing the data from the sensor net and sweeps were making for the navigational charts. Suddenly, AI tagged certain radio waves as artificial in origin."

Ronin nodded. All of them were familiar with the surprising amount of radio wave activity in space. Most of it was just background clutter.

Jonsey continued, his deep, bass voice easily filling the room with sound. "The waves initially seemed to be intermittent like everything else out there, but the AI found this and cleaned up the signal as best it could. It's an audio broadcast, but at this distance it's pretty scattered. AI, replay the audio signal." Jonsey's face was dead serious as he ordered the AI to play the recording.

The AI had also taken the liberty of suppressing the background hiss and crackle, so the playback was surprisingly easy to understand. "November three niner … approach … devous (static) … hundred hours." The AI played the recording on a loop four times before stopping it.

The five of them looked at each other for a few moments before Delacroix spoke first. "AI, what are the odds that is an ancient message from Earth?"

The AI had already asked itself the same thing. "The odds against detecting any coherent remnant of a communication originating from Earth at this distance are so remote as to be the next closest thing to impossible. Interstellar interference would have scattered it beyond any reasonable possibility of recognition long before it reached here."

Anticipating the next question, the AI continued. "As you no doubt have noticed, the words in the communication were spoken in American."

Ronin nodded. They had definitely noticed.

"Delacroix, thoughts? Is this a stray message from an ancient spacecraft that passed by long ago?" Mueller asked.

Delacroix nodded, but not confidently. "Yes, AI estimates it could be. It also believes it could just as likely have originated from the Megrez system up ahead. Lieutenant Russo and Chief Jonesy didn't intercept the message fragment until they had jumped five light years ahead of our current position. The scattering of the fragment made determining the direction of origin impossible."

"You didn't detect anything on the first four jumps? Only after the fifth jump?" Ronin asked Russo.

"Yesssir. We maxed out at one light year on each jump, and then ran our scans. Jonsey's board didn't light up until after jump five. The AI analyzed it while we finished our charting scans, then we decided to jump back instead of continuing on to jumps six and beyond. The other Bulldog teams were too far away to reach on the wireless, so they don't know we've returned," Russo responded.

Ronin nodded. "Good call. Teams one, two and five should be back in a few hours. Go down to the ready room and debrief with Lieutenant Sunderland. He's waiting for you down there and we'll talk about what to do with this information in the interim."

Russo and Jonesy both rose and left while Ronin turned to Mueller and Delacroix before speaking. "Well, I know we're looking for the Lost Colonies but that was unexpected. We've only been gone for a few weeks."

Mueller leaned back in her seat. "Yes, but maybe we just got lucky and found one of them right away? And will we be able to survey the jump gate on this end even if we could find it? Does it still exist?"

Delacroix sighed softly and likewise leaned back. His blue eyes blazed in stark contrast to his raven black hair as he intently looked at both Ronin and Mueller.

"Am I correct in assuming our navigational surveying has been suspended in favor of our primary mission objective and that *Cerberus* will start our pre-planned interstellar skulking about?" Delacroix asked. He already knew the answer, but asked the question anyway.

Ronin smiled as he recognized what Delacroix was doing. "Yes. Once our birds return to the nest, begin the skulking about as you so eloquently put it. Prep the Bulldogs for extreme long range missions. I'll talk to Lieutenant Alphonso in Fabrication to prepare and coat each Bulldog in diamond black skin for maximum stealth. When last we discussed it, it would only take a few hours per Bulldog." When he finished, Ronin rose from his seat to leave.

Mueller and Pierre did likewise. "We'll hold this position for now, so let's designate these coordinates Foxtrot Station. If we find nothing, we'll move on, otherwise, we stay here for the time being."

CHAPTER 8

FABRICATION

Instead of talking with Lt. Kristoff Alphonso over a commlink, Ronin and Mueller decided to visit him in the ship's new Fabrication Department. The Eastern-Mediterranean-born Alphonso triple majored in college with a combination of Computer Design, Mechanical Engineering, and Robotics. After the ship's power system was upgraded from fusion, the far smaller dark matter system opened up a lot of room that was primarily repurposed to create Fabrication. Kristoff now headed up that full department.

Ronin and Mueller stopped abruptly in surprise as they entered Fabrication. Staring them in the face was a Marine in what appeared to be some sort of modified exosuit.

"All right, Toshi, just hold still for a few more moments while we finish calibrating the skin on this beastie." Alphonso was saying distractedly.

Everyone held still while Alphonso, who was hunched over a screen readout with his back turned to Ronin and Mueller, finished making adjustments with a few mouse clicks. "There! Finished. Let's shoot a gun at you and see how it feels."

As he said that, Gunnery Sergeant Toshi Kanagawa looked at Ronin and Mueller with a "Please save me from this absolute madman" look on his face.

Kanagawa's look was so pathetic, Ronin and Mueller burst out laughing, which got the startled Alphonso's attention. "Captain, Commander! I'm sorry, I didn't realize you were standing there. What can I do for you?"

Motioning towards Kanagawa, Ronin asked, "That the new liquid armor exosuit skin?"

Alphonso nodded excitedly. "Yessir." Alphonso said, drawling out the word as was common among the crew. "Gunnery Sergeant Kanagawa was 'volunteered' to test it out. Seems we had no shortage of Marines lining up to shoot him with their carbines for the testing phase, but oddly no one wanted to be the guy getting shot at," Alphonso said with such an exaggerated air of not understanding why, that Kanagawa just rolled his eyes and shook his head.

"Ugh. Now I may have to ask my people to please shoot me and just put me outta my misery so I don't have to listen to any more of your bad jokes," Kanagawa quipped.

Alphonso laughed evilly. "You already got a big enough target painted on you when Lieutenant Gustav volunteered you and asked if anyone wanted to take some free shots once we got you all gussied up," Alphonso said, causing Kanagawa to laugh ruefully.

"Yeah, I never figured if I had to face a firing squad, it would be my own team demanding to be the shooters," Kanagawa joked.

Alphonso made one final adjustment, and then turned to face Ronin and Mueller with his full attention. "So, what brings you down here, Captain?" he asked.

Ronin wasted no more time. "*Bulldog 3* returned early from its navigational charting mission, and we need the Bulldogs to do some quiet, long range scouting. How soon can you coat the Bulldogs in the diamond black metal skin? Last time you thought it would be three hours," asked.

"Yessir. We figure three hours for the first bird, and hope the experience gained on the first bird enables us to reduce the time needed for the following shuttles," Alphonso replied.

Ronin nodded. "Good. I need you to get started on *Bulldog 3* right away since it's the only bird in the nest at the moment. Expect to cover all four of the Bulldogs when they return from their current mission."

Alphonso nodded. "Very good, sir. I'll get a team started on it immediately. Give us an hour to mix up the coating, and then they'll get down to the hangar bay and make it happen."

CHAPTER 9

SCOUTS

Alphonso removed his goggles to admire his team's handiwork. *Bulldog 3* sat alone in the hangar bay, blacker than night now. Alphonso checked the time and announced, "Two hours and forty-five minutes. Good work, people!"

The fabrication team that had been crawling all over *Bulldog 3* broke out into applause, whooping and hollering. A broadly smiling Alphonso opened a commlink: "Alphonso to Captain Ronin. *Bulldog 3* has been re-skinned and is ready for flight ops."

Up on the bridge, Ronin quickly acknowledged Alphonso's status report and opened a link to the ship's CAG. "Lieutenant Sunderland, this is the Captain. Lieutenant Alphonso reports *Bulldog 3* has been re-skinned and is ready for flight ops. Let's get them into the launch bay and out into the dark."

"Roger that, Captain. I've already got my flight crew in the ready room. They'll be away in ten minutes," Sunderland responded through his collar node as he walked from his office to the pilot ready room. As he entered the room where Russo and Jonesy were seated, he said without preamble, "All right, you two. Your sweet ride has now been pimped out in black, with all the chrome, sporty pinstripes and flames you could ever want."

Russo and Jonsey looked at each other. "You thinking what I'm thinking?" Jonsey said with a huge grin that contrasted his white teeth against his very dark skin.

"We're styling the hottest babe magnet in the universe! Let's go cruise for chicks!" Russo responded with a matching grin.

Sunderland set a record with his eye-rolling, but he couldn't resist. "I really hate you guys. You two couldn't pick up chicks even if they were just actual farm animals."

Russo and Jonsey roared with laughter, which was echoed by Sunderland's chuckling. "All right. Down to business. You know the drill. Long range reconnaissance. If you make jumps all the way to Megrez system, stay ghosted and on the outskirts. Scoop up all the data you can. Any trouble, jump away immediately. You find anything big, gather what you can, then run home to mama. Questions?"

Russo and Jonsey both shook their heads. Sunderland dismissed them, saying, "Then your chariot awaits, gentlemen. Time to get after it."

Minutes later, they were seated in *Bulldog 3* down in the launch bay. "Launch control, our board is green, ready for launch," said Russo over the commlink.

The launch officer quickly responded, "*Bulldog 3*, launch control. You are cleared for launch."

Moments later they quickly shot out into space. After putting some distance between themselves and *Cerberus*, Russo announced it was time to see what deep space had to offer. "Jump one in three. Two. One. Jumping."

The now dark black Bulldog vanished with almost no jump flare.

CHAPTER 10

CROWD CONTROL

Seaver's comm buzzed with an incoming message, interrupting what was so far an unexpectedly boring morning.

"Admiral, we've received a request from the Armored Cavalry units moving into the Borderlands to provide live optics due to the fighting that broke out. I've granted the request and we are live with the video now."

Seaver put down the coffee mug from which he had been sipping. "Thanks, Chief Centon. Keep me apprised of any new developments."

After Seaver closed the comm, he opened a window on his monitor to watch the live stream. *The God's Eye view itself*, he thought. He could see smoke obscuring parts of the Borderlands and several armored units burning and smoldering. *Those Cargo Class lowlifes need to get some comeuppance from this. Put them back in their place*, he thought as he watched.

Down at the Orbital Optics desk, Abernathy watched the same comm feed. Her reaction was one of horror as she watched the armored cavalry and special forces battle her people.

"Louise, are you alright?" asked Kutsler. He was very concerned about her, and had become sensitive to the plight of Cargo Class folks who were getting attacked for wanting equal rights.

"Yes. No. I don't know!" whispered Abernathy with a traumatized shake of her head. "They're so heavily outgunned!" Tears welled up in her eyes as her mind raged. *I hate the Officers!* she thought.

CHAPTER 11

BULLDOG 3

"There sure is a lot of weird stuff about the Megrez system," Jonsey muttered for the tenth time as he watched the screen in front of him. They arrived in system a week ago, after duly making a series of jumps and surveys before reaching Megrez.

"You can say that again! At least once we arrived, it wasn't hard to identify where those communications we intercepted came from," replied Russo without looking. He was busy running his own survey. "Look, here comes that huge ship again."

Their high resolution optics clearly displayed a giant ship in orbit around a planet with a blue atmosphere and white clouds tinged with a slightly orange hue. "AI, you sure about the size of that monster yet?" asked Jonsey, as he eyed the silvery monster circling the planet.

"Making the final measurements on this orbit, Chief," responded the AI, as they watched the display. "Its dimensions are approximately ten times the size of *Cerberus*. Assuming the dimensions are consistent with Confederation Navy standards for tonnage and metallic composition, that ship could weigh about 1,000,000 tons or more."

Finally! thought Russo. It seemed to take a long time to scale out that ship. It was enormous, but so far, they hadn't seen much activity involving the thing except for various ship to surface traffic and some faintly detectable repair work that was underway. Hidden in the system's asteroid belt, they were too far away to detect specific communications emanating from the vessel.

"AI, what level of confidence do you have if we jump back and report we've found a planet that appears to have been a massively terraformed gas dwarf?" Jonsey asked. He wanted to give *Cerberus* a reasonably comprehensive survey upon their return and this was one of the biggest anomalies about the system.

"I am 68 percent confident this atmosphere was once similar to Saturn's in composition, and should be 75 percent hydrogen and 25 percent helium. Although difficult to tell at this distance, its oceans appear to be quite recent in origin and lacking in both depth and a matured coastline definition. There also appear to be large structures at the poles which might have been confused with mountains except that they share an identical optical profile which suggests an artificial origin."

"Michael, any change in their comms traffic?" Russo asked.

"No. Still heavy traffic. Most of it is broadcast in the clear but a small percentage is still encrypted. We haven't been able to crack the encryption code as it's pretty advanced. The comms in the clear and their other stray broadcasts have made it abundantly clear the inhabitants speak American, too," Jonsey replied.

"I'm calling it. We've collected plenty to establish a high probability that we've found an advanced human colony. We just haven't determined which colony it is, so we can't yet definitely identify it as Forrestal, Celestra or Solara. Nor did we stumble across a jump gate. Not that we know of anyway. Not that we knew what to look for, but we looked anyway," Russo said. "It's time to return to the nest."

CHAPTER 12

FOXTROT STATION

onin sighed as he sat at his desk in the ready room, drumming his fingers in boredom as he checked the time again. Sarah and Edward were about to return to the family's quarters after a long day at school, and he was ready to go back and have a little family time while things on the ship were quiet.

That boredom evaporated quickly when an update popped up on his screen. Seconds later, his commlink node chimed with an incoming message.

"Captain, *Bulldog 3* has returned. They are requesting priority landing in the hangar and an immediate briefing with you and Commander Mueller," said Lieutenant Delgado.

Dan's eyebrows shot up at hearing that sequence of information. "Acknowledged. Have them meet us in the main conference room. Bring in Lieutenants Delacroix, Sunderland and LeCroy, too." Ronin stood up and immediately headed for the conference room. *This promises to be interesting*, he thought as he walked.

Minutes later, the seven were seated together in the main conference room. With a look and nod from Ronin to begin, a scruffy-looking Russo spoke first. After a week on a Bulldog which lacks showers, he and Jonsey were pretty ripe and unshaven.

"Captain, Commander, Lieutenants. Thank you for seeing us so soon. We were pretty sure you wouldn't want to wait for this to filter up through the ranks and would want us available for questions immediately. AI, please play the video report we've prepared. If I may, I ask you please hold your questions until the end as this is a BLUF report."

Everyone in the room knew BLUF stood for Bottom Line Up Front.

The room darkened and a holo appeared over the middle of the table and played a video, which Jonsey live narrated with deep voice because he knew the presentation was being recorded by the conference room's security system. "This is a BLUF report. Bulldog 3 observed what strongly appears to be an established human colony in the Megrez system. As you can see from this video, in that system there is an enormous spacecraft orbiting a planet that our AI determined would ordinarily be a planet that is a rare gas dwarf. Instead of an atmosphere we would have expected to resemble the 75 percent hydrogen and 25 percent helium composition of Saturn's, this planet has an atmo similar to Earth's. Instead, the atmosphere we would have expected to resemble the 75 percent hydrogen and 25 percent helium composition of Saturn's atmo, this planet has an atmo similar to Earth's. We believe it to have been extensively terraformed by these two massive structures with identical optical profiles at each pole. AI suggests their size, precise pole centering and identical profiles indicates an artificial origin. AI also theorized the structures may have had something to do with the terraforming, but that isn't substantiated by much at this time." The video images were timed to show images corresponding to Jonsey's narration.

Jonsey cleared his throat and took a sip of water before continuing his narration. "We observed plenty of activity in-system, but the vast majority of it seems to correlate to commercial mining and communication activities. Other than this massive ship in orbit which AI estimates to be ten times the size of *Cerberus*, all observed spacecraft appear to be fusion powered and are relatively small by our standards. There have been no observed military actions, although the AI indicates numerous satellites orbiting the planet are armed. Alarmingly, those armaments are directed towards the planetary surface and not out into space. We also did not observe anything we would suspect to be a jump gate."

Jonsey paused while the video showed still images of armed satellites in orbit, and then moved on to one of the biggest bombshells. "Lastly, the kicker for us in figuring we are looking at a human colony is from these recordings. There are plenty of communications being broadcast in the clear in that neighborhood, and all of it seemed to be in this language." He went silent while the recorded audio of a newscast filled the room.

> Crew members were shocked at the display of disrespectful behavior of the Cargo Class towards the Officers during the Landing Day festivities in downtown First City today. Reports of Cargo Class rioting and looting presaged a law enforcement crackdown in the Borderlands that seeks to restore order and safety on the outskirts of the city proper. All citizens are urged to remain indoors until the current unrest settles and the perpetrators of these crimes are brought to justice. In other news today...

Jonsey stopped the recording. "As you can hear, that was broadcast in the clear and was obviously spoken in plain American. The accent is a bit odd to our ears, but the AI says it matches that of ancient recordings found on Earth and it is actually our own accents that have changed in the interim." Jonsey brought the lights back up before asking, "Questions?"

Ronin wasted no time. "How long did you observe this system?"

"About seven days, Captain," responded Russo, nodding towards Ronin.

LeCroy was next. "Any signs you were detected?"

Jonsey handled this one. "None that we could identify, Lieutenant. We did not approach closer than the asteroid belt we hid in. We also felt the planetary authorities weren't overly vigilant in watching the skies given the weapons posture of the armed satellites as they only faced down towards the surface. Something is causing that posture, and we don't yet know what it is other than the recording we played that mentioned riots."

Ronin looked toward Lieutenant Sunderland. "CAG, I think we should recall the other Bulldogs earlier than planned. How soon can you send *Bulldog 3* out to retrieve them? Obviously I'm assuming they didn't stray far from the preplanned jump coordinates so *Bulldog 3* has a better chance of jumping within the communications range of each flight crew."

Sunderland leaned back and eyed his scruffy, smelly *Bulldog 3* crew at the table. They certainly smelled ripe from a week away from *Cerberus*, and were badly in need of showers and shaves. "Aye, Captain, if they be willing. They don't took over tired, but I'd recommend they get cleaned up while the deck crews get their bird off the landing bay, restocked and back into the launch bay," he said in a heavy brogue, his bright blue eyes looking at his guys with some amusement. *The lads look like they're up for another round*, Sunderland thought to himself.

That was all Ronin needed to hear. He too could see that Russo and Jonsey could barely contain their excitement. "Russo. Jonsey. You heard 'im. Boss-man says you need a good scrubbing and a shave. Grab some chow after that, and get back to your bird." Sunderland said.

The grinning pair stood and replied with "Yessirs" and quickly headed to the showers. Russo held out a fist to Jonsey to bump once they were in the passageway, grinning as he said, "I feel the need." Then together they said at the same time, "The need, to feed!" You could hear their stomachs growling as they walked.

After they left, Ronin leaned forward and clasped his hands while resting elbows on the table and looking at the others. "Well? Obviously we're going to pay the system a visit. Recommendations?"

Mueller, who hadn't said a word so far, went first as the second highest rank in the room. "I recommend we jump to the same observation distance as did *Bulldog 3*, but in a different section of the system's belt just in case they had been detected and there's a greeting party that showed up after they left. From there, plot out how best to conduct some more surveying of the system by having the Bulldogs place a drone sensor net. Gather more information from there before we make more decisions."

They all nodded, each having thought much the same thing. They all wanted more information before jumping into orbit uninvited.

LeCroy went next. "I also recommend we put a few observation drones into orbit. We can have the Bulldogs launch them from a distance, and fly them into place using the kinetic speed they have from the Bulldogs so they won't have engine flares that might be spotted."

Ronin nodded. Another good idea. He added, "I'd like to position a few drones with weapons packages that same way, too. I want something nearby all the weapons satellites we might discover before *Cerberus* joins the party around the planet. What about that giant ship?"

LeCroy had been scanning the data on the huge ship and spoke first. "Captain, the current optics on the ship isn't the greatest, but so far AI feels that ship has few, if any, armaments. While we can't be sure, AI hasn't analyzed anything in the optical recordings that it felt constitutes a threat to *Cerberus*. In fact, the AI on *Cerberus* thinks it may not be a warship at all. It thinks it could be some sort of ancient generation ship."

"It does?" said Sunderland, who was startled by the AI's conclusions. "AI, how do you figure that? There's nothing in the old legends about a generation ship, is there?" he asked.

"You are correct the legends and known histories are silent about the existence of human generation ships or any colony missions using them, Lieutenant Sunderland; however, we know very little about the era of space exploration from prior to the discovery of jump gates because of the loss of records and worldwide civilizational collapse during The Fall.

"Based on radiocarbon dating of old relics found in the ruins of the Johnson Space Center, our scientists have speculated a belief that such era spans approximately two or three centuries of human spaceflight. They have not been able to more precisely date the period because of interference from the radioactive ruins of Houston itself. That interference introduces too many variables to be more precise under current dating methodologies."

Pausing for a moment, the AI continued just as Ronin started wondering if the pause was a shrewdly employed dramatic moment. "Despite the lack of ancient historical records, many scientists in the last century toyed with the characteristics a generational ship might need if humanity was to return to the stars without a faster than light way of getting there in the absence of locating jump gates. Those characteristics generally were a very large size, a simple design that lends itself to hauling large machinery or dismantling, and an advanced AI to run the ship and educate the children who are created when the DNA cargo is combined after arrival and preparation of the colony by the AI."

Now it was Ronin's turn to sound startled. "What? The ship wouldn't have a crew or colonists during transit?" It wasn't a problem that he'd devoted any time to thinking about before.

"Not unless the technical issues about sustaining a human population in space for centuries at a time could be solved, Captain. The extreme risks that any malfunction or damage could prove fatal to a living colony in transit are drastically higher than merely transporting the raw genetic material and incubating them into children that the ship's AI can educate after the arrival. Logically, a small preselected number would also be born and raised prior to arrival who could serve as the overseers of the colonization prior to the ship's arrival at their destination. That would maximize both the abilities of a small human crew and the AI for the most optimum chance of success."

After the AI finished, they all looked at each other for a few moments before Ronin spoke.

"All right. Working theory at the moment is we're approaching a lost human colony from a generation ship instead of Forrestal, Celestra or Solara, but we keep our eyes peeled for a gate in case this turns out to be one of those three instead. LeCroy, I want to see your plan to neutralize their satellite network, weapons or otherwise, as soon as you're done with it. CAG, when your Bulldog crews arrive back at the nest, make sure they're rested and ready for some more stealth work when *Cerberus* arrives in system. Also, make sure your Tomcat pilots know the tactical situation before we jump in so they're prepared for what we might face." Ronin paused as he looked at each of them. "Anything else?" he asked.

There wasn't, so they stood and split up in different directions to make it happen.

CHAPTER 13

PHANTOM CONTACT

Abernathy was busy pretending to be busy. In reality, she was watching the video feed from the satellites trained on the action in the Borderlands, so she just projected the appearance of being busy to discourage anyone from interrupting.

"Any change in the action?" Kutsler asked as he leaned over to see the video on Louise's screen. Kutsler wasn't fooled by Abernathy, but he certainly wouldn't spill the beans on her either.

"No. Just a lot of fire and smoke obscuring the picture. Infrared just shows a lot of hotspots," Louise replied glumly. She was still horrified at watching her Class take a beating.

Someday we'll be able to fight back. We won't have to take it anymore, she vowed under her breath so she wouldn't get into trouble for such seditious talk. She always got moodier when the Cargo were on the receiving end of a beat-down to put them in their place.

A light began flashing on Kutsler's screen, accompanied by a soft beeping. "Proximity alarm," Ryan muttered as he brought up the alarm report on his screen.

Louise glanced over as Ryan began reading the report. Proximity alarms weren't unheard of so they didn't see much reason to get excited.

"Optical cameras reporting possible intermittent contact in high orbit," Ryan noted, with rising interest in his voice. "It's not on a collision course with The Ark or any satellites. It's really strange. We can't seem to get a radar lock on it or get an image of it," he muttered.

While Louise fiddled with the cameras for the planet's satellite net to try to get a view of the unidentified flying object, Seaver had taken up a position standing behind them. "Any luck, Kutsler?" he asked as Louise brought more cameras on line and Ryan tried to get a better radar lock.

"Negative. The cameras just can't seem to find it and the radar keeps ghosting in and out, Admiral," Ryan responded. Several more minutes passed before the system's alarm suddenly stopped.

"Admiral, the contact is gone," Ryan said as he looked up at Seaver.

"Nonsense! Rocks in space just don't disappear. We should be able to track along its predicted trajectory," Seaver responded, annoyed that they had lost the track. Losing a possible meteorite wouldn't look good on his reports if it ended up damaging something.

"Radar lost it entirely, sir. Our systems tried scanning all along every projected trajectory," Ryan responded a little defensively.

"Are you sure it wasn't from user error..." Seaver began saying when Louise interrupted him.

"Admiral, look at this!" she said.

Wallace was about to dress down the impertinent Cargo girl for daring to interrupt an Officer when he noticed the screen she hadn't taken her eyes from.

Forgetting to give Abernathy the admonishment she earned for interrupting him, Seaver simply stared at a computer-enhanced partial image. Whatever it was, it was pitch black. The image also showed something that was much more important.

It had straight, uniform edges. The kind of edges that do not occur naturally.

Nearly a minute passed while the three of them stared at the image.

"Kutsler. What does our computer think about the possibility that this is a remnant of the original colonization of Terra Station?" Seaver asked.

The answer came swiftly. "Admiral, the system says it is 65 percent sure that matches no known configuration of any equipment on The Ark's manifest."

Seaver looked at Ryan, confused. "Why only 65 percent?"

Ryan was ready with the answer. "There isn't enough of the object in the picture to be surer than that, sir."

Seaver nodded. "Alright. Send this picture and a quick report to my desk. I'll submit it upstairs and we can let the big brains think about it for a while."

Ryan nodded and a few seconds later, it was on its way.

As Seaver sat back down at his desk overlooking the space control center, his mind was puzzling what they'd seen while he wondered what to write in his report. *What WAS that, if not some old junk from the colonization nearly four centuries ago?* he asked himself. It was clearly not just a piece of rock.

CHAPTER 14

BULLDOG 3

"Think they finally saw us?" Jonsey asked as he stretched. In the small cabin of their Bulldog, his exceptionally deep voice tended to be a bit booming.

"You tell me, buddy. I'm just a dumb bus driver," Russo replied, sounding a bit bored. "You're the one with all the pretty toys and gadgets back there."

Jonsey grinned broadly, his white teeth contrasting to his nearly coal black skin as he reached out to adjust something on his board. "AI says they're finally picking up what they think is an unidentified, intermittent contact. Our drones are reporting that the nearest satellites are now pointing their optics and radar towards our position."

"Geez. About time they finally noticed someone was lurking out here. We practically had to put on a fireworks display before we finally got their attention," Russo quipped.

Jonsey made a few more scans and readings. "We're done here. Our drone net is in place, and we distracted them from whatever action they were taking down on the surface. Time to jump back."

Russo nodded, and jumped the Bulldog back to *Cerberus*.

CHAPTER 15

SPACE CONTROL CENTER

"**A**dmiral, this is Abernathy at the Orbital Optics Desk. We're picking up another intermittent signal."

Seaver immediately sprang up and walked quickly to where the Cargo girl was busy trying to get a clearer picture of the new possible contact. Seaver had spent the last few hours wondering what that last contact had been. He had come up with several possible answers, but that's all.

"Is it a meteor shower or something?" Seaver asked as he arrived. He wanted to eliminate any mundane explanations from his list of possible answers.

"Negative, Admiral. And it just appeared, as if from nowhere," she replied without looking away from the video feed of Satellite 27, which she had oriented towards the contact.

They both watched the feed closely. "There's something there, all right," muttered Seaver as he realized that scanning for the stars that were blotted out made it easier to track the otherwise unseen object.

Suddenly, there was no there, there. Literally. Without warning, the inky blackness was filled with visible stars again.

"What happened?" Seaver asked.

"Just like that last time," Abernathy said. "Suddenly, whatever we're tracking just vanishes. It doesn't make sense, Admiral."

Just as Seaver was going to take out his annoyance on Abernathy for being unable to do her job, Kutsler's board lit up. "Contact! Multiple contacts this time!" he nearly yelled.

"How many?" Seaver asked.

"Four," Kutsler responded. "All CBDR, constant bearings and decreasing range." He rapidly entered commands on his board before he looked up and froze as the optical report updated itself to show the object trajectories had now suddenly changed.

"Admiral, all four contacts are changing their headings. And they're slowing down."

CHAPTER 16

CERBERUS

The situation report was informative. "Captain Ronin, the data collected by the Bulldogs and the drone 'net now positioned around the planet is extensive. The locals call the planet Terra Station. Its society appears to be structured into three classes: The Officer elites, the middle class Crew, and the lowest class called the Cargo. The Cargo Class appears to function as serfs with few rights, while the Officers can do what they like within few boundaries.

"The data taps on the massive ship in orbit reveal it is called The Ark. It is a sub-light Generation ship that arrived in orbit 402 Earth-years ago. The Ark's voyage began approximately 175 years prior to the discovery of the Jump Gate in our solar system; however, the uncertainty in precisely dating the departure date relative to the discovery of the Jump Gates is due to the lack of records surviving The Fall. The ship was launched by Interstellar Colony Corporation, which was based in the old United States. We have no records of such an entity in our limited databases.

"The Ark is unarmed and our sensors estimate its age as exceeding 900 years. Cargo Class persons were transported as raw genetic material who were birthed in the millions after arrival and terraforming of the planet. The Ark's logs reveal there was a mutiny by the Crew Class, who were small in number and in hibernation. The Crew Class was awakened ten years prior to arrival at Terra Station. The leaders of the mutiny became the Officer Class, while the remainder became the Crew Class.

Ronin looked around at the faces gathered in the main conference room. The ship's top officers were listening intently to the AI report while watching various holo images that were projected over the center of the table and corresponded to the subjects of the report.

The AI continued its report. "While arrival at Terra Station was just over 400 years ago, terraforming took over a century. Actual settlement began before the completion of terraforming and the remains of the environment domes can be seen around what was once the outskirts of the capital, which is named 'First City.' Due to the millions of Cargo Class who were birthed, the planetary population quickly exceeded 500 million, although there is civil unrest due to the inequitable rights of the Cargo Class citizens. Because of the unrest, most of the planet's lightly armed military is focused on quelling the Cargo."

Ronin again looked around after the AI finished the report. "I want your departments to map out how that impacts the First Contact protocols cooked up by the Fleet. CAG, I especially want to see both a defensive posture for the protection of *Cerberus*, coupled with a first strike capability. The iron fist in a velvet glove approach. Reports to my desk in six hours. Questions?"

There were none at the moment.

"All right, dismissed."

The conference room quickly emptied. As Ronin and Mueller walked back to the bridge, they talked about what they had just watched.

"I'm pretty sure the anthropologists back at Fleet headquarters didn't predict a scenario like this one," Mueller said. "They've been focused on finding colonies from a later era, with more of a historical record connecting them to Earth."

Ronin nodded thoughtfully. "Weirdly, this colony may have both a closer and more mythologized connection to pre-Fall Earth at the same time."

Mueller raised an eyebrow as they both came to a stop, prompting Ronin to finish his thought.

"Closer, because for them less time has seemed to elapse since the colony has only existed for less than half as long as the colonies we thought we were looking for. But since the mutineers selected what bits of historical records to pass along to the newborn colonists, that lack of context mixed with whatever stories they cooked up also made Earth more of a myth than had ever been a reality."

Now it was Mueller's turn to nod thoughtfully. "I hadn't thought of it that way. The much earlier time in which The Ark's voyage began tends to make you think the colony is likewise much older, when for them it's much younger instead. Another variable to keep in mind, Dan, is we don't know how advanced their technology is. Some of it could be more advanced than our own."

"Thanks to The Fall, yes. There is no way for us to definitively know where we are at in relation to each other until after we make contact." As Ronin finished saying this, they continued to the bridge.

CHAPTER 17

SPACE CONTROL CENTER

"**S**lowing down?" Seaver asked loudly as he loomed over Kutsler's seat at the Orbital Weapons desk. *The implications of THAT were stunning.*

Kutsler and Seaver looked at each other for a few moments with fear in their eyes. Abernathy turned her head and watched the two of them.

Seaver grabbed his phone and called Esmeralda Centon. "Get Central Military Command on the line," he commanded when she answered on the first ring. Centon connected him immediately.

Seaver listened intently as the phone rang several times before someone answered. "Dispatch, Lieutenant Cavanaugh speaking. How can I help you?"

Seaver grimaced at the young voice of an Officer Class person actually answering the phone like some sort of lower class flunky, but Centon must have bypassed lesser functionaries and connected directly to his office.

"This is Admiral Wallace Seaver at the Space Control Center. I need to speak to Secretary Ellis, immediately."

"I'm sorry, Admiral. The Secretary is indisposed and requested not to be disturbed," came the prompt response.

"Then *disturb* him!" roared Seaver into the phone, causing every head in the control center to suddenly turn and look at him with wide eyes. "This is a Priority One Communication."

The anger in Seaver's voice and identification of the priority level caused Cavanaugh to stutter a bit in his response. "Uh, yes, Admiral. Right away. Please hold."

Wallace didn't have to wait long. Soon he heard the annoyed voice of Secretary Stanton Ellis.

"Wallace, this better be important, like a 'message from earth' or something."

"It just might be, Mr. Secretary. We're attempting to track four unidentified objects in orbit. Mr. Secretary, these objects have altered their headings and speed. So far we are unable to get an accurate fix on them or train optical satellites on them. It's like they're ghosts."

There was dead silence for a few moments, before Ellis responded. "I'll scramble some reconnaissance planes so we can get a better look at them. Coordinate your efforts with a liaison who will contact you shortly. "

"Understood, Mr. Secretary."

CHAPTER 18

BULLDOG 3

"**S**canners showing aircraft inbound, this position," Jonsey reported intently. "They appear to be capable of reaching orbital altitudes."

Russo nodded silently. His finger remained poised above the button to jump the assault shuttle away at the first sign of trouble.

"OK, range is 30 miles. Presumably they have radios capable of working at that distance. Initiating communications, now." Jonsey announced as he entered the commands on his board.

* * *

"*Eagle One, Eagle Two.* The UFOs still don't appear on my radar," said Air Sergeant Jeremiah Baker from the cockpit of *Eagle Two* as he held position off the starboard wing of *Eagle One.*

"*Eagle Two,* that's affirm," responded Air Sergeant David Hoffman. "We might have to get close enough for a visual sighting with our Mark Ones."

Hoffman knew Baker would understand his tongue-in-cheek reference to using their eyeballs. "We should be close enough to see something by now. *Eagle Two,* do you..." Hoffman started to say when a new voice overrode the channel.

"Attention Terra Station reconnaissance ships. Attention Terra Station reconnaissance ships. Are you receiving this message?"

Hoffman and Baker both turned to look at each other in surprise from their respective cockpits. The unidentified voice spoke with a strange sounding accent.

"This is Air Sergeant David Hoffman of Eagle Flight. Identify yourself and state why you are on an encrypted military frequency," Hoffman said, stating his reply as a command, not a question.

"This is Flight Officer Michael Jonsey of the Confederate Navy. You are approaching our position."

Hoffman was shocked to be addressed by an Officer in such a disrespectful way over the radio. *And who is the Confederate Navy? This had to be a trick.*

"There is no such thing as the Confederate Navy. Clear the line." As Hoffman ordered Jonsey to abandon the line, both planes cleared the atmosphere and approached the orbital coordinates they had been ordered to investigate.

"Don't believe me? Would you like me to turn on our exterior lights for you?"

The accent in the voice was unlike anything Hoffman or Baker had ever heard.

Hoffman had enough of the games. "Citizen, you are ordered to clear this line and submit yourself to custody of the nearest sheriff's office for prosecution."

The only answer suddenly appeared ahead in the darkness as a previously unseen spacecraft lit up bright searchlights.

As the shocked pilots continued closing on the UFO, the strangely accented voice said, "There ain't too many sheriffs around these here parts, boys."

CHAPTER 19

SPACE CONTROL CENTER

"ETA at the UFO?" Seaver asked in a commanding voice.

Kutsler glanced at the timer on his screen before responding. "Fifty two seconds, Admiral. You want me to push the wireless feed from the planes over the speakers?" Kutsler looked up at Seaver, who was standing over him.

"Do it." The speakers crackled for a moment before the pilot frequency was located.

"Citizen, you are ordered to clear this line and submit yourself to custody of the nearest sheriff's office for prosecution."

Kutsler and Seaver looked at each other with bemused expressions at such an odd expression, but their faces expressed complete shock moments later when they heard the reply, "There ain't too many sheriff's around these here parts, boys."

Just then, both Kutsler and Abernathy's screens revealed an object lighting up in orbit.

"What IS that?" Seaver murmured as all eyes stared at the bright point of light.

"Sir, we still can't get a radar lock on it," Kutsler reported after a swift check of his targeting systems.

Aboard Eagle Flight, the reactions were of similarly shocked silence.

BULLDOG 3

"**I** think you've messed with their heads now, 'flight officer,'" an amused Russo remarked, causing Jonsey to snicker. "Good thing the captain temporarily promoted you just so they would think you're some kind of elite officer citizen."

Jonsey roared with his deep, booming laugh. "Yeah, just remember when we return to *Cerberus* that I'm a Chief, because I still work for a living."

Now Russo burst out into fits of laughter.

Soon the two settled down. They could see their visitors were getting within visual range now. Jonsey decided it was time to transmit since they're getting eyeballed. "Now that you've seen us for yourselves, we would like you to escort us to a landing site on your planet. We have an emissary from our government to Terra Station aboard."

Seconds passed while the pilots of Eagle Flight communicated with their Central Military Command. "Unidentified vessel, you are ordered to follow us. We've been directed to ask who is the emissary and what 'government' do they claim to represent."

"Eagle Flight, the emissary is Ambassador Prisha Gadre. She represents the Confederate States of Earth."

CHAPTER 21

SPACE CONTROL CENTER

"It's got to be some kind of trick. There are no records of a Confederate States of Earth in either the public or encrypted databanks," Kutsler said to Seaver and Abernathy as they discussed the new development.

"There are also no records of independent space flight capability among the Cargo or Crew here on Terra Station, and Officers have shown little interest in space other than mining operations. There are a few large corporations with minor capability, but they're all contractors with the government," Seaver replied. "How soon until their arrival at O'Reilly Airport in First City?"

Kutsler checked his tablet. "Twelve minutes, sir. They're being directed to a secure landing pad on the outskirts where the military can control the situation. The military decided to provide transportation for the emissary to the capital building, since the existence of that ship in orbit gave them pause about dismissing the legitimacy of the claim over the wireless."

Seaver drummed his fingers while he thought for a few moments. "Where are the other three UFOs?" he demanded.

"We lost contact with them at the same time we learned of this ambassador. They just vanished simultaneously from our attempts to track them," Kutsler responded.

Abernathy decided now was an appropriate time to add a small tidbit. "They vanished from all optics that were pointed their way at the same time. One second there they were, and the next they weren't."

Seaver raised an eyebrow as he looked at Abernathy and nodded thoughtfully without commenting for a few moments as he processed what she said.

"I wonder where they went?" he asked.

CHAPTER 22

CERBERUS

"Bulldogs 1, 2 and 5 have returned, Captain. They're lining up to land in the hangar bay now," reported Delacroix as his eyes remained glued to his scanner screens.

"Very well. How long until *Bulldog 3* lands on the planet's surface?" Ronin responded.

"Twelve minutes at current speed and predicted landing site at the civilian airport," LeCroy noted from the tactical station.

Mueller moved to stand next to Ronin at his seat. "How upset will our other ambassadors be to not have been picked first?" she said, with a wry smile tugging the corner of her mouth upwards.

Ronin snorted a soft laugh. "They're going to hate on Gadre for a long time, but they all had a 25 percent chance at being first. It's just by chance that *Bulldog 3* keeps drawing the Luck Card this trip."

"The first ambassador to one of the Lost Colonies, even if it was a colony we didn't know existed. That's definitely a career-making opportunity of a lifetime," Mueller murmured.

Ronin nodded thoughtfully. "Hopefully that colony's societal structure can handle the news. The data our drones and sensors brought us doesn't give me much confidence. That rigidly enforced caste or class system seems to introduce a level of instability that isn't terribly comforting. The violence used to quell the Cargo Class a few hours ago was far above the level of a mere police action."

None of this was new. They'd been devising an approach to the planet's very unique situation for days. The violence against the Cargo Class had prompted Ronin to issue a Go Order earlier than he wanted to, but the officers on *Cerberus* agreed sending the Bulldogs into orbit to attract attention might stop the slaughter on the surface.

"I hope your dress uniform is cleaned and pressed. You just know their 'Officer' class will want to meet the captain of the ship from Earth," Mueller said in her best, fake-sounding sweet voice.

Ronin just rolled his eyes at her and shook his head with a small laugh when his commlink node on his collar chimed. "Ronin here," he said as he activated the node.

"Captain Ronin, this is Dr. Winston Wright. I've just learned the ship is prepared for an armed response if threatened. Was I misinformed?" said the ship's head diplomat.

Ronin and Mueller traded confused looks. Neither of them had worked with a Protocol Officer before, and Ronin had told Mueller about his earlier call from Wright over the size of their assigned work-space. *Cerberus* never needed a diplomatic corps before, and they had since found Wright to be both pompous and prickly.

"Dr. Wright, that is correct. This ship will defend itself if attacked," Ronin replied, remembering to use the man's academic title because he insisted on being called by it for some reason. Ronin reflected on Wright's insistence. *What he fails to realize is that reminding me to use his academic titles and degrees, which mean very little to me, just reinforces my sense of him as unjustifiably conceited about having obtained a piece of paper to hang on a wall somewhere.*

"Captain, I must protest. This is a diplomatic mission. If we approach another sovereign planet like armed warmongers, we will incite violence. You should know better than that. Diplomacy by the experts is called for here," Wright intoned pompously.

Mueller tried her best to stifle a smile as she rolled her eyes. Ronin shook his head slightly as he rubbed his forehead with a pained look on his face.

"Doctor, I don't know if you've noticed but *Cerberus* has guns, lots of guns in fact, because she is a heavily armed warship. Nobody in their right mind would confuse *Cerberus* for anything but a warship," Ronin replied somewhat snarkily despite trying his best to placate the difficult man.

"Captain Ronin, it is my considered conclusion you are causing a war with a peaceful people. I must inform your superiors of my opinion on the matter," Wright replied testily.

Now it was Ronin's turn to roll his eyes. "Well, doctor, seeing as we are eighty-one light years from Earth, I'll worry about the impact of your message in about eight decades or so. Ronin out."

As he closed the commlink, the bridge crew who overheard the conversation shot subtle glances at each other. Threatening to tattle on a famous ship captain and cluelessly trying to tell him how to run his ship during a dangerous deep space mission wasn't the brightest idea.

CHAPTER 23

FIRST CONTACT

Ambassador Prisha Gadre anxiously waited for the Bulldog to land as she felt it decelerate. The butterflies in her stomach were threatening to overwhelm the forced look of calm serenity pasted on her face. *I'm just a 30-year-old anthropologist with some diplomacy training. I'm way too young to be doing this,* she thought, fighting the panic welling up inside.

She tried to distract herself by thinking of her family. Gadre had grown up in a small, close-knit family in New Mumbai, India. *If only my mother could see me now. And to think she was panicking at the mere thought of me boarding* Cerberus *when it was orbiting Earth. Now I'm about to work on establishing diplomatic relations with a Lost Colony that's eighty-one light years away!*

She was jarred from her thoughts by the settling of the Bulldog skids on the tarmac, and sudden decrease in engine noise. Russo turned around and said, "Remember, gravity here is .75 Gs of Earth's. Don't reveal that to them in case you need to use that to your advantage sometime."

Nodding to Russo, Jonsey then turned to Gadre. "Showtime, Ambassador. I'll be right at your side."

They both unbuckled and stood up. "Let's do this," she said.

When Jonsey activated the rear hatch to open, bright sunshine immediately flooded in. Outside Gadre could see a small delegation. Her attention was immediately drawn to the single civilian standing front and center of the gathered group of military officers.

She descended the Bulldog's ramp and walked towards the civilian, Jonsey discretely following a few steps behind her. The civilian was tall, with white hair, and immaculately dressed in what Gadre noted was a business suit that was the fashion on Earth many centuries ago. She had seen attire like that in ancient pictures as she studied for her college anthropology degree. The Fall and the passage of centuries had ended fashions like that.

Gadre stopped a few steps from the civilian. He cleared his throat, and spoke first. "Welcome to Terra Station. Can you understand our language?"

Gadre smiled broadly. "Yes. I speak American. It's my native language."

The gathered officers and the civilian appeared confused.

"I'm sorry, did I say something wrong?" asked Gadre.

The civilian cocked an eyebrow at her and responded, "You called the language 'American,' right? We know the language by the name 'English' here."

Gadre nodded. "A lot has changed, and a long time has passed, since your ancestors left Earth. My name is Prisha Gadre. I am the Confederation ambassador. And you are..."

"Ambassador Gadre, very good to meet you. I am Tobias Wilson, of the Officer Class. I am the Terra Station representative who has been appointed by the other Officers to interact with you. May I ask who your companion is?" he asked, nodding towards Jonsey with a tip of his head.

Jonsey stepped forward. "Flight Officer Michael Jonsey. Pleased to make your acquaintance." Jonsey reached out to shake hands with Tobias without thinking about whether the protocol existed on this planet.

Both eyebrows shooting up at the unusual gesture for polite society on this planet, Tobias nonetheless had the refined manners to shake the hand of the hulking flight officer. "A pleasure to meet you, Flight Officer Jonsey. If I may, perhaps we could retire to more comfortable surroundings than this hot cement tarmac? We have transportation waiting," Tobias said, gesturing to a wheeled ground vehicle that was waiting with several other vehicles behind the delegation.

Both Gadre and Jonsey nodded and followed Tobias and the others. It did not escape the attention of the military officers in the delegation that the rear hatch on the Bulldog had closed and locked itself behind them.

Gadre and Jonsey were seated in the rear of a large black vehicle facing Tobias. Tobias pressed a button to close the privacy window separating the passengers from the driver, and the driver began to accelerate towards the road. "May I inquire from where you are from? We have no database records of a ship like yours, or of a Confederate Navy."

With a glance at Jonsey, Gadre figured she would just tell him. "We're both from Earth. I was born and raised in New Mumbai, India. Flight Officer Jonsey was born and raised in Yazoo City, Mississippi."

Jonsey nodded slightly to acknowledge the statement.

"We have so many questions, it's hard to decide where to begin. I think perhaps our society's top question is, Why did it take so long for Earth to follow The Ark ship to Terra Station? Our ancient records have references to planned follow up missions by Interstellar Colony Corporation. We've heard nothing since long before Landing Day."

Gadre presumed everything she and Jonsey said and did was being recorded, and her answer to this particular question had been pre-approved by Captain Ronin before they departed from *Cerberus*. "Mr. Wilson, sometime after your colony mission departed, humanity on Earth was nearly ended by the biological and nuclear warfare we now call The Fall. It was started by the deliberate release of an engineered virus, which lead to a nuclear response. As civilization was collapsing, the combatants ended the hostilities by signing the Treaty of Midway in an attempt to save our race from extinction. They were nearly too late, and most places on the planet returned to barbarism save for a few small cities which survived relatively intact. Those cities retained much of our technology and led our people to re-establish of a new civilization much faster than it would have taken otherwise."

Tobias looked quite stunned at this unexpected history lesson, but recovered his composure quickly. "Please, Ambassador, call me Tobias. I think we should move to a first name basis as I expect us to have many informal discussions in the near future."

Gadre nodded. "Agreed. Please call us me Prisha. May I ask where we are going?"

Tobias quickly replied. "Oh! My apologies. We are heading to the planetary Space Control Center. We didn't have a first contact protocol to fall back on since so many years elapsed with nothing from Earth, or anywhere else I might add, that I'm afraid we did not know where to take you. Smarter folks came up with this destination as it is equipped with any advanced capabilities we may need, and there is a resort and spa very near to it for your lodging." Tobias didn't add that both the Space Control Center and the resort also happened to be secure facilities for the Officer Class where the military would be able to control whether anyone would be able to access the two of them.

The trip to the Space Control Center was short because it was, naturally enough, in close proximity to the airport and could serve as an emergency air traffic control center during an emergency. As they pulled up to the front entrance of the main building, Gadre could see a larger delegation of mixed civilian and military awaiting their arrival.

"Don't worry about trying to remember everyone's names at first. It's going to be a bit overwhelming, I should expect."

Tobias was trying to be kind, but Gadre thought he sounded a bit snobbish. *He doesn't appear to be aware that we have a printed bio computer embedded in our skin. Jonsey and I will have perfect recall of every face, name, and thing we see or hear because of it,* Gadre thought as she decided keeping that little fact a secret was prudent, as Captain Ronin had suggested to her earlier. Instead, they merely nodded their thanks.

As their vehicle pulled to a stop and the doors opened for them, the delegates more or less arranged themselves into a rough approximation of a receiving line. Tobias raised his hands to command everyone's attention.

"Everyone, your attention, please. I'd like to introduce our guests from Earth. Ambassador Prisha Gadre and Flight Officer Michael Jonsey. They speak English as their native language; however, the name of the language on Earth has evolved from English to American, due to significant events on Earth that occurred after our ancestors' departure.

"Please introduce yourselves as they make their way into the building. We can all gather in the main conference room for food and refreshments while we get acquainted. As everyone here can well imagine, we have a lot of catching up to do!"

Tobias then turned his head to Gadre and Jonsey while gesturing with a sweep of his hand towards the entrance with a dramatic flair. "Madam Ambassador. Flight Officer Jonsey. If you would be so kind. After you!"

Navigating the short distance to the front door to the delegates was supposed to be relatively quick. It wasn't. It took forty minutes because everyone wanted a chance to meet and speak with the folks who seemed to have sprung from the old legends about the mother planet. Tobias kept his impatience in check while deftly keeping them moving after a short time with each person.

Finally, they were in the building, so the crowd migrated to the large conference room. The noise immediately filled the room as the attendees carried on small conversations while they picked over the tables overflowing with hors d'oeuvres. Gadre and Jonsey shared a quick glance, wondering whether they should join the food line.

As soon as the smell of coffee, real coffee, hit them, they left behind their inhibitions and joined the line. While they were eyeing the pastries, Gadre quietly asked Tobias, "The colonists brought coffee plant seeds along with them?"

Tobias nodded. "They did indeed! It's one of the plants that grew best in the soil and climate of this planet's equatorial band. I hope you'll find everything to your liking."

They certainly did. It was all delicious.

After the guests and dignitaries had seated themselves at the front table, Tobias stood and approached the podium. The noise level dropped to nothing and all eyes turned towards him. "I'd like to welcome you all to the control center conference room, and extend a special welcome to our guests of honor.

"For centuries, Terra Station has awaited the next contact from our motherland, Earth, and the follow-up missions from the Interstellar Colony Corporation. And no one came. From our short conversation in the car on the drive here, now we know the reason why. War. War on Earth. A war so terrible, it is simply called The Fall.

"The Fall almost completely destroyed the planet's civilization, and nearly wiped out humanity on Earth. But our race survived and rebuilt. Now they have returned, and sought out their children here on Terra Station."

Tobias looked over the assembled faces for a few moments after he said that before continuing. "Thank you for indulging me for a few moments. And now I would invite Ambassador Gadre to share a few comments." Tobias slightly turned to Gadre and gestured to her as he said this.

Gadre stood and joined Tobias, shaking hands with him before he returned to his empty seat next to Gadre's. "Thank you for the warm welcome, Tobias. Earth suffered terribly due to The Fall. Most of our historical records were lost. All the governments collapsed due to damage from biological weapons, or from nuclear weapons. Oftentimes, from both. The major cities of the planet were lost, and our race struggled to survive. Disease, nuclear winter, starvation, and pestilence were the tools of The Reaper. But all was not lost. A few smaller cities survived. They retained much of our technology. These cities eventually brought our people back from the brink.

"Once it took root, the new civilization on Earth spread quickly and banished barbarism once again. This was humanity's chance to begin anew, and leave behind the sins of our past. Sins like slavery, dividing our peoples by race and economic class and pitting them against one another regardless whether the intent for doing so sounded pure, and so on." Gadre paused to take a sip of water before continuing.

"Ours is a hybrid form of Confederation, but each member state is a signatory to a federal set of universal human rights and commerce between them. All people are created equal, and enjoy the same rights as one another. All are free to enjoy the fruits of their own labors. To live according to their drive and abilities. All contribute to the common good, but only in equal shares to one another. No one person is taxed at a higher rate than any other because to do so is inequitable and leads to abuse. No preferential treatment is given in the legal system. Just as all have equal rights, all must have equal duties and responsibilities or society slowly becomes unbalanced."

As she spoke about the human rights of the Confederacy, Gadre observed the faces in the assembled representatives. Most had pasted on a noncommittal game face, but a few appeared shocked. *The Captain's prediction was right, these are all Officer Class. Our concept of equality and rights is completely foreign to an elitist caste like the Officers.*

CHAPTER 24

SPACE CONTROL CENTER

veryone is equal? Is this true? How can that be? Louise wondered. She was shocked as she and Ryan watched the proceedings. Louise had hacked into the security system so they could witness the historic event.

"Louise, is this being broadcast to the public?" Ryan whispered. She shook her head.

"No, it's a closed circuit. I'm recording it, though."

Ryan's eyes opened wide as he looked at her.

"If they catch us with that, the Officers will send us both to jail or worse," Ryan replied.

"I've used as many anonymizers and firewalls as I could, but this is too important to let the Officers keep it from everyone else!" Louise whispered uneasily.

They kept watching.

CHAPTER 25

CONFERENCE ROOM, SPACE CONTROL CENTER

"Ambassador Gadre, we understand your ship is just a shuttle as were the other radar contacts. Can you tell me where the main ship is?" Tobias asked at the beginning of the question and answer segment. It was a top-priority question of utmost importance to the government of Terra Station.

"Yes and no. Our ship is called *Cerberus*. After our shuttles launched, *Cerberus* moved to an undisclosed location for mission security reasons. At this point, I just know the ship is somewhere in a very big solar system."

The next question came from a military person in the main audience. Judging from the amount of braid and ribbons, Jonsey figured the guy was pretty high ranking.

"Madam Ambassador, is the purpose of your mission to establish diplomatic relations with Terra Station?" The speaker remained standing after asking the question.

Gadre shook her head. "No, sir, not specifically. Our mission is to investigate and seek out the Lost Colonies. Legend says they were on the other end of a Jump Gate that may have led to the Baidam Constellation. Your star, Megrez, was the center of the constellation and is the closest to Earth. So Megrez was our first stop."

Gadre's reply clearly created more questions, and the high ranker used his prerogative to ask some follow-up questions.

"Madam Ambassador, how many Lost Colonies are there? Our records indicate our Colony mission was preceded by no others."

Gadre could only nod slightly. "My apologies, but I need to level set expectations here. We were looking for the colonies of Forrestal, Celestra, and Solara. The surviving records on Earth made no mention of any past missions to Megrez. We didn't know you were here."

That answer caused a ripple of low murmuring from everyone. All their lives they had lived with the belief that someday, Earth would come looking for them. Instead, they had been forgotten. Lost in both time and, unlike those other colonies, also lost to memory.

"Ambassador Gadre, forgive me for interrupting, but this is all quite difficult to wrap our heads around. May I ask you what is a *jump gate*? I've never heard the term before." Tobias asked the question partly to get her to elicit more information, and partly to regain control of the proceedings and keep them moving along.

"Jump gate spaceflight came into existence after your colony mission departed Earth. We're not sure how long after. The other colonies were already habitable planets. The theory among the scientists aboard *Cerberus* is their discovery may have initially disrupted Interstellar Colony Corporation's intent to follow up with more long-range missions to Megrez for several decades because suddenly there were three habitable planets that could be reached in mere months instead of centuries like it took The Ark to traverse the distance to Megrez.

"To use an analogy, the accessibility of those worlds took up all the oxygen in the room. And then The Fall happened." Gadre sidestepped mentioning that Jump Gates and related technology were lost to history. *We don't even know if the gates were a natural phenomenon, or how to find one if any exist. Or even really what they actually were other than a shortcut to another location. But I can't let on for strategic reasons that* Cerberus *has a FTL jump drive, just in case things go poorly on Terra Station,* Gadre reminded herself.

Tobias and the officer who asked the questions shared a brief, knowing glance as Gadre spoke. There was still time. Due to sheer distance, Tobias felt certain Earth wasn't aware that Terra Station existed because *Cerberus* likely was far outside of the ship's communication range. Tobias tilted his head down towards the high ranker, who was a general. The general took the hint to continue the line of questioning.

"Madam Ambassador. If I may, I will ask for the staff to activate the screen on the wall behind you for a moment. You mentioned Megrez is the closest star in the Baidam Constellation and it is in the center of the constellation. I'd like to show you a historical picture of the constellation as taken by The Ark when it was en route to Megrez. Our ancient records from Earth called this constellation the Big Dipper."

The wall screen lit up with a picture of the Big Dipper.

Gadre and Jonsey looked at the screen. "Yes, ma'am. That's the Baidam Constellation alright," Jonsey murmured.

She looked back at the general. "The 'Big Dipper, you say? It appears the name of the constellation has changed over time."

CHAPTER 26

BULLDOG 3

usso sat at Jonsey's station monitoring the situation outside as he listened to the proceedings. They were being transmitted by the secret commlink that had been bio-imprinted under Jonsey's skin for this mission.

"I wish you were here, big fella," he murmured to his rearseater Jonsey, as he trained the optics on the team of soldiers who were outside. *What are you boys up to?* he asked himself.

They were busy erecting some sort of machine.

CHAPTER 27

RESORT

After a long, exhausting day, Tobias escorted Gadre and Jonsey to their rooms at the nearby resort. The two had no trouble hiding their surprise over how plush their rooms were.

"Big day tomorrow, Prisha," said Tobias after he showed Gadre around. "As you can imagine, we are quite excited for the arrival of your ship. This will be the biggest day on this planet since Landing Day!"

Gadre nodded tiredly. "Thank you for all your able assistance today, Tobias. I'm so glad everyone was so understanding about why we didn't just bring *Cerberus* into orbit unannounced instead of sending us first. We could only imagine the alarm that would have caused!"

It was Tobias' turn to nod. "Yes, it certainly would. That was prudent thinking to give our people time to get used to the idea we aren't alone any longer."

He moved toward the exit and turned to speak after opening the door. "It was a long day for all of us, and I should imagine tomorrow will likewise be rather long. Is an 8 a.m. breakfast agreeable to you? I'll be along to collect you and Flight Officer Jonsey shortly before then."

Gadre simply said, "Yes, that works well for us. Thank you, Tobias."

After Tobias shut the door behind him, Gadre looked around slowly, using her eyes more than anything else.

Captain Ronin said to assume we are under constant surveillance, even here in our lodging chambers. She walked to the large window on the far side of her suite and pushed the heavy drapes aside to reveal a spectacular view of the lake situated between her room at the top of the resort tower and the space control center. *I wonder why we really haven't met any of the colony's civilian leaders yet?*

* * *

Standing at the window in his suite, Jonsey was taking in the same view as Gadre. *Easily defendable location, no unauthorized access in or out. They've got us corralled up here in what amounts to a plush prison,* he thought as his eyes took in the vista. *If there's any shooting, we're sitting ducks,* he noted sourly.

With nothing else to do at the moment, Jonsey decided to get some rack time. *Ain't no good if I'm too tired to think straight. Just got to trust the plan, and hope Captain Ronin was right. And keep quiet, because someone's listening.*

CHAPTER 28

SPACE CONTROL CENTER

Tobias returned to the conference room of the space control center. He had been summoned there after delivering their new guests to their rooms at the resort.

"Tobias, I won't keep you as we're all tired and tomorrow won't be easy. I wanted to make sure we're on the same page about the threat *Cerberus* poses to our people's way of life, though," stated Secretary Ellis.

Tobias nodded. "Yes, Mr. Secretary. I understand the threat. Are our military assets positioned to deal with the ship when it arrives, or has the plan changed since last I was brought up to speed?"

Ellis looked at Tobias for a few moments before responding. "Yes. The Council has decided to eliminate *Cerberus* when it appears in orbit. The Confederation's ideals represent an existential threat to our civilization and, since Earth in all likelihood does not know we're here, we can keep it that way by shooting *Cerberus* down from orbit."

Tobias stared off into the distance, not registering what he was looking at. He suddenly thought of something that could be important. "The ambassador has not said what drive technology the ship uses. We've subtly tried to pull it out of her or Flight Officer Jonsey, who accompanied her to the surface. Neither has provided any clues."

Ellis nodded now. "It's an important point. The Council feels the ship travels quickly due to these 'jump gates' that were mentioned as gateways to the other Lost Colonies. Some hints the ambassador dropped suggests the gates must be located outside the gravity well of a planet. If *Cerberus* is in orbit around Terra Station, she won't be able to escape.

Ideally we would like to disable the ship and acquire the jump gate drives for our own uses, but at a minimum we will have to destroy the ship if we cannot disable her."

"Do I keep the conference going until *Cerberus* arrives? We don't know precisely when that is yet," Tobias asked.

"Yes. And you might not even be aware whether that hostilities have commenced for some time," Ellis noted darkly. "Just keep up the charade until you do."

CHAPTER 29

CERBERUS

"Captain, burst message traffic from Chief Jonsey ... I mean Flight Officer Jonsey. Sorry Captain, I keep forgetting the new ranks you made up for the Bulldog rearseaters on this mission," said Lt. Maria Delgado from her communications station on the bridge.

Ronin glanced over at her. "You're not the only one, Delgado. This is the first time I can recall where we ever needed to make up a new rank to help accomplish mission priorities. What's Jonsey have to say?"

"Message says code word Kursk, Captain." Delgado looked at Ronin with a raised eyebrow as she said this.

Ronin's eyebrows shot up and his snapped his head around to look at Cmdr. Diane Mueller, who was already looking at him with the same questioning expression on her face.

Before the Bulldogs deployed to Terra Station, Dan created a list of code words for the burst message commlinks when the flight crews would report in. The code word, Kursk, named after the enemy ship Kursk that *Cerberus* ambushed and captured during the war, meant to expect a possibly hostile reception or an ambush.

"Lieutenant Delacroix, are you tracking any more launches from the surface?" Dan asked, glancing over at the sensor station.

"No, sir. Still over 100 satellites and other things that were launched several hours ago. Since then, our drone net hasn't reported any new contacts," Delacroix replied. "Lieutenant LeCroy has them all plotted into Tacnet and the skies are otherwise clear."

Mueller had walked over to stand next to Ronin's command chair so they could confer quietly.

"War fighting assets being pre-positioned. Our Bulldog is surrounded, and our delegates have been sequestered in a secure location. Diane, do you agree this fits the potentially hostile situational profile?" Dan asked.

"Yessir. I don't see how it doesn't. Jonsey's latest report with the code word for the situation only confirms my thoughts about it. We jump into orbit, and we're jumping into what surely looks to be a trap," Diane said quietly.

"My thoughts, exactly," Dan replied. "So, I'm thinking we do the expected thing and spring their trap. But we do it in a way they can't anticipate."

Dan had Diane's complete attention now.

"Do we? What are you thinking?" she asked.

"Have you heard of a Trojan Horse?" Dan asked.

CHAPTER 30

SPACE CONTROL CENTER

"How long have they been conferencing?" asked Ryan quietly when he returned to his station.

Louise glanced over at him. "Hours. They started this morning right after breakfast," she whispered. "I don't like having those military policemen stationed here now." She lifted her chin and pointed to where the MPs had been standing guard inside the control center since yesterday.

Ryan's eyes traveled to where the MPs had posted themselves. "They're Officers, not just some traffic cops. That must mean something's up for them to be here."

Louise just nodded slightly without taking her eyes off her screen. "They can't see my screen from where they're standing so I'm still letting my system record what's going on in the conference room," she whispered so softly that Ryan had to strain to hear her. Ryan let a mere nod suffice as his reply.

Both of them were wearing the same clothes they wore the day before. "I really wish they would have allowed us to go home," Louise muttered under her breath.

Ryan whispered back, "No way would they allow a potential security breach by letting us go home. We're trapped here for the duration."

Several minutes later, Admiral Seaver approached their desks. "Abernathy, keep your systems scanning for any new objects in orbit. We're expecting the delegate's ship to arrive sometime today."

Louise just looked at Seaver before replying, "Yes sir." She hid her irritation well and Seaver moved on. *First you don't allow me to go home, or a fresh change of clothes. Now you're telling me how to do a job you don't know how to do yourself,* she thought, shaking her head and keeping her gripes to herself.

After Seaver returned to his office for a few moments, Louise subtly glanced around to see if anyone was watching. Everyone was busy. She decided now was the time to get the truth out. She pressed a few buttons and called up a small terminal window on her screen so she could bypass the operating system and access the server directly.

With another subtle glance around to confirm no one was paying attention, Louise entered a short series of commands and a password that had been prearranged for her. Machine coding quickly scrolled through that window, and Louise closed the window a few seconds later.

"What did you just do?" whispered Ryan. Louise thought he hadn't seen it.

"Nothing. Just running a scan through the terminal instead of the graphics interface because it's quicker," Louise lied. *No sense implicating Ryan if I'm found out,* she thought.

She watched the tiny completion bar on her screen for a few moments before it, too, disappeared when the transmission was complete. Louise risked another subtle glance around. No one was paying attention to her.

Done! Now the Cargo Class has a copy of the complete video from yesterday. The Officers won't be able to control the information about Earth and the freedoms they have there. Louise was sure that video would create a stir within the ranks of the Cargo population.

Louise returned to her tasks of adjusting the orbital scanning for the ship, although her mind wandered. *What was the name of that ship again? Cerberus, I think the ambassador called it. Seems odd for the ship of a diplomatic envoy to be named after the mythical hound who guards the underworld with three heads representing the past, present and future.*

The orbital scans continued to show clear skies.

CHAPTER 31

CERBERUS

"Dad, why was school canceled today?" Edward asked sleepily as he wandered out of his small bedroom into the family quarter's common area. Dan looked up, steaming coffee mug halfway to his lips.

"Well, I suppose I can spill the beans as the secret won't be a secret in a few hours. Remember I told you we found an interesting planet to investigate?" Dan said, setting the mug down on the small table.

Edward nodded as he curled up next to Dan on the couch. Dan smiled at the sight of his son's messy bed head and wrapped his arm around the little guy.

"It turns out to be a Lost Colony of Earth, but it was more lost than we anticipated on this mission," Dan began to explain, when he saw Edward forming one of those confused, 'my parent has lost his marbles' expressions that parents have seen on their children's faces since parents first began having children long ago.

"Dad, that doesn't make sense!" Edward exclaimed, waking up more as he said it.

"Let me finish! It's a colony that predates discovery of the legendary jump gates. Their ancestors arrived from Earth hundreds of years ago in a sub-light generation ship. All records of this colony mission were lost in The Fall, so the Confederation on Earth didn't know the colony was here. Today we're going to orbit the planet and try to establish a relationship with the colony." As he said this, Dan grabbed his mug for another sip.

"So school was canceled just for that? Or is there something else causing school to be canceled? School is only canceled when families need to stay in their quarters, like during a battle or something," Edward asked, looking up at his father.

Impressed with his son's deductive reasoning, Dan decided to be blunt with him. "Something happened during the colonization which created an unjust and unstable society. While we have seen unjust and violent societies before, like the Collective, our opinion is this society is relatively unstable and we're not sure if we will receive a hostile reception by the group that controls the planet."

"I hope not," Edward replied before rising to forage for food in the kitchen.

* * *

"How hostile do you think?" Diane asked Karl as they ate breakfast in the small kitchenette in their quarters.

Karl managed to respond in between bites of his bagel. "Our simulations keep calculating the odds of an armed response at greater than 80 percent. If that society down there wasn't ruled by a small, privileged elite class with a history of maintaining its grip on power through the military, those odds drop drastically."

Diane nodded. "That makes sense, both from a historical perspective and a tactical perspective. Every unjust civilization on Earth that we found historical records for eventually collapsed. They all featured a privileged elite who suppressed the other classes with military power or by controlling the political and educational institutions. These elite would eventually forget they needed the support of those non-privileged classes to maintain their society.

"Suppressing the non-privileged and shutting them out from improving their lives also left those classes or castes with little incentive to defend that society or take steps to continue it because only the privileged would benefit. Unjust civilizations would eventually collapse from within unless they were toppled by an outside force first."

Their discussion was interrupted for a few moments by the appearance of Sonya, their daughter, who hugged Karl before crawling up into Diane's lap. As Sonya's head snuggled up under her chin, Diane found herself reminded of why she fights. *My family. My friends. My shipmates. Whatever it takes to protect them*, she thought.

"The captain has taken your team's calculations to heart and he agrees this is a dangerous situation," Diane said as she brushed away a stray strand of Sonya's blonde hair. "We've got a plan to act accordingly."

Karl nodded thoughtfully. "After first contact by our Bulldog shuttles, the planetary military quickly encrypted its communications with an advanced mathematical protocol. My team has been working with the AI to try to crack the code but we haven't had any success yet."

"It's a good thing we scooped up all that data before first contact. It helped us form an overall strategy and game out our tactical responses to different scenarios. There's always the unknown to worry about, but it beats going in blind," Diane responded.

GUESS WHO'S COMING TO VISIT?

Captain Ronin sat in his command chair. The atmosphere on the bridge was expectant as the prime crew had just relieved their backups and started their shifts in anticipation of arriving in orbit around Terra Station.

"Captain, final scans have re-confirmed the furthest extent of the planetary satellite detection net remains unchanged. We can still jump in close without being seen," Lt. Delacroix said from the scanning station.

"Acknowledged. Lieutenant LeCroy?" Ronin said tersely, looking from the scanning station to the tactical station as he did so.

"Known targets plotted in Tacnet. Drone sensor net is in place and data commlinks to Tacnet are operational, Captain," LeCroy responded, looking at Ronin as he said it.

With a nod, Ronin then turned to the weapons station. "Lieutenant Anzio?" he asked.

Anzio was waiting for her turn. "Weapons systems online. Rail gun turrets are pre-positioned for rapid response, and firing solutions have been fed to the targeting systems. Missiles are loaded in their launch tubes."

Ronin thumbed the commlink node on his chair arm. "Lieutenant Sunderland, report status."

Sunderland responded immediately. "Remaining Bulldogs ready for launch. Tomcat pilots are geared up and in the pilot ready room if they're needed."

Ronin nodded, even though the CAG couldn't see it over the commlink. "Launch Bulldogs and advise Lieutenant LeCroy when they're away," he replied to Sunderland.

"Roger that." Sunderland closed the commlink node at his neck by tapping it briefly, and then opened another commlink. "Bulldogs, you are cleared for immediate launch. Good luck and good hunting." Sunderland said, saying the traditional words for pilots being sent into a possibly hostile situation.

After he said this, Sunderland looked up from his spot behind the podium at the head of the ready room and focused his attention on his Tomcat pilots who were in their seats. "The clock is running. The Bulldogs are jumping out to loiter at Epsilon Station in case they're needed. *Cerberus* is jumping in an hour's easy cruise from the planet's orbit. That means we stay ready to man our planes until further notice."

Back on the bridge, Mueller had moved to stand next to Ronin before she spoke. "All stations report ready for action, Captain. The ship is at Alert Two, and the Tomcat pilots are remaining in the ready room as ordered."

More quietly, Mueller then softly said to Ronin so only he could hear, "It feels odd that we're springing a trap on purpose."

Ronin's eyebrows shot up, and he nodded thoughtfully. "It sure does. Step into my parlor, said the spider to the fly," he said as they shared a knowing glance.

"Lieutenant Perez, execute jump," Ronin ordered.

Perez had been waiting for the order. "Roger that, jumping now," he responded to Ronin.

Cerberus jumped from its hiding place in the asteroid belt and reappeared near Terra Station.

"Jump complete, Captain. We're in the planet's solar shadow on the night side," reported Perez.

"Any signs we've been detected?" Mueller asked.

Delacroix already was scanning, looking for any signs they'd been seen. "Negative, Commander. Scopes are clear and no signs of sensors yet."

"All right. Let's get the ship dressed up before we arrive in orbit. Execute image projection," Ronin ordered.

Within a few moments, the dangerous looking, dark black warship hull of *Cerberus* was swiftly transformed into what appeared to be a bright white, much smaller transport vessel.

"Projection complete, Captain. We look like a boxy, bright, white-colored diplomatic ship now," reported LeCroy. "We should trip the planet's sensor net in thirty-five minutes at present speed," he added.

CHAPTER 33

SPACE CONTROL CENTER

"Admiral Seaver, this is Ensign Alvarez in Communications. We've detected an unauthorized transmission originating from the control center operations room."

Wallace looked up from the report he was reading at his desk. Leaning forward in his seat, he asked, "Seaver here. What sort of transmission?"

"Admiral, there's still a copy of it in the communications buffer. It's a video of yesterday's proceedings with the ambassador. It was sent from the Orbital Optics desk after someone hacked our security protocols. The recipient is an unregistered address out in the Borderlands," Alvarez quickly summarized.

His anger quickly threatened to overwhelm him. "Who sent it?" he replied, already entertaining strong suspicions about the answer.

"The logon belongs to a Cargo Class worker named Louise Abernathy," Alvarez said.

"Thank you, Ensign. I'll deal with it on my end. Retain all your records on the transmission until notified otherwise," Seaver ordered.

Seaver sat back in his seat to think it over for a moment. It didn't take him long to decide what to do with a traitorous Cargo servant. He leaned forward and tapped a button to open a new line. "Chief Centon, contact the military police and have several armed soldiers sent to my office immediately."

"Right away, admiral," came her crisp response.

Because they were already providing heightened security due to the arrival of Ambassador Gadre and Flight Officer Jonsey, the MPs (military police) arrived at Seaver's office within minutes.

"Admiral, how may we be of service?" asked the lieutenant in charge of the detachment.

* * *

"Why are there MPs in the admiral's office?" Ryan whispered. He could see them in Seaver's office through the glass wall overlooking the main floor of the control center.

Louise's quickly glanced up towards Seaver's office. *They know!* she thought, watching them look down at where she was seated.

Half keeping an eye on the MPs as they moved towards her seat, Louise's hands quickly opened another terminal and she abandoned all pretense of just doing her job. When the command line appeared in the terminal, Louise typed the secret code words "Gods eye" and pressed "Enter" just as the MPs took up a position surrounding her.

"Louise Abernathy, raise your hands and step away from your station!" announced the lieutenant.

Moving slowly, Louise raised her hands and complied while her eyes watched the terminal window close itself.

As she turned, Admiral Seaver was standing there behind the MPs. He spoke first. "Ms. Abernathy, you're under arrest for treason and espionage."

CHAPTER 34

TERRA STATION ORBIT

"Captain, we are entering orbit. Their satellite net should be alerting the planetary government by now," announced Lt. Delacroix.

"Not much of a planetary sensor net," murmured Mueller to Ronin as she stood next to his command chair.

Ronin shook his head slightly, agreeing with Mueller. "Nope. Pretty weak stuff. Since they haven't had to worry about combat or meaningful traffic in the solar system, the lack of an effective sensor net isn't really surprising. The need just hasn't been there," he replied.

"Captain, we're detecting burst message traffic between their ground control and multiple satellites. It's mostly encrypted, but our AI confirms they've seen us," announced Lieutenant LeCroy, who was monitoring communications as part of his tactical duties for this mission.

"Acknowledged. Lieutenant Perez, keep our jump drive spun up in case things get ugly," Ronin ordered, even keeping the jump drive spun up was part of the mission planning. Ronin wasn't feeling comfortable having every weapon system on an entire planet pointed at his ship.

"Aye aye, Captain," Perez responded.

"Captain, we've detected dozens of targeting systems that have locked onto *Cerberus*. They include both from the satellites and those down on the surface," reported LeCroy excitedly. "Plotting them onto Tacnet as they appear," LeCroy added.

* * *

"No!" screamed Louise as she fought the military police who were trying to get a hold of her.

"Take her! She's just a Cargo servant, don't worry about hurting her," ordered Seaver.

While the MPs struggled to grab Louise, a loud chime suddenly originated from Louise's orbital optics station. "What is it? What did she do?" yelled Seaver over the combined racket of the struggle and the electronic chiming.

Ryan shoved them all aside and leaned over Louise's station before responding. "Admiral, there's a large ship entering orbit!" Ryan's words had the effect of a loud thunderclap in the control center as all eyes turned to look at him and the room fell silent.

"Put it on the main screen. Now!" ordered Seaver.

Ryan pushed a few buttons, and suddenly the room's main screen showed a large, white ship that was generally rectangular and blocky looking. They could clearly see a hanger in the middle of the bottom for docking the smaller ship that brought the ambassador and flight officer down to the surface.

Just then, Chief Esmeralda Centon entered the room. "Admiral, Secretary Ellis is on the line!" she said. Like everyone else in the room, Centon's eyes were riveted to the image on the screen in the front of the room.

Seaver looked at Centon for a moment, then shifted his gaze to the lieutenant commanding the MPs. "Take the Cargo girl away and put her into the brig," he ordered. Looking back at Centon, he said, "Thank you, Chief Centon. Follow me."

"Seaver here," he said as he arrived at his desk. On his screen was a video of Secretary Ellis.

"Seaver, the Council has ordered the planetary defenses to open fire on *Cerberus*. Do you have the Cargo spy in custody?" Ellis asked without preamble.

"Yes, Mr. Secretary. An Ensign in the Communications area reported they detected a transmission from the Orbital Optics desk to an unregistered recipient in the Borderlands. The military police just seized her and are transporting her to the brig per my orders," Wallace replied.

"Admiral, we believe that unauthorized communications leak will create a storm of protests by the Cargo Class. After we polish off *Cerberus*, how soon can your satellites pivot to a support role for our ground units?" Ellis asked while giving Seaver a hard look.

"I estimate between one and two hours, Mr. Secretary. Variables include whether we need satellites to dodge any debris, whether any of them are damaged or destroyed, whether the command and control structure sustains any damage, and so on," Seaver reported quickly.

Ellis nodded. "Understood. That will be satisfactory. Keep your satellites locked on *Cerberus* for now. You won't have to guess when the fireworks start. Ellis out."

CHAPTER 35

THE BRIG

Military police surrounded Louise as they escorted her into the campus building containing the brig. She looked around ruefully as the doors to the secured area started to swing open. *I'll never even get to say goodbye to my folks,* she thought sadly. *Or see Ryan again. I'll just be disappeared like all the others were before me.* The handcuffs behind her back weighed heavily against her wrists.

Just as the metal double doors finished opening, the MP to her right suddenly pushed her down to the ground as he fired his sidearm into the MP on her other side. The pistol roared with a low booming sound, with flame spurting from the barrel.

The unexpected weapon's report deafened Louise and left her momentarily stunned. She heard several more shots from the projectile pistol, and from inside the brig. Just as she started to squirm away, there was an explosion in the brig that seemed to shake the entire building.

"Come on! We've got to get out of here before they have time to regroup," the remaining MP said after he holstered his weapon and began unlocking her handcuffs.

"Uh, whaa!" was about all Louise mustered to say through the fog in her brain from the sudden violence.

The huge MP didn't waste time explaining as he quickly lifted Louise to her feet with a great deal of strength. "You're not the only Cargo Class who infiltrated those bastards. They didn't know there were sleeper agents from the Cargo Class. Follow me if you want to live," he said as he half pulled Louise in the direction he wanted her to go.

She soon shook of the mental fog as they hurried out of the building. "Where to?" Louise asked as they both walked quickly, but not so quickly as to attract undue attention at the same time.

"Motor pool. We have a ride waiting for us there," said the still unnamed MP as he looked around subtly.

"What's your name?" Louise asked as they turned a corner and began heading towards a large building with an assortment of olive green vehicles parked in neat rows next to it.

"No names. It's better for both of us if one is captured if neither of us knows the other's name."

Startled, Louise asked "You don't know my name?"

"No. Just that I was to become active after your God's Eye message and break you out of here before you were locked away. When we get to that building, go around the corner to the right of us. There is a door. The door code is 1645a. Your driver is waiting inside," said the MP.

Once they reached the building, they heard a massive detonation far behind them.

"What on earth was that?" Louise said as she punched in the door code while the MP turned to look in the direction of the explosion. A fireball was turning into a huge, mushroom cloud shaped cloud of fire, smoke and debris about a mile away that stretched thousands of feet up into the air.

"My God. The war has started!" was all he said.

CHAPTER 36

THE RESORT

"I'm sorry to disturb you, Ambassador Gadre. You'll have to come with us. It's for your own protection," said a hulking Military Policeman to Gadre after she opened the door to her suite at the resort.

A look of alarm appeared on her face. "Why? What's happened?" she asked quickly.

"I don't really know beyond some sort of general unrest in the area," the MP responded to her question. "My orders are to escort you and Flight Officer Jonsey to a secure location until whatever is going on blows over."

Gadre looked at the small detachment of MPs. There were six of them. Quickly concluding she obviously wouldn't be able to resist their charms if they became insistent, it was time to play along and initiate Plan B and hope Captain Ronin had also gone to Plan B.

In their pre-mission preparations, the captain had devised a series of goals and actions if the situation became hostile or more dangerous. Together, those instructions had been designated Plan B.

"Well, I'm glad you handsome men are here, then. Please lead the way," she said, deliberately putting them at ease. *Pilot Officer Russo, Plan B, in custody. I say again, Plan B, in custody. Confirm*, she subvocalized, sending the message via the commlink that had been bio-imprinted under her skin.

Acknowledged. Plan B is in effect and you have been captured, came Russo's reply from *Bulldog 3*.

CHAPTER 37

BULLDOG 3

Russo tapped the node attached to his collar to close the commlink after he responded to Gadre. He was already seated in his pilot's seat and had been nervously eyeing the troops outside because they were obviously getting ready to fire the large weapon that had been positioned outside the Bulldog.

Russo furiously began tapping buttons on his boards. *You will NOT shoot that thing at me!* he thought angrily as he skipped the normal start up procedures and brought the main drive online. *I wish Plan B just had me using the jump drive to disappear from here instead of driving away using the main thrusters. Too bad the Captain said we had to hide our jump capability for strategic reasons,* he thought.

Seconds later, his boards were green and just as he hit full power, the weapon fired, but the aim was spoilt by the suddenly departing shuttle.

As *Bulldog 3* rocketed skyward several dozen feet, the engine blast from its sudden departure knocked the weapon over as well as toppling the small team of troopers manning it. Russo noticed the interior of the shuttle seemed a bit warmer as he hugged the dirt with his bird.

No damage, thank goodness! he thought as followed the terrain from a dangerously low altitude at speeds that were clearly unsafe. No sign of pursuit yet, he noted as he looked for a spot to hide the plane. *There!* Russo spotted a fog bank as he approached the edge of the ocean.

Russo double checked to confirm the jump drive was spun up as he drove his bird right into the thick fog. Seconds later, *Bulldog 3* jumped away.

CHAPTER 38

ORBITAL AMBUSH

"**A**dmiral! Targeting complete. Ready to fire, sir." Ryan couldn't believe what he was saying, but the glare of heavily armed MPs convinced him to do his job without drawing attention to himself. *Why would we attack a spacecraft from Earth?* he wondered.

"Acknowledged. Stand by," Seaver said. He was standing behind Ryan, listening to a phone pressed against his ear. "Yes sir, we're ready on this end," he suddenly said into the phone. "Roger that. Commence firing," Seaver responded to whoever was on the other end of the line.

Seaver ended the call and looked at Ryan. "Open fire," he simply said.

"Firing now," responded Ryan with a heavy heart. *All my life I've wanted Earth to contact our colony, and now we're shooting at the first ship to arrive. I can't believe this*, he thought as he entered the command to unleash the satellite weaponry.

"Damage assessment?" Seaver asked, though it was really an order.

"Checking now, sir." On the main screen, Ryan replayed the video from the moment they fired at *Cerberus* through the time of impact, according to his satellite targeting system. Other than a few fleeting moments of image shimmer, there didn't appear to be any effect at all.

Confusion rapidly spread across the faces of everyone present. All eyes in the room simply stared at the image on the screen, expecting to see some sort of damage.

"Did we hit it?" Seaver finally asked.

"My readings say we did, Admiral. I'm going to superimpose color into the projectile tracks on the replay to confirm," Ryan responded.

Ryan also took the liberty of zooming in on *Cerberus* for the replay and slowing down the video playback. This time the projectiles from the satellite-borne weapons were visible. The image shimmer they saw the first time was definitely from the distortion caused by the passage of high speed missiles and kinetic weapons unleashed by the satellites. Dozens of the now brightly colored 'tracks' appeared to intersect with the gleaming white hull of *Cerberus*.

Immediately after he entered the commands, he switched screens at his desk to get a big picture view of the situation. His system lit up with a new wave of missile tracks. "Sir, we're tracking over a hundred outbound missiles. The defense system says their impact window is 45 seconds to 90 seconds, depending upon where each missile was fired from."

"Why doesn't *Cerberus* show any damage? We hit it with enough firepower to end everyone inside it," Seaver murmured, loud enough for Ryan to overhear. Neither of them had any answers.

CHAPTER 39

CERBERUS

"**S**tatus?" said Ronin, although the question was really said as an order in an unintentional mimicking of Admiral Seaver's commands given in the Space Control Center.

"Projection holding steady, ten miles off our port side," responded LeCroy. "Tacnet has plotted the positions of all the weapons satellites and missile sites that fired on the decoy *Cerberus*," he added.

Seconds later, Lieutenant Delgado spoke. "Captain, message drone from *Bulldog 3* has arrived. *Bulldog 3* has jumped to the rendezvous point out in the belt, and Pilot Officer Russo is reporting he received the following message from Ambassador Gadre: 'Pilot Officer Russo, Plan B, in custody.'"

Ronin nodded while he and Mueller, who was standing next to him, exchanged glances. "Acknowledged. Plan B and two crew members captured," he responded, more for the benefit of the bridge crew than anything else.

"Lieutenant LeCroy, are those missiles still tracking for our decoy?" Mueller asked.

"Yes, Commander. The first of them arrive in 30 seconds. Lieutenant Anzio is standing by with the firing solution for jump bomb deployment," LeCroy responded, while glancing over to Lieutenant Anzio, who nodded to confirm she was ready.

"Jump bomb launch window in 10 seconds," Anzio added.

The seconds passed quickly. "Jump bomb away," Anzio stated excitedly.

On the screen showing the image of the white decoy image that the planet's military believed to be *Cerberus*, there was a tremendous flash of light and multiple explosions as the inbound missile payloads detonated from the force of the blast.

"Decoy *Cerberus* destroyed, Captain. Won't be long until they figure out they were shooting at a fake," Lieutenant Delacroix reported without looking up from his scanning screens.

CHAPTER 40

SPACE CONTROL CENTER

As everyone on the main floor of the control center watched the image of *Cerberus* on the main screen, there was a huge flash that momentarily blinded the optical resolution.

"Missile impact. Sensors reporting multiple denotations," said Ryan quietly.

The optical resolution restored itself. There was nothing left but some small pieces of debris on the screen.

Seaver, whose face registered satisfaction that the enemy ship was hit, was the only one to react. "It appears *Cerberus* is destroyed," he announced. "Scan for confirmation. There's got to be debris we can capture for analysis," he added, looking down at Ryan.

Ryan nodded and began scanning. Minutes later, sounding very confused, he said, "Admiral, the only debris present seems to be from the missiles. That's not possible, is it? Why can't we find anything from the ship?"

"It isn't possible. Something's wrong!" Seaver cried just as the control center was slightly rocked by a massive explosion miles away from their location. Shocked, Seaver and Ryan looked at one another with surprised faces. Several other distant explosions followed in the next few seconds.

Ryan flipped the feed on the front screen to show an overhead view First City and the surrounding area. They were horrified to see several large mushroom clouds rising into the atmosphere from areas outside the city.

"We've been nuked! Where are they coming from?" cried Seaver.

CHAPTER 41

CERBERUS

"**A**way the anti-satellite missiles. Let's take down their orbital network," ordered Ronin.

Lieutenant Anzio responded quickly without looking up from her boards and screens. "Missiles leaving the tubes now." Then she added, "Firing solutions for the railgun rounds were spot on. Railgun rounds have destroyed their targets on the planet."

"On screen," Ronin ordered. The main view screen on the bridge soon showed a view from orbit.

"Looks like we dropped a bunch of nukes on them instead of railgun rounds," murmured Commander Mueller. She stood next to Ronin, who was still seated in command chair. Ronin glanced up at her with raised eyebrows.

"It certainly does, doesn't it? The newly upgunned turret batteries pack a much bigger wallop than before. Too bad we won't stick around to admire our handiwork," Ronin responded.

They fell silent as they watched the railgun impacts on the planet's surface, their quiet reverie eventually broken by Lieutenant Delacroix announcing the number of impacts.

"AI reports 367 railgun impacts on surface targets. There is now too much dust accumulated in the debris in the atmosphere to make additional damage assessments at this time."

As expected, thought Ronin about the amount of atmospheric dust as he merely nodded towards Delacroix in response.

More minutes passed, the quiet on the bridge only broken by the sounds of the ship. Finally, the next step was about to come to pass. "Captain, the first wave of missiles are about the make contact with the satellites!" said LeCroy excitedly.

Both Ronin and Mueller looked at LeCroy expectantly.

"Our missiles tracked straight and true. Dozens of satellites are being destroyed," LeCroy finally reported.

CHAPTER 42

SPACE CONTROL CENTER

Seaver stood behind Ryan in the control center as they both stared in horror at the satellite imagery displayed on the front screen.

"My God, they creamed us!" Ryan murmured softly before catching himself. He cleared his throat and tried to sound more professional. "Impacts appear to be kinetic strike weapons only. Non-nuclear detonations, Admiral."

Seaver reluctantly tore his eyes away from the massive scale of destruction he was witnessing. "NON-nuclear you say?" Seaver emphasized "non," because he thought those sure looked like the normal mushroom clouds of a nuclear strike like those in the ancient database records. His eyes flicked back to the front screen for a moment before continuing. "With that sort of power from a kinetic strike, apparently adding nuclear detonations would probably just be redundant anyway. Why didn't we detect any weapons systems on *Cerberus*?"

Ryan shrugged before answering. "Unknown, Admiral. It's possible we didn't know what to look for, but I suspect there was another ship in high orbit."

"What? How do you figure?" Seaver exclaimed in a somewhat annoyed tone of voice.

"Based on the data we've received from the kinetic strikes, a retrograde trajectory analysis that is not yet complete suggests those projectiles originated about ten miles away from where we saw *Cerberus*," Ryan replied, not taking his eyes off the secondary screen where the analysis was still being updated.

Before Seaver could respond, the screen image at the front of the room suddenly went black.

"No! No, no, no, no!" said Ryan, his panicked tone rising as he rapidly began switching satellite feeds. Each time he found an active feed, it would black out seconds later.

Seaver decided to keep quiet while Ryan scrambled to find active satellite feeds. He didn't have to stay quiet for long. Ryan soon turned to look at him with a shocked look on his face.

"Well? Have they scrambled our satellite network?" Seaver asked imperiously.

Ryan shook his head. "No, Admiral. Not scrambled, shot it down. It appears all our satellites have been destroyed."

Seaver's eyebrows shot up. That was not the response he had been expecting.

"ALL of them? How is that possible?" Seaver demanded.

"Yes, sir. Everything. Even the weather satellites. The only thing we have left in orbit is The Ark," Ryan stated.

CHAPTER 43

THE OFFICERS COUNCIL

"Did we destroy *Cerberus* or not, Mr. Secretary?" demanded the Speaker of the Officer's Council, Dennis Hayward. The Speaker was wasting no time on preamble or pleasantries in this emergency meeting.

Stanton Ellis felt the eyes of the Council boring into him. He cleared his throat slightly before responding.

"Mr. Speaker, we do not believe *Cerberus* was destroyed, or even damaged," Ellis said in a deliberate manner, choosing his words carefully. "Based on a retrograde trajectory analysis of the kinetic strikes from orbit and other data collected from observatories at both poles, we believe the representation of *Cerberus* we saw and attacked was merely a decoy."

"How is it possible that we all saw a decoy? Where is the real ship, Mr. Secretary?" asked the Speaker.

"Mr. Speaker, we do not know the answer to either question. What we do know is that ship is out there, somewhere, and right now *Cerberus* rules our skies," Ellis said. This statement caused a low rumble among the Officers that were assembled and seated behind the table where Ellis was seated, facing the Council.

Ellis decided to forge ahead with his report. "We cannot be sure, but we believe *Cerberus* is the only ship from Earth that is currently lurking in our solar system. Furthermore, it is the defense ministry's conjecture that *Cerberus* may still be in orbit somewhere but for some reason we cannot locate her. Of greater concern is the opinion in the defense ministry that the visual representation we saw likely looks nothing like the real *Cerberus*. My staff has been studying the images closely and they identified nothing that would suggest that ship carried the sort of armaments which hit our planet and wiped out our satellites."

The Speaker leaned forward in his seat and interlocking his fingers in front of him. The Speaker's eyes narrowed slightly before he asked his next question.

"Secretary Ellis. Just what kind of ship does your staff believe arrived from Earth?" the Speaker asked, but it sounded more like a threat the way he said it.

"Mr. Speaker, the defense ministry does not believe *Cerberus* is a diplomatic vessel. Nor does the ministry believe *Cerberus* is a scientific or exploration vessel, nor a colony ship. Judging from the firepower and other capabilities we witnessed, we believe *Cerberus* is a warship. And she's a powerful warship at that. Just being named '*Cerberus*' should have been a clue about the true nature of the ship," Ellis said plainly.

"What do you mean? I do not recognize the word," said the Speaker.

Ellis cleared his throat slightly to be heard more clearly. "Sir, *Cerberus* is an ancient Greek name for the hound of Hades. It was a multi-headed dog who enthusiastically guards the gates of the Underworld to prevent the dead from leaving. Hardly the name one would expect to be given to the ship of a diplomatic envoy."

Ellis decided to risk saying more. "Despite being a powerful warship, I do not believe *Cerberus* arrived in our system with the intent to engage in combat. WE did that by luring the ship into our orbit and firing upon them. *Cerberus'* Captain somehow figured out our plans and devised a strategy whereupon we revealed both our ill intentions and the locations of our military assets. Now that both sides have exchanged shots and we were thoroughly outplayed, we have to adapt our strategy to use our remaining assets to our advantage when *Cerberus* decides to make the next move."

"How do you know *Cerberus* will be making the next move? Why not our military instead?" asked the Speaker, now using a more thoughtful tone.

"*Cerberus*'s counterstrike wiped out most of our significant offensive capabilities, Mr. Speaker. At that moment, we lost the war in space. If *Cerberus* decides to go on the offensive, the only theater of combat that remains is on the planet's surface. This becomes a ground war of attrition, but only if we position our military assets among the civilians on the ground to neutralize the orbital strike capability of their ship. If we do not, *Cerberus* will easily pick them off with the kinetic strike weapons we now know she has." Ellis paused to allow the Council to respond.

The assembled Officers began murmuring again, considering Ellis' words. The Speaker paused to let the Council communicate their thoughts to him through the passing of handwritten notes which he duly reviewed. Ellis just had to sit there and watch the drama play out in front of him for several long minutes.

Finally, the Speaker leaned forward in his seat and clasped his hands on the table as he spoke. "Secretary Ellis, what you propose is highly unorthodox and dangerous. Mingling our military among the Cargo Class, who are as likely to engage in combat with our military forces as *Cerberus*, will be a highly volatile situation for our forces. Unfortunately, it is also the opinion of this Council that we also now lack any other options because the effectiveness of the counterstrike from *Cerberus* took all our other options off the table. We find ourselves in a war for which we are ill prepared and it is our own fault. You are authorized to engage in a ground war as you propose."

Ellis couldn't help but be somewhat surprised at the authorization to mingle military and civilians together to fight the ground war. What he had proposed was a high stakes bet. If he failed, his society would not survive its self-inflicted war against *Cerberus*.

CHAPTER 44

THE CARGO REBELLION

Gadre and Jonsey shared glances as they rode in the back of the same vehicle they had arrived in not long before.

"Where are we going?" Jonsey inquired of the lieutenant in charge of the military police who were escorting them.

The lieutenant shook his head. "Protective custody at one of the bases near the port where your ship landed. It has defensible terrain around it, and if things go bad we can fly you out of there. The decision was rather rushed so it's the best we can offer for now," the lieutenant replied. He didn't sound like he was too upset over the decision as he said it.

Jonsey was about to push a little harder by asking about who they were supposedly being protected from when the shock wave from a thunderous explosion blew both vehicles off the road.

* * *

Jonsey felt a hand roughly shaking him awake.

"Flight Officer Jonsey? Jonsey! Wake up! You've got to go. NOW!" Despite his panicked attempts to wake Jonsey, the lieutenant couldn't help but notice how unusually heavy and solidly built Jonsey seemed to be compared to his physique.

As Jonsey opened his eyes and focused them, right in front of him was the bloody face of the lieutenant who was escorting them. "Ungh. Lieutenant. You're ugly mug is hardly the face I want to see when I wake up."

"Jonsey! Focus! Or you'll die here like me," the lieutenant said.

As he came to a little more, Jonsey suddenly realized they were upside down in a vehicle that was somewhat afire. His eyes snapped open, fully awake now. Gadre was hanging by her seatbelt across from Jonsey, who was also hanging by his seatbelt.

Jonsey's head whipped around to look back at the lieutenant. He was both entangled in his seatbelt, and partially trapped between the roof and floor because it had been crushed down.

Unlocking his seatbelt, he began repeating, "Gotta move. Gotta move. Gotta move." Several times Jonsey's limbs became entangled in the mess as he panicked while the smoke thickened from the rising heat.

The lieutenant couldn't be sure, but he believed he saw Jonsey tear the seatbelts from their moorings on the side of the vehicle. *That's impossible. No human is that strong*, he thought as he watched Jonsey pull an unconscious Gadre from the interior. To his surprise, Jonsey reappeared seconds later.

"Flight Officer Jonsey, I'm trapped. Take the Ambassa..." the lieutenant started to say when Jonsey interrupted him.

"Hang on, my man," Jonsey grunted as he positioned himself upside down in the overturned cab so his feet pointed up to the floor above them.

Jonsey pushed and the crushed section of the vehicle began to separate. Within seconds he had moved it enough to pull the lieutenant free and irresistibly dragged him from the cab of the vehicle.

The lieutenant was shocked at the abnormal strength displayed by Jonsey. Even though he looked large and powerful, Jonsey clearly was significantly stronger than would have seemed possible.

Once outside their wrecked vehicle, Jonsey bent down and easily lifted both the lieutenant and Gadre up onto his shoulders in a double fireman's carry before he moved them away from the wrecked vehicles.

He lifted us as if we weighed no more than small children, the lieutenant thought. His next thought was to look around to assess their situation. As Jonsey set them both down a safe distance from their smoldering vehicle, the ground was rocked slightly when it exploded. Then the ground rocked again, this time from other explosions further away.

"She'll be okay when she wakes up," Jonsey said after checking on Gadre. "What's going on around here?" he asked as sat down on the ground next to the lieutenant, who was shaken up by the incident but otherwise undamaged.

They were in a grassy area about forty yards from the roadside where their vehicles were now burning. Black smoke rose in the air from both the vehicles, and also from several hundred yards further beyond them in what appeared to be a mixed residential and retail area of buildings ranging in height from three to five stories. Sounds of small arms gunfire could be heard, punctuated by the occasional small explosion.

"Rebellion," the lieutenant responded simply.

"Your society's Cargo Class, I presume?" Jonsey asked, but it sounded more like a statement than a question.

The lieutenant nodded. "It's a good bet they're using the distraction provided by the arrival of *Cerberus* as cover for a rebellion."

Before Jonsey could comment, their attention was drawn to a massive blast off to their left in the direction of O'Reilly Airport, where they had been headed before their cars were hit. Even at the distance of ten miles or so, they could feel the concussion and remains of the shock wave from here. It was soon followed by a mushroom cloud rising in the distance.

"I don't know where our Cargo Class could have gotten hands on that kind of firepower," the lieutenant said distractedly.

As another fireball could be seen rising further away from the one at the airport, Jonsey looked closely at the lieutenant because of his odd choice of words. "That's not the Cargo Class, nor is it the planetary satellite network. It's *Cerberus*. The Captain wouldn't initiate an orbital bombardment of Terra Station unless they were fired upon first. But if *Cerberus* didn't pick this fight, that ship surely will finish it." Jonsey's eyes narrowed slightly while he decided to take a chance based on his hunch. "You're actually Cargo Class, aren't you, Lieutenant?" Jonsey asked. It sounded like both a question and a conclusion.

The lieutenant's eyes snapped away from looking at the twin mushroom clouds rising into the sky to look at Jonsey. A thoughtful look appeared on his face as he decided whether to trust Jonsey. Trust won out.

The lieutenant nodded. "Yes. I replaced an unknown Officer Class recruit who was eliminated back at the military academy before anyone got to know him. My mission was to be a Sleeper agent until activated. Today is activation day."

It was a big revelation to take in. Jonsey sat back as he watched the burning vehicles. "What happened to our rides?" he asked with a point of his chin.

"Rocket Propelled Grenades, I suspect. We ran into an ambush for Officer Class vehicles. Standard procedure for those is to strike from a distance, and disappear before the Officers can figure out what happened. Erick, by the way. We don't do last names for security purposes," the lieutenant said.

"Erick? Nice to be introduced. Call me Michael. Or Chief Jonsey, if you like. Or Chief," Jonsey replied, extending a hand for Erick to shake.

"I thought you were a Flight Officer?" Erick asked as they shook.

Jonsey cracked a huge smile. "You're not the only one posing as an Officer for this little field trip. So, Erick, what do we do now?"

"The Cargo Rebellion has begun. We've been preparing for several decades, engaging in skirmishes and so on to test tactics and weaponry. Your arrival simply provided the spark that was needed to start the fire," Erick stated. "I was supposed to walk us into an ambush at the base at the airport to eliminate the rest of the MP team and deliver you to the rebellion leadership. Both fortunately and unfortunately, we encountered another ambush on the way. That's highly unfortunate because Ambassador Gadre is injured and we didn't make it to our real destination. It's also highly fortunate, because we didn't make it to our former destination because it looks like everything and everyone there got vaporized. Now I have to go with our secondary plans to get you to them," he added.

The smoky columns extending into the sky spoke for themselves about how lucky they were not to have arrived at the airport.

Jonsey couldn't help himself. "Well then, Erick. Take me to your leader," he said with a quirky grin as Gadre gingerly lifted her head to look at them.

"Welcome back to the land of the living, Ambassador," said Erick, still grinning at Jonsey's quip that was straight out of cheesy old novels about aliens arriving on Earth.

"Anybody get the number of the bus that ran us over?" Gadre said. "What happened?"

Jonsey and Erick brought her up to speed, then Jonsey asked Gadre, "Are you mobile, or do we have to drag your butt all over town?"

She stood and tested her balance. "Just a headache, but my balance seems solid. The lower gravity sure helps. We can run all day in this," Gadre replied.

Erick's eyebrows shot up. "Lower gravity? What are you talking about?" he asked.

Jonsey and Gadre glanced at one another before Jonsey answered for the two of them. "Terra Station only has three quarters of standard Earth gravity," he said.

"What?" exclaimed Erick. "Well, that must explain why you were able to do all those things to get us out of the vehicle before it blew. You're like a superman in this gravity. It's crazy."

The ancient cultural reference to supermen drew a blank look from Jonsey. "Who or what's a superman? You mean like an enhanced Officer or something?"

"Uh. Never mind. I was brought up to speed about the loss of historical and cultural records during The Fall and forgot you might not recognize an old popular culture phenomenon we brought here," Erick replied.

Jonsey grinned. "Ambassador Gadre might be able to give you trouble in an arm wrestling match because her muscles were built for about a quarter more Gs than you have here," Jonsey said with a tilt of the head to Gadre. Gs were the Fleet's commonly used slang to refer to Gravities. Erick looked at her slight build and diminutive stature.

"It seems hard to believe, but today's the day for hard to believe. OK, if you're up for it, to get to the Rebellion leaders we're going to have to go through that," Erick said with an up tilt of his chin pointing towards the mixed use residential and retail area beyond the burning vehicles. "We'll have to move fast and try to avoid the fighting as much as we can.

And I'll need to ditch this military uniform because it'll attract too much attention," he added.

As he helped Gadre off the ground, Jonsey looked at Erick and said, "Let's make it happen."

CHAPTER 45

CERBERUS

"**A**greed. We need to tap into their communications systems to give our AI more data to try to crack their encryption, Commander," said Lieutenant Delgado as she looked up at Mueller, who had moved to stand next to her station on the bridge. "Right now there isn't enough for us to figure out their code, and after our counterstrike, planetary communications by their military dropped to minimal levels."

Overhearing their muted conversation, Ronin walked over to Delgado's station to join them. "We're trying to find a decent point where we can tap into their communication system, but so far the likeliest taps were either destroyed by our railguns or they're too heavily guarded for us to access," Ronin commented.

Delgado looked frustrated, mirroring Ronin's and Mueller's feelings. "Have we captured any military hardware? Satellites? Aircraft? Anything?" Delgado asked.

"No. We've destroyed everything we came across," Mueller replied.

"Captain, if we can't start reading their mail, Plan B will have to be modified again," said Delgado. "Then it will be a lot heavier lift to accomplish the objectives," she added.

"Where are they still operating from?" Dan asked, somewhat rhetorically. He looked at Delacroix as he said it.

Delacroix knew from experience he was being summoned by Ronin and he walked over to join them at Delgado's station.

"Scans confirmed our prediction that they would move their military forces into close proximity to civilian populations to protect them from additional railgun strikes. It might be possible to land a Marine detachment with the objective of capturing a field radio," Delacroix noted.

Mueller shook her head. "Yes, but that's a high risk operation. Unless we can come up with something better from a risk-reward perspective, let's have that be the final option unless another need to do so arises. Where do your scans indicate other active units are?"

"There are a couple of military bases and missile silos we haven't erased yet, but they're likely to be heavily guarded. For our Marines, those will also be hard targets. We saw minimal troops at the poles where those old terraforming units are, but I don't believe the odds of finding the communication gear we need will be in our favor at out of the way places like that," said Delacroix.

Ronin absently rubbed a thumb along the side of his chin and jaw as he considered the situation. "Ideally we would hit an active, but out of date installation down on the planet somewhere. The problem is this colony isn't old enough to have any facilities meeting those criteria," he said thoughtfully.

"Can we lure an aircraft up here?" asked Delgado. "That would have the kind of gear we would need."

"How would we do that? They learned that sort of thing is a suicide run a few hours ago," Delacroix said. "I can't imagine too many of their surviving pilots would want to take a run at us now."

Ronin's eyes lit up at Delacroix's comment. "But a drone would! We already know where their drones routinely fly to," said Ronin.

They all looked at him expectantly.

"Their old colony ship in orbit. It hasn't been a threat to us, but we already know it has a regular contingent of repair droids. Those droids are controlled through the communications array on board the ship. Lieutenant Delgado, would tapping into that array be sufficient?" Ronin asked.

Delgado nodded. "I believe it would be, Captain. I'll confirm with our AI."

Ronin tapped the commlink node at his collar. "Lieutenant Sunderland, this is the Captain. We've got a job opportunity for your Bulldogs and the Marines waiting to board them."

"They'll be glad to be of service, Captain. Where do you want them to land on the planet, and who do you need them to shoot?" came Sunderland's reply.

"Negative, Lieutenant. This is a boarding action on a potentially hostile ship in orbit," Ronin said.

CHAPTER 46

THE ARK

ulldog 1 jumped from Epsilon Station and appeared near the hull of The Ark. "Jump complete," said Pilot Officer Erin Johnson. All they could see was the dark hull since they jumped to the side of the ship facing away from Terra Station, and space. Seconds later the rearseater, Chief Hal Patterson spoke to both Johnson and Gunnery Sergeant Brett Mackey (Bravo 1) over the commlink between the three of them.

"Bulldog 5 has also arrived and is proceeding to their designated boarding zone," Patterson said.

"Gunny, we'll be setting down in thirty seconds near what our drone scans suggest is an airlock," Johnson announced.

Mackey was ready. "Roger that. Thirty seconds." Mackey passed the same information along to Bravo team on another commlink.

Bulldog 1's skids settled against the hull of The Ark and Johnson engaged the magnetic skid locks. "Maglock secure, Bravo 1, you are a go for egress," she said moments later.

"Copy that. Go for egress," Mackey confirmed. He switched commlinks to talk to Bravo team. "Bravo team, egress by the numbers. Magnetism works on this hull metal, so engage your boot maglocks. Let's move out!"

Bravo team was lined up in a double row to exit the Bulldog quickly down the rear ramp. Twenty seconds later, they stood in vacuum on the hull of The Ark.

"Sweet Mother of Pearl, but this is a big lass!" muttered Bravo 6, Private Steve Cupper, in his Scottish accent. Cupper took in the sheer size of The Ark while Bravo 4, Private Carlos Guthrey, attempted to open the airlock hatch. All the Marines except Bravo 4 and 7 held their weapons at the high ready position as they scanned around for threats. Bravo 7 had his hands on the carry handle grip of a strange looking environmental suit about the size of a large dog.

"Shut it, Bravo 6. Bravo 4, status?" asked Bravo 1.

"Making progress. I don't think this hatch has been used for centuries, but the hand wheel in the center is turning slowly. I'm using full power on my exosuit to do it though," replied Bravo 4, grunting a few times during his report over the commlink.

Another minute passed before Guthrey made everyone jump inside their exosuits. "Got it!" he exclaimed, as he pushed the hatch inwards and launched a Butterfly drone inside. It was pitch black inside. Seconds later, Guthrey announced, "There's no greeting party waiting for us. It's empty."

"Bravo team, go go go!" yelled Mackey to get his Marines inside. They secured the outer hatch behind them as Guthrey quickly worked the inner hatch of the airlock. As soon as the outer hatch was sealed, the airlock quickly filled with simultaneously rising levels of light, atmosphere, and gravity. Guthrey and Mackey looked at each other in alarm for a few moments before they realized it was just an automated process of this ship's airlock instead of being a sign there was someone waiting for them.

Once the inner hatch was opened, Bravo 4 sent the Butterfly inside. "Empty! And we have breathable atmosphere inside as well," he said loudly over the commlink. "Bravo 7, I think you can let Cujo out to play."

"Bravo 4, Bravo 7. With pleasure," replied Private Ty Jeffries. He was the handler for Bravo team's war dog.

The team moved out of the airlock into the rest of the ship.

"Bravo 1, the Gs are at 1 Gravity," commented Bravo 2, Corporal Ed Wilson over the team's commlink.

"Yes ... and?" was Mackey's reply. He didn't see the relevance beyond the fact the ship had artificial gravity.

"Bravo 1, the people on Terra Station are adapted to .75 Gs. They're a mismatch for this ship's 1.0 Gs. We see anyone, they might be moving a little slower because of it," Wilson said as he finished his thought.

That brought Mackey to a stop as he stiffened up straighter and looked at Wilson.

"Noted. Gravity mismatch. Good catch, Bravo 2," Mackey said after a moment before continuing on.

The team entered a long corridor that curved away out of sight in both directions as it traversed the shape of the ship's hull. It had pockets of soft blue-green lights, and several sections where the lights obviously did not work any longer. Bravo team took up defensive firing positions to cover the approach from both directions.

"AI, where might we find the tap for the communications array from here?" Mackey inquired on a different commlink than the rest of the team.

"Bravo 1, we identified several possible objectives based on the drone scans of this ship as we have no other records of this vessel. Logically, the bridge is presumed to be near the center of the ship and many communications lines will converge there. The auxiliary bridge, if there is one, is presumed to be aft, near the likely location of Engineering. The remaining location is on the array itself on the surface of the hull, but that is Bulldog 5 and Echo team's objective for this mission," said the AI.

"AI, where is the nearest possible objective for Bravo team?" asked Mackey.

The AI responded visually as well as audibly when a glowing green arrow and range indicator appeared on his helmet screens. "The closer objective is the presumed location of the auxiliary bridge, located approximately a thousand yards down that hallway."

Mackey immediately put that information on the team's Tacnet plot. "Bravo team, listen up! AI says our objective is the auxiliary bridge, aft towards where Engineering is likely to be. Even you slackers can handle a stroll of a thousand yards. We don't know what we'll find, so keep your heads on a swivel," Mackey ordered as the team formed up to move down the corridor.

As they moved, Guthrey flew the tiny Butterfly ahead of them, scanning for trouble.

CHAPTER 47

THE ARK

The Officer in charge of the Crew Class detachment of troopers on board The Ark sighed. Duty on this old relic was tiresome, not to mention physically exhausting to deal with the ship's unusually heavy gravity.

"Lieutenant Richardson, recent encrypted message traffic from Terra Station," said the young Crew Class corporal as he handed him a tablet with the latest messaging. Grant Richardson accepted the tablet and opened up the messages link.

It didn't take long as Terra Station's military was sending very few messages since the Cargo Rebellion began with the attack on *Cerberus*. "Well, Corporal, it would seem the war is not going well and we're on our own up here," Richardson said cynically, before adding, "Like we needed some weenie down on the planet to tell us these things after watching hundreds of mushroom clouds from orbital strikes wipe out most of our facilities."

"Yessir," drawled the Corporal. All of them had seen videos of the failed attack on *Cerberus* followed by that ship's devastating counterstrike. "And no telling where *Cerberus* is lurking now."

"Yes. Some sort of cloaking device, I should imagine. Quite the advantage, that," noted Richardson. He flipped the tablet back to the Corporal, who managed to catch it without dropping the thing in the heavy gravity.

"Lieutenant, are we still going to rotate the pat-" the Corporal started to ask when The Ark's ancient AI interrupted him.

"Intruder alert. Deck fifteen, corridor one, section seventeen. Their direction of travel is towards Engineering."

Both lieutenant and corporal looked at each other with shocked expressions. Neither of them had ever heard The Ark's AI before.

"Corporal, deploy our troopers ahead of them. Repel boarders," ordered Richardson after recovering from the surprise. He stood up to check that his sidearm was still securely holstered. Richardson had never fired it outside practice on the range.

CHAPTER 48

BATTLE OF THE CORRIDOR

Breathing hard in the heavy gravity after they carefully ran to the corridor, Lieutenant Richardson looked around at his troopers who were sweating and likewise breathing hard. They had chosen to ambush the intruders in a darkened area of the corridor extending about twenty yards long where the lights no longer worked. *They won't be able to see us until it's too late*, he thought.

Just as their breathing began to settle down to more normal rates, something small zipped past them almost too fast to see.

Richardson's head snapped around to try to catch a glimpse of whatever it was that just appeared. So did everyone else's.

He broke out into a cold sweat as he was startled by a scream suddenly coming from one of his men, punctuated by some sort of angry sounding growling and snarling. None of them had ever heard those sorts of sounds before.

Richardson's head snapped back to see what was happening. He was completely shocked to see some sort of huge, hairy, four legged beast tearing into a pair of privates at the forward position for their ambush. The blood and gore was horrifying.

"Shoot it!" yelled someone. Richardson wasn't sure who.

"I can't, we'll hit our own guys!" someone else responded.

Richardson was about to order someone to shoot that beast anyway when there was a rapid fire series of strange sounds emanating from down the corridor. They sounded like some combination of electrical "fffft" sounds with a slight undertone buzz. The smell of burnt ozone suddenly filled his nostrils. Based on the scary sounds of metallic ricochet's pinging around him and punching holes in the corridor walls, it didn't take a genius to figure out they were under fire.

"Lieutenant, they're using some sort of primitive projectile weapon!" yelled the Corporal over the sound of the beast that had moved on to the next nearest troopers.

"Return fire! Maximum wattage!" Richardson yelled back.

* * *

"Bravo 1, Cujo has engaged hostiles!" said Bravo 7, Pvt. Ty Jeffries over the team commlink.

Since their distraction worked, Mackey wasted no time ordering his squad into action. "Bravo team, engage the targets as designated on your Tacnet!" He had taken the time to auto lock individual targets for each Marine to ensure fire support.

Bravo team's answering gunfire was frightening in the confined corridor. Enemy combatants began falling rapidly.

"Bravo 1, looks like they don't have an answer for Cujo!" Jeffries noted as he monitored their huge Rottweiler's progress. Cujo was chewing up his fifth victim already.

Before Mackey had a chance to reply, some sort of directed energy beam connected with the new liquid armor skin of his exosuit. His skin immediately began tingling where the beam hit before he could duck behind a bulkhead.

"Bravo 1, are you alright?" yelled Bravo 2 when he realized what happened.

"Your suit started glowing at the point of contact!" added Wilson.

Mackey checked his suit's readouts. "I'm good! Looks like I took a low dose of radiation, but my suit kept out the hard stuff."

* * *

Richardson couldn't believe his eyes as he lowered his weapon. He could swear he finally hit one of those invaders right in the torso of his strange suit that looked like it was made out of some sort of non-reflective black liquid. *He should have been burnt to a crisp with a highly lethal dose! What kind of material IS that?* he thought as he fought to control his rising panic. The black shapes moved so fast in the heavy Gs he couldn't seem to find a target before they disappeared.

Just as he began raising his weapon to fire again, he was bowled over by a violent collision from behind. Cujo had arrived in an angry mass of muscle, fur and teeth.

"Yeargh!" yelled Richardson in a mixture of surprise, fear, and pain as the massive animal began tearing at his legs with its teeth. He tried to scramble away, but it was too fast and powerful, like a four-legged demon.

While he was entertaining Cujo, Richardson failed to notice the few surviving members of his unit who weren't dead or incapacitated had decided to surrender. Even though it only took less than a minute for the invaders to take the survivors prisoner, to Richardson the same period of time seemed to take forever.

Suddenly the devil dog backed off and Richardson, hurt and bleeding, found himself facing the primitive and scary looking muzzles of the enemy's projectile weapons. The beast stood next to one of the black suits and looked ready to attack again. Richardson could barely take his eyes from the monster as he wailed in pain, "What IS that thing?"

* * *

Slightly confused, Mackey and Wilson turned slightly to glance at each other. "What do you mean, 'What is that thing?' It's a war dog," said Mackey using his suit's speaker. The bleeding Officer at his feet was startled by the sudden and strangely accented voice coming from one of the black suits who now held him prisoner. It wasn't what he expected to hear.

"I, I don't know what a 'war dog' is. We don't have those on Terra Station" Richardson stuttered slightly as he said this while one of the other black suited Marines finished disarming him.

Then the Marine who disarmed him reached down and easily lifted Richardson off the ground with one arm. It seemed as effortless as lifting a small sack of potatoes. Richardson couldn't resist the overwhelming strength in his enemy.

As Bravo 6 lifted Richardson up and placed him in handcuffs, it became obvious the lieutenant had soiled himself in addition to being a bleeding mess. "Ah yuck. The lad done pooped himself," said Private Cupper.

Mackey couldn't resist. "Doesn't look like we'll need much encouraging to keep our exosuits sealed up tight, Bravo 6," he noted dryly.

"Aye, Bravo 1, that we won't," Cupper replied, as he roughly spun the shaking officer around to face them while Bravo 4 returned from checking the corpses.

"Bravo 1, Bravo 4. Fifteen tangos are KIA, four are wounded but mobile for now. Six more tangos have surrendered. No further signs of hostiles from our drone screen," reported Guthrey.

"Acknowledged," Mackey said over the Bravo team commlink. Then he noted the obvious for their benefit. "If they don't know what war dogs are, we can use that intel to our advantage. Bravo 2 and Bravo 7, interrogate Cap'n Raygun here and threaten to unleash Cujo if he doesn't tell us about this ship's defensive compliment and where to find a communication tap."

Wilson and Jeffries both grinned inside their black exosuits though no one could see their faces. "With pleasure, Bravo 1!" growled Jeffries as he activated the commlink to Cujo. "Cujo, job opportunity. Come along boy!" he said. Jeffries kicked open a door next to him in the corridor and entered the room beyond with Cujo growling and trotting along at his side. Wilson grabbed the lieutenant by the hair on the back of his head and dragged the now sobbing and pleading lieutenant in behind Wilson and Cujo.

CHAPTER 49

BATTLE ON THE HULL

"Echo 1, Echo 2. No contacts, scopes are clear," said Corporal Adrian Longman to Gunnery Sergeant Kanagawa as they slowly advanced along the hull of The Ark.

"Array is fifty meters, dead ahead," Kanagawa responded while he was simultaneously monitoring Bravo's team commlink.

"Echo team, Echo 1. Be advised, Bravo team is in contact with multiple tangos. They know we're here, so stay frosty," Kanagawa warned over the team's commlink.

It was a good thing Kanagawa did, because the team only managed to cover a few more yards before Tacnet suddenly plotted dozens of tangos of their own to deal with just ahead.

"Contact! Echo team, advance by numbers!" Kanagawa ordered. The team leapfrogged each other by pairs while they closed the distance.

"Why didn't Tacnet spot them sooner?" Echo 2 (Longman) asked. Echo 2 had been tagged with the nickname, the Pirate, during the war. The Pirate didn't realize he'd said it over the commlink as it was more of a rhetorical question to himself.

The answer soon revealed itself. Hidden panels on the hull slid back to reveal drones. Hundreds of them.

"Here they come!" yelled Echo 4 (Private Han Pak). He was situated behind Echo 3 (Private Rhee Lee), Echo team's heavy weapons specialist. They began firing their weapons. Echo 4's standard mag-rail infantry assault carbine pumped out round after round that punched holes in dozens of drones, but the storm of rounds only destroyed a few of them.

Echo 3's much heavier caliber Buzzsaw either blew out much larger holes, or blasted chunks off the machines.

"Echo 1, there's too many of them!" Echo 4 yelled.

"Fallback!" ordered Kanigawa.

"Echo 1, Echo 5. Negative on the fallback. We're surrounded," responded Private David Danfries over the commlink.

Kanagawa's eyes flicked to the Tacnet readout. Echo 5 and 6 were in the middle of a swarm of drones, but other Echo team members were nearby and outside the engagement envelope. *Dang it*, he thought to himself. This was happening too fast.

"Echo 12 through 16, you're closest to Echo 5 and 6. See if you can take some of the heat off them," Kanagawa ordered.

The drones don't appear to have any weapons other than appendages for ripping and tearing, Kanagawa thought as he fired his mag-rail carbine in three round bursts. All the moving drones and their appendages were an optical distraction to target selection. "Echo 2, shoot and scoot!" he yelled over the commlink. Echo 2 needed to move faster to stay ahead of the wave of hostile machinery headed their way.

As Kanagawa ran past Longman, he took up position behind some sort of rectangular shaped bulge in the hull and whipped his rifle back up to lay down more covering fire for Longman's turn to sprint back past Kanagawa while they leapfrogged each other. As he fired on the drones, Kanagawa never saw the one that rose from its hole in the hull behind him.

"Aagh!" Kanagawa managed to say over the pain as he was slammed into the cover he had chosen to hide behind. The pain was incredible.

"Echo 1, status!" yelled Longman as he disengaged his maglock boots and leapt up the side of Kanagawa's cover in the zero G before re-engaging the boots. Longman moved over the top of the cover swiftly when Kanagawa lost consciousness.

"Echo team, Echo 2. I'm advancing into unit command. Echo 1 is down," Longman said over the commlink just as he peeked over the edge to see a drone pinning Kanagawa to the other side of the cover. Longman flipped his fire rate to full auto and poured rounds into the machine, blowing off large chunks of it in the first few seconds. The drone stopped moving and began drifting away.

Longman glanced at Tacnet, noting Echo team's collective casualties. There were too many. He jumped down to lift Echo 1 onto his shoulders to get him to safety when private Pak spoke over the commlink.

"Echo 2, Echo 4. We've captured a live drone and I tapped into its commlink. Sending shut down commands now," said Echo 4, who was also the team's electronic warfare specialist.

Longman peeked around the cover back at the wave of drones that had rapidly been advancing on their position. Pak had shut them all down, and they were drifting in every direction. Some collided with others, changing their direction of travel while others floated free.

"Echo 4, you did it! Echo team, check fire! Check fire! Collect casualties and regroup on me," Longman ordered. This seemed as good a spot as any, he figured.

A dozen KIA, and only six wounded, Longman thought to himself in shock. *They mauled us.*

"Echo 2, Echo 4. The data I downloaded from the drone we captured show those were the ship's repair droids. We stumbled into a drone hive," Pak said as the team gathered to take care of their wounded. Pak sounded shaken by the encounter.

"Acknowledged, Echo 4. Any other threats out there?" Longman asked.

"Negative, Echo 2. They threw everything they had at us," Pak replied.

"Echo 4, have your drones scout and confirm that. Echo 7, take Echo 6 and Echo 20, and get our casualties taken care of. The rest of you, effect any exosuit repairs you need while Echo 4 finishes re-scouting the objective. We'll move out when he's done," Longman ordered. There was a lot to do, and his Marines needed to keep busy.

CHAPTER 50

AUXILIARY BRIDGE

"**Y**ou sure this is the place, Bravo 4?" asked Mackey.

"That's affirm, Bravo 1. This is where Cap'n Raygun said we could tap in. You got a better idea or something?" responded Guthrey as he removed the panel to a workstation marked "Communications."

"No. Just worried a crayon eater like you might get confused by all the wires and glowing buttons," Mackey quipped as he noted Bravo team had finished securing the auxiliary bridge of The Ark without any more fuss. *If you don't count Cap'n Raygun and his skid mark stained arse cowering from Cujo*, he thought wryly.

The captured survivors and their fearless leader, Cap'n Raygun, had been handcuffed and marched along with Bravo team to the auxiliary bridge instead of their original objective. Mackey's eyes swept over them from behind his helmet screen. They were seated along a sidewall with their hands behind their backs. *There's no fight in them*, he noted to himself. *And they don't want to deal with the scary looking men all buttoned up in their black exosuits.*

Guthrey snorted as he responded to Mackey's quip. "Oh, ye of little faith. We're in! Testing our connection now ... " he started saying as Mackey's AI interrupted them on the team commlink.

"Bravo 1, the tap connection here is successful. The hull relay that Echo team just placed has signal acquisition and forwarded the uplink to the drone network we seeded into orbit. Cerberus has confirmed data receipt," said the AI.

"Bravo team, Bravo 1. We've worn out our welcome. We're going to egress back to our ride and get outta here. Bravo 4 take point with your drones. We're taking the prisoners with us," ordered Mackey.

CHAPTER 51

REBEL RUN

Gadre tried her best to keep quiet and not cough from the smoke and dust swirling over her position. They had holed up in a Crew Class department store for a few minutes so Erick could rustle up some new clothes and stash his MP uniform out of sight when they had found themselves trapped inside. An armored cavalry unit commanded by the Officer Class had taken up position outside the store and was busily exchanging fire with the rebels when the store had taken a hit from a rocket propelled grenade.

This doesn't look good, thought Gadre as she peeked at the new hole in the wall of the store from her hiding spot behind a rounder of clothes on a rack positioned well into the store. A noise behind her caught her attention and she glanced that way.

"Here, put these on!" whispered Erick as he handed her some new clothes he had grabbed. "You need to fit in with the population here to avoid attracting attention."

Gadre looked over Erick's change in outfits, and she cocked an eyebrow as she smiled and nodded her approval. "Nice threads!" she noted as she started to don the clothes.

A look of confusion passed over Erick's face. "Don't you think we've got more important things to do than worry about fabric quality?" he replied.

Gadre rolled her eyes a little bit and slightly shook her head. "No, it's slang generally referring to your entire outfit, not to fabric quality."

Erick looked embarrassed for a moment just as Jonsey joined them. "Oh, sorry. I guess that was lost in translation."

Jonsey heard that and couldn't help himself. "I dunno about you two, but I make this outfit look GOOD!" he whispered loudly with a huge, cheesy expression. As he intended, this prompted both Gadre and Erick to look at each other and stifle a pair of small laughs.

Serious now, Erick whispered, "The rebels won't be able to stand toe to toe with that armored cav unit. They'll hit and fade, then repeat the process somewhere else. We just have to wait them out and hope we're not found. Now that we are all dressed like Crew Class, we'll attract a lot less attention from the military." Erick had shortened cavalry to cav, unknowingly truncating the word as many people commonly did.

Even as Erick said this, they heard the engines of the armored vehicles outside rev while the sounds of gunfire suddenly ceased. Through the broken front windows to their right, and the new hole in the wall to their front, they could see men and machines pull out.

Erick nodded, somewhat to himself. "There they go. When they've moved on, follow me."

The three crouched quietly for a few more minutes, and then Erick snuck over to the front of the store. No one was in sight, and he scrambled back to Gadre and Jonsey.

"It's a ghost town out there! Time to move. If we're captured by Cargo rebels, tell them who you are and that you want to meet their leadership, even if they call you a Dreamer, which is just another word for Crew Class. If captured by Officers, just say you're trying to get to your homes in mid-town, which is a Crew neighborhood bordering the Officer Class residential area downtown. If we're captured by Crew, then it might get a bit dicier because it might be difficult to discern where that particular group of Crew's sympathies might lie. Could be with either Cargo or Officers. Might be neither. So I'd suggest just using the mid-town story and seeing how things play out," Erick whispered quickly.

Gadre and Jonsey nodded, neither saying anything as they glanced at each other.

They followed Erick out through the front of the department store. The glass had been shattered from the concussion when the stray RPG round hit the other side of the building. As they stepped back into the daylight, the transformation in the area was shocking. Thirty minutes earlier, it was a reasonably prosperous looking shopping area. Now, windows on the entire block were blown out, scorch marks and impact craters dotted walls for several blocks up the road, small fires burned, and the air was filled with smoke.

"This way!" Erick said as he started jogging in the opposite direction to put some distance between them and the air cavalry units. Both Jonsey and Gadre adopted a skiing like loping stride in the low gravity, so Erick felt a little ridiculous taking two or three steps for every one of their strides.

They disappeared into the city.

CHAPTER 52

DIXIE STATION

"**C**aptain, the Bulldogs carrying Bravo and Echo teams have jumped back into the rendezvous point," said Lieutenant Delgado. "The teams sent a BLUF report. Both Bravo and Echo missions accomplished. Bravo team ... no casualties, ten EPOWs with four wounded but in stable condition. Echo team ... twelve Marines KIA and six badly wounded who need immediate medical attention, included Gunnery Sergeant Kanagawa." Delgado hadn't even noticed she used the acronyms BLUF (Bottom Line Up Front) and EPOW (Enemy Prisoner of War) that are commonly used in the Confederate Navy.

"Acknowledged. Put Doctor Taketa and his medical unit on standby and top priority for Echo's bird in the landing pattern. Send an armed security detachment to meet Bravo team in the landing bay. Debriefing in the main conference room in thirty minutes," Ronin replied, although his orders regarding Taketa were redundant as the medical unit had already been notified.

Ronin turned towards Lieutenant Delacroix and asked, "Any sign we've been spotted yet?"

Delacroix never took his eyes from his screens although he unconsciously dipped his head in a side nod towards Ronin as he answered, "Negative, Captain, scopes are still clear. They've got some intermittent radar operating, but they still don't know where to look."

Within minutes, both Bulldogs arrived in the landing bay. Ronin's collar node commlink chimed with an incoming message. "Captain, this is Lieutenant Sunderland. Both our birds are back in the nest and offloaded."

Ronin had been waiting for that message. "Acknowledged. Stand down the Tomcat pilots. We're jumping the ship out of orbit. Ronin out."

Taking that as her cue, Commander Mueller immediately gave the order. "Lieutenant Perez, execute jump."

Perez nodded. "Aye aye, Commander. Executing jump now," he said as he jumped Cerberus out of orbit.

When they reappeared deep into the system's asteroid belt, Perez announced, "Jump complete. Taking a navigation reading now. We're at the coordinates previously designated as Dixie Station."

"Acknowledged," Mueller said. She looked around at the tired bridge crew before issuing another order.

"Primary bridge crew, call in your backups for shift change. Get some rest," she said loudly.

After the shift change on the bridge, Ronin and Mueller went to the main conference room for the debriefing.

"You look tired," Mueller noted as they walked.

Ronin glanced at her with a humorless half-smile. "Yeah. Long day in the saddle. It sure didn't play out like we hoped, did it?"

Now it was Mueller's turn to smile, somewhat ruefully as she shook her head slightly. "Sure didn't. Would have been nice to be invited down to a nice, getting-to-know each other dinner with some drinks. Instead they come at us with guns blazing. Hard to believe they declared war and tried to take us out as their preferred response."

Ronin nodded thoughtfully. "That was a strategic mistake of epic proportions," he said as they entered the main conference room.

Lieutenants LeCroy, Sunderland and Alphonso were already waiting for them.

"Grab a seat and we'll get started," Mueller ordered as they all found a place to sit around the holotable.

"Lieutenant LeCroy, what's the ship's combat readiness?" Ronin asked.

LeCroy was expecting to go first, so he was ready. "Cerberus is undamaged and stood down to Alert Three for heightened readiness but unmanned action stations. All systems are green. We're pretty low on railgun ordnance due to the orbital bombardment. Food, water and life support are excellent. Ten EPOWs are secured in the brig to keep them from talking about our infantry capabilities, with four of them receiving medical attention injuries ranging from rifle wounds to bites and tearing from Cujo. Medical expects them to make a full recovery, although Medical even noted how frightened the EPOWs were of our war dog after their mauling by Cujo in the corridor of The Ark. Post capture interrogation revealed there are no canines on Terra Station.

"Additional interrogation of our guests will take place forthwith. Both Marine teams successfully placed the data tap and data relay on The Ark. The relay is using The Ark's own communication array to transmit significant signals Intel to our orbital drone net. We will be rotating Bulldogs to gather the data streams sent through our drone net to Epsilon Station, and Bulldog 7 is currently loitering there to scoop up the data for our AI to analyze."

As LeCroy summarized, Lieutenant Gustav, Gunnery Sergeant Mackey and Corporal Longman walked in and quietly took their seats at the table.

"Lieutenant Gustav, what is the status of your teams?" Ronin asked.

Gustav cleared his throat slightly. "Captain, Echo team is down eighteen men and as a result is currently combat ineffective. Gunnery Sergeant Kanagawa is in surgery and is expected to take a few months to recover. Bravo team is unhurt, but needs some rest and to rearm. In the meantime, Gamma team is stood up as the Go-To Team should Marine action be called for."

"Captain, Lieutenant, if I may add something?" said Mackey politely.

"Go ahead, Gunnery Sergeant," said Ronin.

"Captain, I haven't had a chance to review captured enemy weaponry yet with Lieutenant Gustav, but they appear to have been using some sort of X-ray spectrum, hand-held energy weapons. I was hit by one, but our new liquid armor exosuits stopped most of it. I'd like to work with Lieutenant Alphonso to fine tune our armor's resistance."

Everyone looked at Mackey with surprised expressions on their faces.

After a few moments, Ronin nodded. "Navy armories are of the opinion that hand-held energy weapons were impracticable, if not impossible! Excellent idea, and don't forget to work with Lieutenant Gustav to develop some tactics to deal with energy-based weapons."

"Yessir. We'll have a lot to go over," Mackey replied.

"Captain, I'm also going to assign a few of my department's mad scientists to figure out how those X-ray weapons work. It could be a breakthrough on that sort of weaponry if we can reverse engineer it," Alphonso said, speaking for the first time. His eyes gleamed at the chance to get his paws on a working raygun like those he used to daydream about as a kid.

Ronin nodded. "Seeing as we've segued into your department's wheelhouse, Lieutenant Alphonso, after your area fabricates replacement ordnance for the munitions we've expended, I want your people to look into the effectiveness of Cerberus' new black diamond hull coating against X-ray weapons. No telling what else we might encounter during the next engagement."

Alphonso nodded. "Yessir. Speaking of fabricating more ordnance, we still have the two options for obtaining the materials. We can mine it ourselves from the asteroid belt, or we can raid the automated mining and ore processing operation on several asteroids that were identified during the pre-mission planning surveillance. Our fabrication speeds will vary depending upon the availability and quality of the ore. Have you decided which option you prefer?"

Dan nodded slightly as he answered the question. "I have. Since Ambassador Gadre and Flight Officer Jonsey are still down on the planet and the latest auto-report of their status through the drone net noted they are on the run with a representative from the Cargo Class, my thinking is we need to return to orbit for possible fire support missions sooner rather than later. That means we raid the automated facility and take the higher grade materials to replenish our ordnance. Anyone disagree?"

Everyone else at the table responded in the negative. Speed over deliberate action was more prudent given the pace of the war so far, and they all knew it.

Ronin looked at both Sunderland and Gustav. "Lieutenants, conduct the raid with the reserve units, Gamma team and Bulldog 2. Call on anyone you need to get it done. We need that ore, or this will be a fairly short war for Cerberus."

Sunderland and Gustav nodded, responding with a chorus of "Yessirs."

"That takes care of our immediate worries. Let's regroup tomorrow after we rest and mend some wounds. I want to see your reports by midday," Ronin said. With that, the debrief ended. Everyone was tired, and it had been a long day. *Time to get ready for our next steps*, thought Ronin as he stood to leave.

Minutes later, Ronin stopped in his quarters to check in on his kids and to grab some rack time. As the door opened, the rooms were dark and quiet.

Dan walked in quietly, realizing it was the middle of the night for his kids and feeling disappointed they were asleep. *I'm starving. Think I'll rustle up a sandwich before hitting the rack*, he thought as he stopped to pull the ingredients out of the small fridge in their quarters. His eyes spotted a brown bottle with a handwritten tag tied to the neck. Dan pulled the bottle out to see what the tag said.

In Lieutenant Sunderland's handwriting, it said, "*Captain's Decompression Ale*". Figuring that decompression was always a matter of high priority in space, Dan opened the bottle and took a long swallow of the cold beer inside. *Hazy IPA this time. Sunderland missed his calling to be a brew master*, he thought as he took another hit of the delicious new concoction from Sunderland's hidden beer brewing kitchen. *Not that I'm ever going to look too hard to find the thing*, he told himself.

Just as he had finished assembling a serviceable sandwich and was raising it to his mouth for a bite, Dan felt eyes looking at him from behind. He cocked an eyebrow as he craned his head over to look at the owner of those eyes.

"And, why might YOU be up in the middle of the night, kiddo?" Dan said with a small smile as he set the sandwich down.

"Dad! Why are you having a midnight snack?" said his daughter, Sarah, as Dan lifted her up into his arms for a hug.

"Oof! You're getting to be a moose!" Dan said with a small laugh.

Sarah bent back and said, "I'm not a moose. They're big and hairy and smelly!"

That made Dan laugh a little harder. "I was starving since I missed dinner, whenever that was. It was a long, hard day."

* * *

Diane walked into her family's quarters. It was dark and quiet. On the counter in their small kitchenette was a note pointing to the small fridge. It simply said, "Don't forget to eat! Saved you a sandwich!" and had a small smiley face on it.

Just then, Karl walked out of their bedroom, yawning and scratching the side of his head. "Morning! Or is it goodnight?" he said as he wrapped his arms around Diane.

"It's goodnight, I think. What a long day!" Diane said.

"I heard we ended up crossing swords with Terra Station today," Karl said quietly.

"Yeah, we sure did. Cerberus went in posing as a diplomatic vessel but ready for hostilities. We projected our fake image to be miles from our actual location, and they opened up on the decoy ship. We collected all sorts of data on their defense installations, and then dropped the hammer on them all after they opened up on Cerberus' decoy image. We'll be going back soon after we replenish our ordnance and settle on what our next steps will be," Diane replied.

"Hopefully we'll have broken their communication encryption scheme by then, which should help. I'm headed to the lab after a quick shower now that you're here," Karl said.

"Being able to read their mail again would definitely be a plus," Diane noted as she opened the fridge to grab the sandwich.

"Was Lieutenant Sunderland here?" Diane asked, spotting the brown bottle with a handwritten tag labeled, "*Commander's Decompression Ale*". She handed Karl the bottle to open.

"No, I don't know this Sunderland person of which you speak," Karl replied with a smile and in a highly disingenuous tone of voice. "Perhaps it is some stranger with a poorly hidden talent for making good beer whom we should get to know?" Karl said, still grinning, as he opened the bottle. They both took a sip of a light-tasting cherry beer.

"Decompression is an important matter in space," Diane murmured appreciatively after taking another sip.

CHAPTER 53

THE LAB

Karl and the Cerberus AI had been crunching the numbers for hours. "Each time we think we took a step forward, testing it runs into a brick wall. What are we missing?" he asked.

"We have determined the cipher is not a grid leading to another grid because the access point changes each time. Perhaps our approach is to eliminate what it is not?" the AI responded.

"Perhaps. Problem is we've already eliminated all known methods of cryptography and eliminated them. It's not something simple like a Caesar Shift, or a virtual Alberti's Disc. Nor is it a Vigenère square key to a Caesar Shift. It's not an RSA encryption with a public key, either. So what is it?" Karl responded. He was stumped.

"It's also not a block or a stream cipher," the AI helpfully noted.

"AI, I'm thinking this is a pattern cipher that's paired with one of the known ciphers. A pattern that provides the keyword that unlocks the downstream encryption key in a different way each time. And since we've observed the downstream key has shifted a lot, we need to see what that initial pattern corresponds to," Karl said as he leaned back in his seat and put his feet up on his desk and clasped his hands behind his head.

"That is logical based on our current deductions and observations of the data we are now receiving from The Ark. I have not been able to discern an applicable pattern," the AI commented.

"Me either. So what are we missing? You've already checked for various celestial events and found patterns that didn't seem applicable. We've got to keep looking," Karl concluded as he thought over what they had seen in the system. "Maybe it's the occurrence of TWO predictable patterns?"

"AI, list all the predictable patterns we know of. Orbits. Blinking stars visible from the surface. Holidays. Birthdays of prominent persons. Comets. Eclipses. Seasons. Let's start there."

Seconds later, Karl saw a scrolling list appear on the large wall screen in the lab. It kept scrolling down.

Karl shook his head slightly. *Going to need more coffee for this.*

CHAPTER 54

TAKE ME TO YOUR LEADER

"**D**id you transmit our situation to Cerberus?" Gadre quietly asked Jonsey as they hid around a corner and watched Erick scout ahead a half block.

Jonsey glanced at her and nodded. "Yeah, I'm not sure if Cerberus is still in orbit since we haven't seen any more railgun strikes for a while, but my bio circuits definitely made contact with a commlink to a drone. The report will be relayed to wherever the ship is lurking," he said softly.

"In the meantime, we are to make contact with the rebellion as per our Plan B orders," Gadre said, finishing the thought for both of them.

Erick turned and motioned slightly for them to follow. Jonsey and Gadre did their best to look nonchalant as they walked out from behind the corner. There was little sign of damage in this tree-lined neighborhood of three-story brownstone buildings. Gadre noted the generally neat appearance of their surroundings. *This has to be a Crew neighborhood. Not fancy enough for Officers, and not a slum like the Cargo has to live in.*

A few blocks later, still following Erick from a discrete distance, they arrived at the banks of a small river. Erick stopped at a bridge and subtly glanced to his left and right before eyeballing the far side, about a hundred yards or so away from where he stood, where the buildings appeared to be much larger and shabbier. It seemed as though nothing was happening.

"Looks like we're crossing over to the Cargo Class neighborhoods," Jonsey whispered discretely to Gadre as they approached the bridge themselves. "We should cross over before we lose him," he added.

They hurried across, not wanting to stay that exposed for long.

Erick was waiting for them on other side. "Welcome to the Borderlands. We need to keep going for a few more miles."

Nodding without saying anything, Jonsey felt rather than heard the ground shake. He glanced back at the bridge as they began to walk. The ground shook again, hard enough this time to send ripples coursing through the river.

"Hurry! I think the Officers have an armor unit headed this way. We don't want to be here when they arrive," Erick said as he ran to the left where a road intersected with the road along the riverfront. Now the ground was beginning to shake slightly and they could hear the sounds of clanking coming from across the river.

Erick turned the corner and began running with Jonsey and Gadre close behind. They immediately collided with a unit of Cargo rebels, who pointed weapons at Gadre and Erick. Jonsey found himself being grabbed by a rebel who tried to push him up against the wall of the building to their right.

Jonsey, with his greater weight and far greater strength, was an immovable object, clearly surprising the rebel, who had expected at least some degree of give. Jonsey pushed the man's hands away and easily lifted him by the throat using only a single arm.

"Enough! Everyone stand down," yelled a tall rebel who was several years older than the others in the unit.

Jonsey glanced at the tall rebel who seemed to be in charge, and arched an eyebrow in surprise for a second as he took in the number of weapons that were pointed at him. Looking back up at the rebel dangling from his arm, he let the man go.

As the rebel collapsed on the ground, Erick said loudly, "My code name and number is Loki three niner. We need to meet with your commanders."

The tall leader looked at Erick with surprise on his face for a few moments. Long enough for Jonsey to wonder if it was time to make themselves scarce because the rumbling and clanking from across the river was starting to get pretty loud. The leader suddenly turned to one of his men.

"Take them to FOB Charlie. Tell Commander Hunt that Loki three niner wants to see him immediately," said the leader. He turned to face Erick, Jonsey and Gadre. "Follow my man and stick close to him. He will get you to FOB Charlie. Now get outta here before it's too late. Things are about to get ugly."

Gadre looked at Jonsey, who mouthed the words "Forward Operating Base." A civilian like Gadre wasn't as conversant with military acronyms.

Erick and the leader quickly shook hands, then Erick led Gadre and Jonsey through the rebel unit at a run. Their speed picked up when they heard and felt a whooshing, followed by an explosion somewhere behind them.

As they ran, Jonsey noticed the unmistakable signs of combat in the slum. Buildings with holes and scorching. Roads with craters. Smoke and small fires burning in wrecked vehicles, corpses everywhere. The Cargo Rebellion in progress was putting up a stiff fight against the Officer Class.

A few blocks in from the river, they passed several sandbagged emplacements with Cargo rebels firing mortars across the river at the Officers. They would fire a couple of times, then scramble to displace before the Officer's counter battery shells would arrive. *Like a Whack-a-Mole, hit-and-run strategy*, thought Jonsey. *Smart*.

Other than urging them to hurry, their escort didn't say much. He didn't have time. They quickly covered several miles quickly and emerged from the slums into a dead park bordered by a wide boulevard. It was a wasteland of dead, blackened trees and burnt plants, ringed by defensive firepower.

They trotted up to a makeshift gate. Sandbagged emplacements protected fire teams on both sides. Still following their escort, they approached the armed rebel who had positioned himself in front of the gate.

"Halt! State your business," said the rebel, eyeing the four of them warily.

"I'm Corporal Peters, 1st Platoon of the 216th. This is Loki three niner," said Peters, identifying himself for the first time since he started escorting the group and gesturing towards Erick. "They're here to see Commander Hunt."

The guard's eyebrows shot up at hearing Erick's identifier. They'd been briefed about the deep-cover Loki agents, and their activation for the Cargo Rebellion. He nodded quickly, then turned and motioned for another of the rebels to come forward.

Within minutes they had been searched for weapons and escorted into a tent that was clearly serving as some sort of temporary command and control center, based on the amount of communications activity and tactical data displayed on a dozen screens set up inside. There were perhaps twenty people inside the large, dark tent, and the interior was poorly lit by a few bulbs hanging down from the ceiling. Commander Hunt was waiting for them along with his staff.

Hunt was tall and thin, with graying brown hair and brown eyes and a serious expression. He was also all business and didn't have time to waste. "Loki three niner? I'm James Hunt. What do you have for me?" Hunt said by way of introduction.

On their way through the Borderlands Erick had rehearsed what he would say. He got right to it and nodded over his shoulder to Gadre and Jonsey, who were behind him in the gloom of the tent. "Sir, these two people are Ambassador Prisha Gadre and Flight Officer Michael Jonsey from the Cerberus, a ship of the Confederate Navy of Earth. I broke my cover as a military policeman who was tasked to escort them to a secured location controlled by the Officer Class and brought them here. I think you will be interested in what they have to say."

Commander Hunt arched an eyebrow skeptically before he responded. "How do you know they're for real? They could just be another pair of Officer Class spies?"

Hunt's next question was interrupted by a voice from behind him. "Commander, if I may?" asked a female who stood up and walked over to the light where the others stood.

Hunt turned to look at her. She was young, with red hair. "Yes, Miss Abernathy?" he prompted.

The redhead didn't take her eyes from Gadre and Jonsey. "Commander, these are the two representatives from the Cerberus' shuttles that we tracked from the Orbital Optics desk at the Space Control Center. I also hacked into the Center's surveillance system and released the video of them to the rebellion. It's them, sir," Louise's voice shaking a bit as she spoke. She was still trying to wrap her head around how the Cargo Rebellion infiltrated the military and snatched her from their clutches before they ended her life for treason.

Hunt, clearly surprised at the unexpectedly quick confirmation, merely looked over to one of his staff who was already pulling up the video and playing it on a screen next to them. As seconds passed, they all watched in silence.

Clearing his throat slightly, Commander Hunt turned back to Gadre and Jonsey.

"Well, Ambassador Gadre and Flight Officer Jonsey, it seems you arrived at an inconvenient time for everyone. What can I do for you?" he said.

Jonsey replied, "Commander, we were sent here to make contact and establish a relationship with the government of Terra Station. That being said, we devised a Plan B contingency when we observed how unstable the situation was on the surface."

Hunt interrupted Jonsey. "So, what are you telling me, Mr. Jonsey?"

Jonsey continued, "Commander. Plan B was to assist the Cargo Class in overthrowing the government if hostilities commenced due to our arrival."

All conversation in the tent ceased as every head turned to look at Jonsey and Gadre.

"Pardon my slowness in adjusting to the changed circumstances here, but how do you propose to help us? You're all alone down here and we believe Cerberus has left orbit," Hunt stated.

"Yessir, but Cerberus will be back. And we can communicate with the ship, because we seeded a communications and observation network around the planet that can relay messages and data to the ship," Jonsey explained.

Hunt looked impressed. "Presumably you have a safe way of establishing contact then? If we try using our equipment, we might as well light up a 'Drop Bombs Here' sign over our position. The military will beat us like a rented mule the second we expose our operations that way."

Jonsey and Gadre shared a glance, before Gadre answered for the two of them.

"Commander, Cerberus already knows we're here."

CHAPTER 55

CERBERUS

"Captain, all I'm saying is the ethics of overthrowing a sovereign foreign government are dubious at best," said the ship's lead protocol officer, Dr. Winston Wright, ignoring the stares of Commander Mueller, Lieutenant Delacroix, and Captain Ronin. In truth, Captain Ronin's slightly squinting eyes and furrowed eyebrows might be more accurately described as a heated glare. Anyone who wasn't tone deaf would recognize that look as a warning sign to be heeded.

Wright tapped his foot impatiently. He was much more used to dealing with people who were willing to see things his way and listen to reason. Not like these militarized barbarians he was speaking to now.

"I don't think you understand, Captain Ronin. You are committing an act of war against Terra Station. Even potential genocide, with your indiscriminate orbital bombardment. There will be a war crimes tribunal and a possible court martial waiting your return to Earth," Wright declared. His rising voice echoed from the walls of the main conference room.

Ronin's eyebrows went up slightly and his eyes took on a steely look. Deliberately omitting Wright's title, he said, "Mr. Wright, seeing as the planetary military opened fire upon us while we were attempting to establish peaceful contact, your fevered imagination has clouded your judgment."

"Do not question my judgment, Captain, you aren't qualified to..." Wright began to say.

"Mr. Wright! Navy captains are responsible for the safety of their ships. They have VERY broad discretion in how they choose to do so!" thundered Ronin. "You were merely added to this ship's compliment in an advisory capacity. Thus far, your advising has been dangerously uninformed and out of touch with the tactical situation. Now, return to your workspace and try to help this ship complete its mission without placing Cerberus in needless danger."

Wright unwisely tried to speak again when Ronin ended that notion. "Mr. Wright, you are dismissed. Do you need to be escorted to your assigned workspace?" he said with an ominous edge to his voice.

After Wright left, Mueller spoke up first. "I'm sorry, Captain, that guy is a jerk."

Ronin cut her off. "Commander! Not here, please. This isn't the time or place," he said, but this time he spoke with less of an edge and more of a tone of concern.

Mueller seemed very surprised, then she quickly realized from Ronin's expression and tone he wasn't rebuking her. He was protecting her. Delacroix was also present to hear her comment, and her testimony could become relevant if Wright filed a complaint.

Without missing a beat, Lieutenant Delacroix piped up. "I didn't hear a thing, sirs. Even if I and the rest of the crew wholeheartedly agree with Commander Mueller's comments, had she actually said anything. Which she didn't." Delacroix flashed his roguish grin as he spoke.

Ronin and Mueller looked at Delacroix with raised eyebrows in surprise for a moment before simultaneously laughing softly.

Delacroix continued. "The good DOCTOR has already annoyed and irritated the rest of the crew who've been unfortunate enough to have any interactions with him. He isn't taking home the Mr. Popularity trophy from this mission."

They all smiled at Delacroix's comical emphasis on the word "doctor."

"Good to know. Thank you, Pierre," Ronin said, using the lieutenant's first name as a sign he was grateful for his input.

"What's next on our list?" asked Mueller, to keep things moving.

"Our drone net has located the new hiding spots for their remaining combat aircraft, and they've been plotted onto Tacnet by Lieutenant

LeCroy for future reference. So far they aren't flying them anywhere and seem to be relying on drones for surveillance of the Cargo Rebellion. The rebels, for their part, have raised a robust air defense against the military drones and have shot them down faster than the military can find new ones," said Delacroix.

"Find?" Ronin looked confused. He was expecting to hear about manufacturing drones, not finding them.

"Yessir. The military drones were all manufactured in a base that was solely occupied by the Officer Class so they could control the technology and prevent it from falling into the Cargo Class hands. One of our rail-gun strikes ended the base, and all the military's drone construction, in one salvo. No doubt they'll try to replace that manufacturing capability, but since the base had a large percentage of the military's Officer Class on it when we wiped it out, the strike put a big hurt on both their capabilities and available manpower," Delacroix explained.

Right then, Ronin's commlink chimed with a message from the ship's AI. "Captain, Karl Mueller is requesting to see the three of you immediately. He says they've cracked the enemy's encryption code."

The three of them looked at each other with excitement. "Does he want us to meet him in his lab?" Ronin asked.

"Negative. After I informed him of your location, he departed immediately and is en route to the conference room. Mr. Mueller will arrive in two minutes."

"Well, I guess I'd better serve the coffee while we wait for his arrival," Ronin said as he stood up and grabbed the coffee carafe to begin pouring four mugs.

Karl arrived just as Dan finished pouring the last cup.

"Captain, please excuse the interruption!" he said, slightly out of breath. Commander Mueller smiled at seeing her husband try to speak and breathe at the same time.

"Grab a seat, Mr. Mueller. What do you have?

"We finally achieved a breakthrough on unlocking the encryption scheme employed by the Terra Station military, and I wanted to show you what they were using," Karl said. He nodded his thanks for the hot cup of coffee that Ronin handed to him. The long day of code cracking was taking its toll on him.

Karl brought up an image in the center of the holotable. "Thanks to the additional data streams sent from data relays the Marine teams placed on The Ark, we had a sufficient sample size for me and the AI to figure out their encryption key was a pattern cipher that's paired with one of the known ciphers. Sort of a key to the map. The problem was we needed to identify the pattern so we could then figure out what cipher was in use." He paused, drew a breath and sipped his coffee.

"So, what was the pattern? It never seemed to repeat itself," Diane asked.

"Correct. Once the additional data from The Ark began filling in the missing parts, we had a large enough sample to start seeing repetitions show up. The pattern is based on a combination of these parts," Karl said as he manipulated the holo to show The Ark, its orbit, and a highlighted point on the surface of the planet.

Karl then continued his explanation while they looked closely at the holo representation. "It's simpler to show you instead of just trying to explain. This is a mathematical formula based on the date from the colonist's Landing Day, the orbital position of The Ark on the date each message is sent, and whether the day of the month is an even or odd numbered date. Even numbers are added, and odd are subtracted. Once we identified the variables and solved that pattern, we were then able to identify the cipher as a simple Caesar Shift, which was named after an ancient Roman emperor, who used the cipher to protect their military communications. That method is merely a substitution cipher replacing a letter with another letter based on a fixed number of positions down the alphabet."

"So we can read their mail again until they come up with another encryption cipher?" Delacroix asked.

Karl nodded. "Then we'd have to start all over again. Hopefully this dust up doesn't last long enough for them to do that."

"Karl, can you assist Lieutenant Delgado with reading their message traffic? Mueller asked. We're trying to develop a clearer tactical picture of their situation down on the planet."

"I can, but keep in mind this isn't a complete window into their communications strategy down on the surface. It's just information automatically routed to The Ark on a tight beam laser that's relevant to that ship and the troops that were stationed aboard. But, still pretty helpful to us since The Ark functions as their only eyes in the sky right now," Karl noted.

"I'm sure they're wondering why our Marines did a smash and grab on The Ark, but they probably haven't had time to mull over the implications yet. Same for Gamma team's raid at their ore processing facility in the belt a few hours ago," commented Ronin as he opened a commlink to the Fabrication Department while Karl left for the bridge to help Delgado.

"Lieutenant Alphonso, this is the Captain. What's your estimated time to complete fabrication of the replacement munitions?"

The reply was immediate. "Seven hours or so, Captain. And we've had time to look into those rayguns our Marine team captured on The Ark. After we finish fabricating the munitions, we are going to add a small layer of protection to the exterior of the Marine exosuits to better resist the weapons. They're nifty little devices."

Mention of the rayguns brought another concern to Ronin's mind. "Alphonso, any thoughts on whether the Terra Station military has scaled up versions of those rayguns for use against fighters or spacecraft?"

"Yessir," drawled Alphonso. "But our tests regarding the rayguns yielded another benefit that I wanted to mention. The black diamond hull coating disperses the vast majority of the energy and all of the radiation in the beam. Repeated hits tend to heat up the target, so we would have to stay on top of how much heating occurs during a battle."

"Then, hopefully we can eliminate a weapon like that before it becomes a problem," Ronin noted. "Thank you, Lieutenant. Ronin out."

Ronin's commlink node chimed. "Captain, this is Lieutenant LeCroy. We received a message from Jonsey. He and Gadre linked up with the leadership of the Cargo Rebellion. They say the rebels have a great deal of interest in working with Cerberus to end the war and institute a representative republic democracy. They're awaiting your reply."

Ronin looked at both Delacroix and Mueller and responded, "Acknowledged. Tell them we have good copy on their message and to standby for our response later."

"Will do, Captain," said LeCroy, ending the commlink.

"Well, the clock is ticking. When we've ironed out some details, then let's have Lieutenant Delgado communicate our desire to set up a meet and greet with the rebel command elements. We have a lot to discuss," Ronin stated.

CHAPTER 56

SPACE CONTROL CENTER

"Admiral Seaver, we need to know if Cerberus is in orbit or not," said Secretary Ellis. His frustrated tone of voice clearly conveyed his growing impatience as the two of them sat in Seaver's office. "The military is repositioning our assets, but we need to know if they're up there spying on our movements."

Seaver tilted his head and shook it slightly before he replying, "Mr. Secretary, we just don't know. Our defense network thought it had the ship locked in, but that was the decoy BEFORE Cerberus wiped out our satellite network. Now we're left with little more than telescopes on the surface as we try to locate them."

"Whoever the Captain is, he's no fool. A wily opponent who seems to have been several steps ahead of us the entire time," Ellis said.

Leaning back in his chair, Seaver nodded thoughtfully. "The last time our military was on the offensive was when we opened the hostilities, despite not being totally sure Earth was still unaware of our existence or of Cerberus' capabilities. We've been playing defense ever since," he noted.

It was Ellis' turn to nod. "Yes, I think our Council has finally caught on to that little nugget of wisdom. Right now, we have no momentum. We're just reacting to whatever that ship does. We don't have any information to help us out."

"It probably doesn't help to point out that our lack of information is so acute, we still don't even know what Cerberus actually looks like, much less it's true capabilities," Seaver said. Just then, there was a knock on his door.

Frowning at the interruption, Seaver said, "Enter." His aide, Esmeralda Centon, wouldn't have interrupted a meeting with the Secretary unless it was important. And, right now, it seemed as if important information all seemed to be important in a very bad way.

Centon stepped into the room and shut the door behind her. "Excuse me, Admiral, Mr. Secretary. We received reports that rebels attacked the convoy escorting Ambassador Gadre and Flight Officer Jonsey to the secure drone manufacturing base at Little Creek. They're both missing," Centon said.

"Great. That's just great. Now we don't even have those two in our custody to question, either. And it's lucky for them they didn't arrive at Little Creek Base near the airport. Cerberus erased it from the map," Seaver said, shaking his head. "Thank you, Chief Centon. That will be all."

"Sir, there's more, if I may. Other reports suggest there was a raid on The Ark by an unknown, heavily armed force that appeared without notice. It wasn't spotted until it was too late. We're trying to reestablish contact with the units stationed aboard, although we are still receiving drone telemetry. And we've also lost contact with an ore processing station in the asteroid belt."

Perplexed, Seaver and Ellis looked at each other for a moment before Ellis spoke first.

"Assuming those hits are attributable to Cerberus ... how did Cerberus cover so much distance that quickly, and why would they bother?" he asked.

Seaver just shook his head slightly as he replied. "I dunno. Since we don't have a sense of Cerberus' capabilities, we can't even make an educated guess."

"I've never felt so helpless against an adversary before," Ellis said. "If your people can locate that ship, we may have to resort to using the experimental anti-ship cannon," Ellis noted ominously.

CHAPTER 57

BULLDOG 3

"**B**ravo 1, get your guys tucked in back there. We're ready for launch," said Russo, the pilot of *Bulldog 3*, over the commlink to Gunnery Sgt. Brett Mackey.

"That's a good copy. I'll get them wrangled into position," Bravo 1 replied. He switched over to his team's common commlink. "All right, you apes, get your butts buckled in. They're ready to launch this bird," he roared as Bravo team, augmented by the remaining Echo team members, quickly boarded the shuttle and found their seats. With everyone all dressed up in their battle rattle and carrying extra equipment in addition to extra bodies, it was a tight squeeze.

Bravo 1 sat in Jonsey's empty seat and buckled in. He returned to the commlink with the pilot: "Russo, Bravo 1. We're all buttoned up back here."

Instead of responding, the immediate loading of their shuttle into the launch tube served as acknowledgment of the message.

"Bravo 1, our boards are green. Launching in five. Four. Three. Two. One. Launch!" Russo counted down for Bravo 1, who had patched the message through to the rest of the heavy composite team.

The Bulldog shot through the tube out into space. Seconds after departing Cerberus, *Bulldog 3* made the first of its jumps to return from the belt to Terra Station.

* * *

Bulldog 3 appeared low in the night sky of Terra Station with a small jump flare.

"Jump 4, complete!" yelled Russo over the noise to Mackey on their still open commlink. "Atmospheric jump arrivals are always pretty bumpy!" he noted as the shuttle rumbled and decelerated hard. Russo was trying to rapidly minimize the tail of fire that appears behind a Bulldog when it jumps into a planet's lower atmosphere until they can fall below the temperature and speed thresholds that cause it.

Mackey was already working the scanners at Jonsey's station. "I've located the homing beacon. Sending coordinates to your screen now," he said while the ride quickly smoothed out.

"That's good copy, Bravo 1. Turning to match the course now. ETA ten minutes," Russo replied.

Mackey switched over to the team's commlink. "ETA, ten minutes. Get ready."

Soon, Russo had dropped his Bulldog down to the dark surface as he piloted the bird in terrain following mode. It was quiet in the cockpit while he concentrated until Mackey interrupted.

"Russo, Bravo 1. Scanners indicate a possible threat detection about a hundred miles to port. Whoever's over there is trying to acquire our image signature."

"Acknowledged! AI, activate our ECM suite and jam their signal," Russo ordered, bringing their AI into the commlink.

"ECM activated," replied the AI.

The next several minutes passed in tense silence while Russo flew and Mackey eyed the scanners. Both of them jumped when the AI suddenly broke the silence.

"Enemy radar unable to acquire signal lock. We are out of their range now."

"Acknowledged. Bravo 1, ETA two minutes," Russo stated.

Sixty seconds later, Russo suddenly spotted a large 'X' lit up on the ground ahead. It looked like the light was courtesy of small torches on the surface. Russo was waiting until the last second to slow enough to stick the landing. "Bravo 1, we're coming in hot. I see movement around the LZ. We're not taking incoming fire," he announced as the Bulldog set down while Russo dropped the rear ramp.

Mackey stood up immediately and barked, "Bravo and Echo teams, un-ass from this bird! Move it, move it! They're cleared for immediate dust off." The heavy composite team quickly exited with all their extra gear, accompanied by the sound of engine whine as Russo kept the engines running.

At the edge of the dim, flickering firelight provided by the torches were several shadowy figures. As soon as the Marines exited the Bulldog, the biggest of those shadows began walking towards the ramp.

When he approached the shadow close enough to identify Chief Jonsey, Mackey reached out to shake hands. "I knew you were too ugly to kill, Chief," quipped Mackey with a big grin.

Jonsey laughed a deep laugh. "You aren't that lucky, Bravo 1!"

Mackey grew more serious. "Don't forget about your friends down here while you're up there joyriding," he said.

"Give us a shout when you're ready for a lift, Bravo 1," Jonsey replied before he headed up the ramp and hit the button to close it.

Moments later, Jonsey stuck his head in the cockpit where Russo was busily keeping his engines warm. "Hi, honey! Miss me?"

"You were gone? I thought you were finally letting me have some peace and quiet up here," Russo joked without turning to look. He began powering the lift thrusters to raise the shuttle several feet into the air before he engaged the drive engines.

Jonsey was already strapping himself into his seat while he eyed his instruments. "No current threats detected. Skies are clear," he said after a moment over the whine of the main drive's increasing thrust as the Bulldog quickly began to gain speed and departed the area.

Mackey turned to watch *Bulldog 3* lift off and disappear into low into the dark sky as it followed the terrain to a deserted area so they could jump away unseen. Satisfied with the Bulldog's quick dustoff, Mackey saw several more of the shadowy figures approach.

"Ambassador Gadre. Good to see you again, ma'am," Mackey said over his external speaker.

Gadre smiled a broad smile, barely visible in the dim lighting. "Thank you, Bravo 1," she replied, having been reminded by Jonsey to call Mackey by his call sign designation when in the field. She turned and motioned to the tall man standing to her side. "I'd like to introduce you to Commander James Hunt. Commander, this is Gunnery Sergeant Brett Mackey, call sign Bravo 1."

Mackey and Hunt quickly shook hands.

"Gunnery Sergeant, we need to depart this area before we're spotted by any observation drones. Are your men..." Hunt began saying when he caught sight of a large, four footed animal with Private Jeffries and stared at them. "What ... is THAT?" Hunt exclaimed.

Mackey turned slightly, and opened a commlink. "Bravo 7, Bravo 1. Can the two of you come over here? Need to make an introduction."

Grinning under his face shield, Jeffries brought the requested team member over to them. "Bravo 7 reporting as ordered, Gunnery Sergeant."

Mackey activated his external speaker again. "Commander Hunt, this is Bravo 7, Private Ty Jeffries. He is the handler for Private Cujo, our team's war dog. Over there is Echo 6, Private Julio Gonzales and Echo team's war dog, Barqhest. I've been advised no one on Terra Station has ever seen a dog before."

Without taking his wide eyes off Cujo, Hunt shook his head slightly. "That's a negative. I've never even heard of a dog. What do they do?"

Jeffries answered Hunt's question while Cujo sat still, with his tongue hanging out and head tilted slightly as he returned Hunt's gaze. "Well, Commander, he does quite a lot. He excels at sniffing out danger, helps us identify friend from foe, is an outstanding tracker, and in this lower gravity he is even more fearsome at fighting than usual."

Hunt's eyebrows shot up. "Lower gravity?"

Mackey answered, "The gravity of Terra Station is three-fourths of Earth."

Hunt nodded thoughtfully. "That explains Loki three niner's report noting the incredible strength of Flight Officer Jonsey during their escape from military custody. He said it was off the charts."

"Agreed. It would seem to be that way," Mackey replied. Changing subjects, Mackey asked, "Your message indicated you have several places to hole up?"

Hunt answered quickly. "Yes we do, which is why we chose this area as the LZ. There are several blocks of large ruins near here and we took the time to outfit the area with jamming devices and heat signature diffusers. Once we get under cover there, we can work on our next steps."

Hunt turned to yell at some of the shadows who remained at the perimeter of the flickering light. "Let's move out!"

Mackey switched to the team commlink. "Bravo and Echo teams, mount up. We're moving out to a more secure location."

CHAPTER 58

CERBERUS

"**D**oc says you'll be fully recovered in a few weeks," Ronin said to Gunnery Sergeant Kanagawa. The two were in the ship's sickbay, where Kanagawa still lay in a bed recovering from his wounds.

"Thank you, Captain. After Doc Taketa patched me back together again, he pumped me full of his medical nanites and whatever else black magic he has lying around here."

"In your case, Gunnery Sergeant, it was more a matter of hammering out your dents and dings, and buffing out the scratches in our body shop," said a grinning Lt. Hirohito Taketa, the ship's chief medical officer. Taketa was casually looking over Kanagawa's vitals on a tablet while standing at the foot of the bed.

"Some car crash. You should see the other guy," Kanagawa quipped, before turning serious. "Lieutenant Gustav was visiting earlier. Said the next op was going to be underway soon?"

Dan nodded. "Yep. He put together a composite heavy team by rolling Echo into Bravo, and outfitting them for a straight-up firefight. No breaching equipment or any of that. *Bulldog 3* delivered them dirtside and now they're in contact with the Cargo Rebellion. Gustav is now in orbit aboard *Bulldog 3* with Gamma team, which is this mission's QRF. He's monitoring the situation from there as a combined command and control element and eyes in the sky.

"As you know, a QRF is a Quick Reaction Force capable of responding rapidly to developing situations to assist other units when needed. QRFs are not often used for Marine combat missions due to the sheer distances involved in space," Ronin said, mainly for Taketa's benefit as Kanagawa would know the meaning already.

Despite merely nodding, Kanagawa's face couldn't help but show his disappointment. "Sorry, Toshi, I'm not going to let you out to play with your friends for a few weeks," said Taketa, nipping Kanagawa's notion of escaping Taketa's clutches in the bud.

* * *

How do I get myself mixed up in this stuff? wondered Gamma 1, Gunnery Sergeant Brett Blackwater. He was cleaning his mag-rail carbine for the fifth time. Testing the feed, magazine, power charges, everything. *And it's always hurry up, and wait, wait, wait,* he thought grumpily. Right now the enemy was boredom.

Blackwater was leaning against the outer hull of *Bulldog 3*. Jonsey sat next to him, intently monitoring the data streaming in from their drone net. The data included Tacnet information from the deployment on the surface, communication intercepts, optics, and scans in various wavelengths. Lieutenant Gustav sat next to him and likewise monitored the information flowing in.

As always, Confederation Marines found very dark ways to entertain themselves. "Hey Gamma 1. Which limb would you rather lose?" asked Gamma 2, Cpl. Jefferson Langley, to start the dark entertainment. "I bet Gamma 1 would rather lose a leg. The Corps can always issue you another one," he challenged.

Blackwater was an old hand at this game, although he hadn't played it with any of the guys on his current team. He smiled coldly as he replied, "Definitely. I'd rather lose both legs so they can give me those mechanical replacements. Then it'd be even easier to run your big butt into the ground," he said.

Before Langley could top that, Lieutenant Gustav surprised them all by loudly saying, "Wow. I was thinking Gamma 1 would give up an arm, so he could beat you to death with it. Disappointing."

Cries of "whoa, whoa, whoa," "ooohhhs," and "ahhhs" simultaneously filled the air. Eyebrows arched at the unexpected dig from the lieutenant, Blackwater felt obligated to top them all.

"Aw geez, Lieutenant. I only need just the one arm to beat down Gamma 2. Using two would just be unfair," Blackwater said, causing the bored Marines to give us some more whoops.

CHAPTER 59

BATTLE OF THE BRIDGE

"**B**ravo 1, Echo 4. There's movement on the perimeter," said Private Pak over the composite team commlink." Pak had positioned himself inside a burned-out building a block back from the buildings adjacent to the river. He was in the slums of the Borderlands, using his drones to monitor the enemy formation on the other side of the river. Commander Hunt had asked the Marines for their help to stop the Loyalist faction of the military from establishing a beachhead in the Borderlands at this river crossing.

"That's good copy, Echo 4. Keep us apprised. All Marines stay frosty until ordered otherwise," Bravo 1 replied from his position next to Hunt. Mackey and a two-man fire team were positioned inside the buildings next to the river, and the rest of the Marines were monitoring the video feeds from Pak's Butterfly drones over the Tacnet.

"C'mon boys, show yourselves. Nothing to worry about over here," Pak muttered to himself. Several minutes passed before movement occurred again. "Gotcha," Pak said to himself.

A shadowy figure on the opposite riverbank reappeared, and turned and motioned for others who were still unseen to follow him. "Bravo 1, Echo 4. One Tango in sight. Appears to be the point man for a unit that's still not in visual,"

Pak decided to fly his tiny drone closer to get a better visual on what was going on. That's when he felt the ground start to shudder slightly. It was followed by more shudders.

The team commlink opened up with the voice of Lieutenant Gustav. "Bravo 1, LT. Be advised, orbital surveillance shows some sort of armor moving towards your position from across the river. We've plotted them on Tacnet. Multiple routes, still bogies. How copy?"

Mackey replied immediately as the ground shuddering was causing him to become very concerned. "LT, Bravo 1. That's good copy. We still can't see 'em," he transmitted.

Pak's drone quickly crossed the river and hovered above the corner of a building rooftop. The entire riverfront on that side of the river was lined by five-story structures.

The new images his drones sent were alarming. "Bravo 1, Echo 4. Unknown bogeys are tangos," he said as he forwarded the images confirming the identity of the bogeys to the team's Tacnet.

"Acknowledged. Loyalist armor and infantry approaching. Bravo and Echo, do not fire until I give the order," said Bravo 1 said, using the new term "Loyalist" he had assigned during his team's briefing as a handy label to identify the opposing military.

The shuddering increased in intensity as the placid river water began to be disturbed with ripples from the vibrations. Suddenly, a loud rumbling could be heard that was quickly followed by something long and narrow slowly thrusting up through the river water.

"Bravo 1, LT. We're now seeing the appearance of the underwater access bridge Commander Hunt advised us about. Can you confirm?"

The teams had been pre-positioned to guard against the underwater bridge. The Loyalist military had built the bridge decades ago as a hidden route into the Borderlands so they would always have a way to surprise the Cargo Class during times of civilian unrest. It was designed to pop up through the water to allow armored units to cross over. The Loyalists didn't realize the Cargo Rebellion was well aware of its existence.

"LT, Bravo 1, that's affirm. Loyalist infantry and tanks are lining up to cross into the Borderlands."

Within minutes, a squad of infantry troops crossed over to secure the landing on the near side. They quickly got behind the available cover while they scouted for trouble.

While watching the video feed from Pak's drones, Bravo and Echo stayed hidden. They didn't have to wait long, as two tanks began crossing side by side, with several more pairs following them.

Mackey waited until they were near the middle of the span, and then he shouted "Marines, light 'em up!" over the commlink. The scattered Marine fire teams seemingly opened fire from everywhere at once.

Unheard above the cacophony, mortar shells from Commander Hunt's mobile artillery units whooshed in from above. Their arrival was punctuated by loud explosions that sprayed shrapnel into the infantry on the bridge.

The infantry on the bridge either dropped from being hit, or hid behind whatever cover they could find before the survivors returned fire. The amount of energy returned across the river by the Loyalist infantry was incredible.

The ambient temperatures on the Marine's side of the river rapidly escalated. "Bravo 5, Bravo 1, shift fire to the buildings across the street and let the mortars and snipers suppress the infantry on the bridge for now. Their infantry rayguns are heating everything up over here. Our thermals are becoming useless," Mackey ordered.

Bravo 5, the team's heavy weapons specialist, Pvt. Terry Allison, didn't have time to respond, he just repositioned his Buzzsaw and began raking the buildings wherever he saw movement. Unlike the standard Marine mag-rail carbine, the Buzzsaw was a heavy Marine infantry assault rifle with much larger rounds that used liquid propellant for a far higher rate of fire than a mag-rail carbine was capable of. The reason it is called the Buzzsaw quickly becomes obvious to the uninitiated because the high rate of fire tended to blur together into a throaty *brrrt* sound.

After unleashing several volleys from the same position that punched right through the walls on the buildings facing them, Allison knew he was almost out of time. "Bravo 1, Bravo 5, displacing!" he called over the commlink. Movement was life, and while Allison wasn't too bothered by the increasing temperatures of the walls he was positioned behind, due to the enemy rayguns being relatively ineffective against the protection of his exosuit, seeing the long barrels of several tank turrets turn his way was another matter entirely.

Allison didn't realize he was counting under his breath as he scrambled to get out of the building. *Five. Six. Se* ... As he ran through the doorway at the rear of the structure on the facing away from the river, a powerful explosion sent him tumbling the rest of the way into the street. Unlike the infantry's raygun weapons, the tanks were clearly using projectile ordnance.

Mackey saw Allison's Tacnet icon switch from green to yellow. "Bravo 5, Bravo 1. Say status?" he called over the commlink. "Bravo 5, say status?" he repeated moments later. He was met by silence as he watched the icon for the Echo team's medic quickly shift position to run over to check on Allison.

"Bravo 1, Echo 7. Bravo 5 is down, but his exosuit has him stabilized for now. I'm going to move him to a safer location," Private Nancy Dos reported after a few minutes.

"Echo 7, Bravo 1. Is his weapon operational?" Mackey asked Dos before she had a chance to move Allison.

"Bravo 1, Echo 7. It's operational," came Dos' reply.

"That's a good copy, Echo 7. Bravo 2, you're closest to their position. Can you retrieve the Buzzsaw?" Mackey asked. He had just arrived at a position behind a retaining wall on the roof of a building and popped his head over the top to get a better angle on the infantry who were still on this side of the river.

"Bravo 1, Bravo 2. Already moving. ETA thirty seconds!" said Bravo 2, Cpl. Ed Wilson. The sound of his voice betrayed his exertion as he moved quickly.

Mackey didn't have to explain the importance of getting the Buzzsaw back in the game. Suddenly he heard the enemy tanks start to move again, and the image on his Tacnet from the Butterfly surveillance drone was concerning.

"Echo 3. Tanks on the bridge headed your way," said Mackey, after knocking down another infantryman with a well-aimed shot from his mag-rail carbine.

"Bravo 1, Echo 3. In position. Taking a shot," responded Pvt. Rhee Lee, the heavy weapons specialist of Echo team.

From his position, Mackey could hear the whoosh and boom from Echo 4's rocket grenade. The building shuddered from the blast.

"Bravo 1, Echo 3. Negative damage. Repositioning for another shot," reported Lee. He wasn't going to risk having the building he was occupying blown up while he was still in it.

Lee wasn't disappointed by his decision to fire and move. By the time he ran into the next building, he could feel his last position take multiple hits from the tanks. *Fortunately all the dust and smoke is helping my cover*, he thought as he slid to a stop behind a wall next to a window opening that provided a different angle on the tanks that were approaching their end of the bridge.

Taking advantage of the dust and smoke, Lee leaned over the window opening and locked in his weapon. "Bravo 1, Echo 3. Shot two!" he announced over the noise as he pulled the trigger. Lee again scrambled to get out of the building before the return fire arrived.

The lead tank slowed to a slight crawl. Lee hit the left tread with his rocket grenade, but didn't cause enough damage to stop it.

"Bravo 1, Echo 3. Minor tread damage. Repositioning!" Lee said as he scrambled out of the building. Seconds later, the building was hit multiple times from the tanks and collapsed into a smoking, dusty pile of bricks.

"Echo 3, are you all right?" yelled Mackey, forgetting to identify himself as he, too, displaced from his latest position.

"Bravo 1, Echo 3. I'm fine. All my cover is gone. Moving back to Point Alamo," Lee responded as he returned to the rally point Mackey designated prior to the engagement. As the first Marine forced to occupy Point Alamo, it was his job to provide covering fire for those following behind unless he received other orders.

"Bravo 1, Bravo 2. Our rocket grenades don't have enough punch to penetrate their armor!" said Wilson over the sound of gunfire. He was firing and moving every few minutes to keep the Loyalists from zeroing in on his position.

Mackey turned to look at Commander Hunt. "Their armor is pushing through. Do your men have any explosives to take out that bridge?" he asked.

Hunt shook his head. "No, we're using most of our explosives in the mortars!" he replied.

Just as the lead tank with the damaged tread was slowly reaching the near side of the bridge, a bright streak of blue-colored fire shot out from the fifth floor window of a distant building. The building was several hundred yards away, slightly around a curve of the river that gave the occupants a better view of the now visible bridge. The Pirate, Cpl. Adrian Longman (Echo 2), had set up a sniper hide in the interior of the building to cover the location where the hypervelocity rounds from his Stinger sniper rifle were originating. A heavy-caliber, magnet rail-gun with an exceptionally high-velocity self-guided round, the Stinger emitted no telltale flash to give away the shooter's position. Longman had taken full advantage of those characteristics and his rifle's Airburst Mode to pour metallic slivers into Loyalists hiding behind cover while he methodically took the Loyalist infantry out of the game.

The blue fire streak was faster than the naked eye could follow and left an observer with a faint impression of having seen the angry strike of a powerful lightning bolt. The sound of it tearing through the atmosphere trailed well behind, even in the short distance of a few hundred yards, but paled in comparison to the boom when the rocket collided against the side of the leading tank. The impact event was so powerful, it seemed as if it blew right through the far side of the heavy tank and knocking it on its side as if it weighed far less than its 75 tons.

After the thunderous crash and flashy blue light streak, the heads of every combatant turned to see where the new threat came from.

LOYALISTS

"**M**ajor Cartwright, they were clearly waiting to ambush us!" said Lt. Evan Peugot as he spoke to Maj. Percy Cartwright over the field radio. "We're pushing on to the far side of the bridge, but the rebels downed 40 percent of the battalion just on the opening volley. The leading company is already combat ineffective. We've never seen that degree of accuracy or those much deadlier weapons by the Cargo Class before," he added.

"Lieutenant, I'm sure you're mistaken. The Cargo Class doesn't have the firepower to stop our units from making the crossing. They may have somehow known about the underwater bridge, but we will prevail. Stop your whining. Have the armor provide covering fire while you move your men across the river. Cargo doesn't have the breeding or pedigree to make a stand against the military," Cartwright said condescendingly. "Report back to me when you're on the other side."

Easy for you to say, Peugot thought angrily, *safe in your luxury tower downtown, twenty miles away, while shells are raining down all around us and a hailstorm of bullets is taking down my men. Idiot.*

Peugot turned to his aide. "Sergeant Timson, order the tanks to provide covering fire for the infantry crossing!" he said curtly. No need to be polite to some Crew Class infantry sergeant that had gotyen assigned for this operation.

"Right away, sir," responded Timson, who was all business and professionalism despite getting stuck without another clueless lieutenant from the Officer Class.

Timson gave the orders to the tanks before turning his attention back to the infantry troops attempting to cross this infernal bridge under heavy fire. "Charlie Company, say status?" he called on their field radio. There was no response, so he tried again. *Maybe they can't hear me over all the noise*, he thought.

"Charlie Company, this is Sergeant Timson. Say status!" he repeated. Still no response. Timson decided to try another company. "Easy Company, status report," he called, growing more worried by the second. "Easy Company, say status!" he tried again. Still nothing.

Timson's growing sense of unease exploded into outright alarm when Foxtrot and Golf Companies likewise failed to respond. Timson finally got ahold of a corporal in India Company. "India Company, say status?"

"This is Private Dunhill. We are under fire and pulling back with heavy casualties!" said the panicked voice on the radio that Timson could barely hear over the sounds of combat.

"Private Dunhill, this is Sergeant Timson. Where is your commanding officer?" Timson shouted into the headset, hoping to be heard above the explosive sounds of the battle on the other end.

"Dead. All dead! I'm in charge of the company now, what's left of it!" Dunhill responded.

"Private Dunhill, you are to regroup your company and lead them across that bridge!" Timson shouted. There was no reply, so Timson tried again. "Dunhill, take your men across that bridge! Can you hear me?" he shouted into the field radio. Still no reply. "Son, if you can hear me but can't respond, double click your talk button," he said, quieter this time. Surprisingly, the line lit up with another panicked voice screaming, "They're dead! Everyone's dead. What do I..."

Timson heard a gurgling sound, then the line went silent.

"Timson to Major Cartwright, please respond," Timson called, trying to remain calm.

"Cartwright here. Have you taken the other side of the bridge, Sergeant?"

"Negative sir. Charlie, Easy, Foxtrot, Golf and India Companies have been massacred. We need more men! The tanks are nearly across and they don't have any infantry support," reported Timson.

"Massacred? That's impossible! Sergeant, they're just lowborn rebels. They can't stand toe to toe with our tanks. Our tanks will have to clear the Cargo Class out for our infantry instead. Have them..."

The rest of his orders went unheard as a bright bluish, impossibly fast streak of fire shrieked out from a building down by the bend of the river and plowed straight through the lead tank and tipping it on its side. The impact event was so powerful that it shook everything in the vicinity and its noise drowned out the sounds of combat.

"What the?" yelled Timson when he saw it happen.

CHAPTER 61

THE BLEED

I *have got to get me more of these!* Longman thought excitedly as he picked himself up off the floor. The recoil from the weapon he just unleashed had sent him tumbling backwards, and the launch tube lay on the floor with smoke rising from it. Longman ran back to the window he had fired through and peeked around the window frame to see what happened.

The blue streak left behind by the super propellant was nothing more than a rapidly dissipating contrail of smoke in the light breeze of the day. Longman could see what appeared to be an overturned, burning tank blocking the bridge with its bulk, but it was difficult to tell from the distance through the smoke.

"Echo 2, Bravo 1. What was THAT?" Mackey's voice was nearly drowned out by the overwhelming sounds of a Buzzsaw being fired near his position.

"Bravo 1, Echo 2. That was a Firefly," Longman replied.

Mackey's face scrunched up in a look of confusion. "Echo 2, what's a Firefly, and do you have any more ammo for it?"

"It's an experimental armor piercing weapon that Lieutenant Alphonso was tinkering with. I only have one more rocket for it," Longman said.

"Echo 2, LT. Lieutenant Alphonso failed to inform command about having made available any new toys for this engagement," came the voice of Lieutenant Gustav, overriding the channel and identifying himself by the callsign, pronounced 'El-Tee'. *It's important for commanders to be aware of their team's equipment packages so they make decisions that align with their capabilities*, thought Gustav with annoyance and concern that he might have missed something important.

Longman grinned as he loaded the remaining rocket into the tube. He didn't have long to loose the next one before the tanks zeroed on his position.

"I'm guessing Lieutenant Alphonso failed to inform the command element because he is unaware the Firefly was tactically acquired by Echo 2 for this away mission, sir," Longman said as he finished reloading and raised the Firefly to his shoulder.

"Echo 2, Bravo 1. Tactically acquired, huh? Can you see the main pillar of the bridge from your position?" Mackey asked. Mackey's voice sounded somewhat amused.

"That's a roger, Bravo 1. You want I should hit it with the remaining rocket?" Longman asked.

Mackey definitely wanted that. "Affirmative Echo 2, take it out."

"That's a good copy, Bravo 1. Taking the shot," Longman confirmed.

Focusing on the Firefly's targeting cross hairs that appeared on his visor, Longman quickly acquired the main pillar of the bridge and pulled the trigger.

Good thing Alphonso outfitted it with a Fire and Forget system instead of a guide wire. The shooter is too busy getting knocked on their arse to keep eyes on the target after launch, thought Longman, picking himself up off the floor. Again.

It was time to move. Longman needed to displace before those remaining tanks dusted his position.

Mackey knew Longman was too busy scrambling to assess the result of his second shot so he figured he would tell him instead and they could watch the replay from Pak's Butterfly drones later. "Echo 2, good shot. The bridge is down and the Loyalists are withdrawing. Meet us at Point Alamo." The bridge continued crumbling into the river as he said it.

* * *

"The Loyalists took a beating at the bridge. Our post-battle assessments suggest they lost about 150 KIA, plus about a hundred wounded, plus several tanks when the bridge underneath them fell. Marine casualties were light, with three wounded, no KIA. Rebel casualties were two dozen KIA, and about the same in wounded. Our corpsmen are treating the wounded in the field hospital," said Mackey to Hunt as they walked to Hunt's command post. "The biggest problem is the only thing we had that was capable of stopping their armor was an experimental weapon that Echo 2 lifted from the mad scientists in ship's Fabrication Department."

"Can they make more of them?" Hunt asked, a look of concern on his face. Without those, stopping the next armor incursion will be problematic at best.

"Yes. Although whether they will arrive in time is unknown. Lieutenant Alphonso was quite surprised some nefarious Marine breached his security system without leaving a trace. Naturally, we have no idea the Pirate did it and we're not going to tell Alphonso who it was," Mackey noted dryly.

As they entered the tent, the gloomy interior swallowed them like a cave. Mackey's visor automatically adjusted for the light levels, so he barely noticed.

The two walked over to a large table covered with maps. Hunt pulled over a map of First City and pointed at the downtown area as he began to speak. "We have been on defense throughout the entire resistance. Trading land for time, which is fine, up to a point. That's because the Officer Class occupies the city centers, while the Crew Class is sandwiched into rings around the Officers. Cargo Class occupies the rest of the planet, at least strategically, so Cargo Class has plenty of land to trade. Officers and Crew only own the ground under their feet, while the rest is ours by default. It's similar to the dilemma faced by the British during the American Revolution."

"American Revolution? Who were they revolting against and why were the British involved?" Mackey asked. He'd never heard of an American Revolution.

Hunt looked at him in surprise. "You don't know about the American Revolution? Didn't you say you were from Alabama?" Hunt asked.

"I'm from Alabama, yes. But remember when I mentioned we were unaware of the existence of Terra Station because of The Fall?" Mackey replied.

Hunt nodded. "Yes, but we didn't get a chance to discuss what The Fall was and there hasn't been time to thoroughly review the video feeds copied from the Space Control Center by Louise Abernathy where Ambassador Gadre explained what that was. Events have been moving too quickly."

Mackey gave Hunt a quick synopsis. "The Fall was so bad, even after the Treaty of Midway was signed we lost almost all the records of our own history because civilization completely collapsed and most of our population centers turned into death zones. Humanity struggled to adapt to a plague and a nuclear winter in order to survive. It was a disaster of such magnitude that what once was, is often no more. We were even shocked to learn that the name of the language we are both speaking now is different between the two planets. You call it English, while now on Earth it came to be called American. No one knows why."

They both stopped for a moment when an aide handed them steaming cups of coffee. Mackey continued, "So, what's the story on the American Revolution?"

Hunt set his mug down. "The quick version that is relevant here are different parts of North America was settled by the British and the French. There was a population of various native tribes already present as well. After a time, the rule of the British became untenable to the British colonists and they rebelled against the heavy-handed rule of the British.

"The colonists lacked the resources to fight the British using the same tactics employed by the British. Once the colonists realized they couldn't win that way and the war wasn't going well, they realized they needed a new strategy. They finally figured out that they didn't need to fight and hold ground because they were supported by the people actually living on the land.

"The British only held the ground under their boots because they lacked the support of the majority of the people who lived there. Most of the rebels' strategy eventually centered around making it too expensive for the British to keep projecting force. Finally the British people tired of the cost of the war, and their King ended hostilities when their trapped forces surrendered."

Mackey nodded. "Yes, that same scenario does seem to apply here as well. When you asked for our participation, it was our speculation that the battle of the bridge wasn't merely to test the Loyalists and keep them out of the Borderlands, it was to bleed them and reduce their appetite for war. The Cargo Rebellion wins by making it too expensive for the Loyalists to win."

Hunt nodded in agreement. "Exactly, my friend. It's the only way we can succeed using the resources we have at our disposal."

"So what's next? Sounds like you're contemplating some offensive action," Mackey said.

"Indeed we are. Since the Loyalists are bunched up in their towers down in the city centers, we thought to take the fight to them in order to bring about the realization they are vulnerable and victory will be too costly," Hunt noted. "We believe the Officer Class will demand more military protection once they realize how vulnerable they are. Hopefully this would draw away military resources from other areas, and tie them up guarding non-critical assets."

Mackey smiled broadly. "I like it. Cause a change in their defensive posture by reacting to a feint or diversion. May I recommend a game plan based on our ability to cause chaos and mayhem?"

Hunt smiled broadly now. "I thought you'd never ask."

CHAPTER 62

MARINES OF CHAOS

ulldogs 1 and 2 appeared in orbit at the designated coordinates. "Nice of you guys to drop by. Did you bring the party favors?" said Gamma 1 over the commlink.

"*Gamma 1, Bulldog 1. That we did. Lieutenant Alphonso still can't figure out how his security was breached, but his people went into overdrive to make you some nice toys,*" replied Chief Hal Patterson, the rear-seater for *Bulldog 1*.

"Now that you're here, we can laser commlink you the arrival coordinates. We're jumping in low to a blind spot in their airspace, then flying to the drop zone using the terrain following mode to avoid any curiosity about our atmospheric flame trails after the jump. We jump in one minute," Lieutenant Gustav ordered.

"That's good copy, LT, Jump in 1 mike," came the reply from *Bulldog 1.*

While Bulldog 2 remained in orbit to maintain an orbital overwatch, Bulldogs 1 and 3 soon jumped away.

They reappeared over a mountain valley at about the same height as the neighboring mountain peaks. Their small jump flares were immediately engulfed by a flame trail that began the second the cold air came into contact with the friction of their speed. Both Bulldogs appeared to be a flaming pair of comets plummeting into the desolate valley before the shuttle pilots halted their pyrotechnic descent.

"*Bulldog 1, Bulldog 3*. Follow us," said Russo over the commlink as his shuttle shot forward through the dark valley while the mountain tops still clung to that last glimpse of sunlight before night set in.

The pilots quickly flew low over the darkening landscape using their terrain following scanners. They stayed off the commlinks, observing radio silence as they streaked out of the valley at several times the speed of sound.

Several hours into their nap of the earth night flight, Jonsey's deep voice broke the extended silence in the cabin of *Bulldog 3*. "Energy signatures detected. Random search patterns. They haven't seen us yet."

Russo was quick to acknowledge. "That's good copy. Send to *Bulldog 1* via laser commlink. Plot their sources on Tacnet so we can avoid them as long as possible."

Anticipating the request, Jonsey had already uploaded the data into the Tacnet so both Bulldogs could avoid them accordingly.

As they approached First City, the number of energy sources seeking aircraft multiplied in number rapidly. The rapidly rising numbers corresponded to an increasing number of course changes by Russo to stay dark on the enemy search screens.

Jonsey again broke the silence. "Incoming data message from Bravo 1. The away team and rebel commandos assaulted and destroyed multiple scanner emplacements at the locations now marked on Tacnet. The gap in scanner coverage leads directly to First City. Our insertion point is called Downers Park in the center of First City. He says to land there and debark our freeloading hitchhikers."

"Freeloading hitchhikers?" roared Gustav, who couldn't help but hear Jonsey in the crowded shuttle as he was standing right behind him.

Grinning madly, Jonsey added, "Yessir. Bravo 1 also said he's — and I quote –'excited to get an honest day's work out of the lot of you.'"

Gustav and Blackwater exchanged incredulous looks before Blackwater muttered, "The man's got balls, I gotta give him that."

Gustav snorted, which got Jonsey's attention. "Tell Bravo 1 the Marines are here, and tell him we'd be delighted to see him in Downers Park. That is, if he can find time in his busy schedule of naps and sun tanning."

Jonsey's grin threatened to crack his face open. "Oh, yessir. With pleasure!"

* * *

Bulldogs 1 and 3 came in hot. Each of them streaked into the downtown of First City, flying between tall buildings to arrive over Downers Park where they quickly landed at the beacon activated by the away team.

Engines whining even at zero thrust because they were still running, the rear ramps to each shuttle dropped simultaneously and Gamma team quickly hopped out. Marines that had been waiting on the ground lifted several wounded Marines and rebels on stretchers, and they passed the exiting Gamma team as they hauled the wounded on to the shuttles.

It was a frenzied few minutes on the ground in the park as Marines quickly moved men, ordnance and equipment in and out of the Bulldogs before the ramps raised again.

"*Bulldog 3, Bulldog 1.* That's it, ready for departure," said the pilot of *Bulldog 1*, Erin Johnson as she increased the lift and thrust of her engines to take off again.

"*Bulldog 1, Bulldog 3.* That's affirm. We're ghost riding from here," responded Russo, using the slang to indicate they were heading back to the Cerberus nest.

Both shuttles rocketed away, leaving the city behind.

"1s, LT. Tacnet shows Loyalist movement our direction from the south end of the park. Let's not be here when they arrive," Gustav called to the sergeants of the away team, Blackwater and Mackey.

"LT, Bravo 1. That's good copy. We've distributed the party favors among each team and are moving to our rebel rally points with the Cargo squads," responded Mackey. He was rapidly traveling to the northeast park entrance with Bravo team as they used their powered exosuits to bound ahead in the lower gravity.

Gustav caught up to Blackwater, as Gamma team likewise raced towards the park's northwest entrance. The pursuing Loyalists never had a chance to catch up.

RALLY POINT GREEN

"Nice of you guys to drop by. Enjoy the tea and crumpets?" wise-cracked Hunt over a commlink as he watched the Marines approach his position with startling speed. Hunt and his people were dressed in some expensive business suits they'd tactically acquired from an Officer Class clothing boutique a few blocks away from the insertion point in Downers Park. The ringing of the burglary alarm could faintly be heard even at this distance.

Seconds later, Bravo 1 landed a few feet from Hunt on his final bound. "You cleaned up nice. Almost civilized looking now," commented Mackey over his external speaker.

Hunt smiled at the joke. "It was hard to believe when you said my people would have to be lookouts for this mission because we couldn't keep up with you. Now I see you weren't exaggerating even slightly, which is somewhat disconcerting. And that mobility is not just from the lower gravity, is it?" Hunt replied, turning serious very quickly.

"That's correct. You just wouldn't be able to do it, but you're people are perfect for dressing like the locals and keeping an eye out while we hit and run," Mackey said.

Before either of them could say anything further, the ground shook from a heavy impact. Mackey turned to see a large fireball rising behind them in the park. The shockwave shattered all the glass in the facades of the skyscrapers lining the outer edge of the park.

"Without the damage, it kind of looks like an old picture of Central Park in New York City that I saw once," Mackey muttered. "Before the city was destroyed."

"1s, LT. Loyalist units in the park were hit from Bulldog 2 in orbit using some of their smaller munitions. You're cleared to engage any enemy you encounter," called Gustav over the commlink to the team sergeants.

Without the Loyalist units biting at their heels, the mission fully changed from an insert and hide, to a hit-and-run mission.

Mackey looked up at the skyscrapers they were standing next to. "This looks like as good of a place to start as any. Bravo team, disperse."

As Bravo team did so, Mackey donned a large vest over his exosuit that Hunt's people had made for him. Designed to look like a local policeman's vest, it said, "Police Department" in bright neon green lettering.

Without need for verbal acknowledgments, Mackey could see his men quickly spread out on Tacnet, which also noted each Marine's respective elevation because several of them were scaling the outsides of the buildings.

While they did that, Mackey opened the front entrance of the nearest building and walked into a scene of pandemonium. He activated his external speakers so the crowd of Officer Class civilians that had gathered in the atrium could hear him. "Clear the building. You have two minutes to evacuate. The rebels are coming. Clear the building. You have two minutes to evacuate. The rebels are coming."

Frightened by the strangely dressed police officer, the Officers in the building surged towards the exits, followed closely by their Crew retinue and enablers.

"Nicely done, Bravo 1. I've never seen Officers in such a hurry before," Hunt remarked wryly over the commlink while Mackey hurried to the next building so he could repeat his performance.

When the streets were filled with panicky people in their pajamas, Mackey decided the time was right. "Bravo team, Bravo 1. Execute Phase One."

The Bravo team Marines, who were likewise wearing fake Police vests over their exosuits, went into action. Broken shards of glass fell far to the ground from where the Marines who scaled the outsides of the buildings had been waiting for the order to go inside. They smashed the windows and climbed in. Other Marines who were positioned on the ground shot out all the light sources to make the streets go dark. Then they, too, entered the buildings to make a mess of things.

Bravo 5 (Private Allison), now recovered from his injuries in the prior engagement at the Battle of the Bridge, was the first Marine to reach the elevators on the ground floor of a building. "Bravo 1, Bravo 5. Setting the lift charges now," he called over the commlink.

Seconds later, another report. "Bravo 1, Bravo 6. I've reached the utilities room of my building. Setting the charges now," Private Cupper wasted no time in attaching explosives to the power, backup generator, and water and air systems of the building he had broken into.

Other reports quickly followed. Bravo team Marines rigged nearly everything needed to make the Officer's residential skyscrapers uninhabitable for ten separate blocks. Marines on the upper floors rigged all relays for each habitation system as well, which ensured no one would be able to reside in the buildings for quite some time.

Mackey glanced at the elapsed time counter inside his visor. Fifteen minutes had passed since their glorious arrival, and now the sounds of sirens could be heard over the screams of the panicked Officers outside.

"Bravo 1, this is Hunt. My people have spotted the military responders. Ten blocks away, but slowed by the people in the streets. We're detonating the car bombs parked in the streets at Point Car Bomb to slow them down now."

That was all he needed to know. "Bravo team, time's up. Execute Phase Two and meet at Rally Point Green. We've worn out our welcome."

Acknowledgments flooded in from the unit.

CHAPTER 63

MARINES OF MAYHEM

"**G**amma 1, LT. Bravo is heading back to Rally Point Green. We'll begin our withdrawal soon," Gustav called over the commlink, while the sounds of gunfire could be heard loudly over the channel.

"LT, Gamma 1. Acknowledged. We're still in contact with the Loyalists over here," Blackwater responded between volleys of rifle fire.

Both sections of Gamma had been split into two elements by Gustav for the engagement. Blackwater's element had forward deployed to intercept the Loyalist's military responders at Point Car Bomb and slow them down even further.

"Commander Hunt's car bombs stopped them cold, Gamma 1 but it won't last. His people say tanks will hit your location in 2 mikes," Gustav said.

"That's good copy, LT. Contact in 2 mikes," Blackwater confirmed.

Blackwater could already hear and feel the rumbling of the Loyalist armor approaching down the boulevard leading to his position. The ground had begun shaking slightly with their weight, which caused obvious confusion among the Officer Class citizens who Bravo team had already evacuated out into the streets.

Soon the tanks were plotted on Tacnet, which was relatively redundant for Gamma team as they were positioned half a dozen stories up in the buildings lining the street. Gamma 3 (Private Louis Caron) peered down at the armored units from inside the room he occupied. Caron opened a commlink. "Gamma 1, Gamma 3. In position. Tacnet has an accurate plot from the overhead drones. Thirty tanks, mixed with emergency vehicles. Speed now approximately three miles per hour."

Blackwater smiled. *Three miles an hour*, he thought. *Sitting ducks, but they're still too far away.* "Stay frosty, Gamma 3. You're the forward observer for now, let them pass by your position until they're all in range. Bravo's about to be the rabbit for the bad guys to chase," he ordered.

"That's good copy, Gamma 1. Eyeballs only until ordered otherwise," responded Caron.

The armor slowly clanked to a stop. *C'mon laddies, stop dilly dallying*, thought Blackwater as he watched the Tacnet.

* * *

The streets were crowded with panicked Officers, their servants, and a mix of civilian and military vehicles. *What a mess!* thought Captain Lawrence Devaney disgustedly as he rode in the lead tank, numbered 225. *No dignity. Officers in their nightclothes and robes, little more than common refugees. Only Cargo Class animals would stoop low enough to do this to civilians,* he concluded.

Devaney was from one of the original families of Officers that founded First City. They were a proud family, and treated their servants well in his opinion, even providing them quarters to sleep in instead of expecting them to sleep on the floor in the servant's work areas like lesser Officer's families normally demanded of their staffs. A product of the prestigious and exclusive Primrose University which catered to the elite Officers and churned out the cream of Terra Station's society, Devaney enjoyed being on the fast track to the Officer's Council that ruled the planet.

"Captain Devaney, do we continue to hold position?" asked the tank's driver, Sergeant McNully. He was a Crew Class tank driver from a respectable family of business owners in another city.

"Yes, sergeant. I don't like this situation. Too many Officers on the streets to move forward safely," responded Devaney. "We haven't located the rebels..."

A large explosion erupted several blocks ahead and drowned out the rest of Devaney's sentence. The power went out, darkening the street-lights and lights from the buildings along the street. Smoke and fire billowed, making it very difficult to see in the confusion.

"Found 'em, Captain!" remarked McNully dryly, shouting to be heard over the noise from screaming civilians who surged forward outside the tank.

"Take us in, Sergeant. We have to protect the Officers from these maniacs!" ordered Devaney, who had now obviously decided to disregard the possibility of running over fleeing civilians.

In response, the tank lurched forward, heedless of the civilians and other vehicles still in the road. They would just have to get out of their way or be crushed by Tank 225.

"Tank 225, you're getting too far in front of your infantry support!" came a call over the radio. It was Major Cartwright. *The man has been skittish ever since the rebels repulsed his armor at the bridge to the Borderlands. He was too timid then, and he's too timid now,* thought Devaney with disgust.

When Devaney didn't bother to acknowledge Cartwright's communication, Sergeant McNully glanced nervously back at him. "Sir? Should we..." McNully began to ask when Devaney curtly cut him off.

Devaney haughtily looked down at McNully. "Nonsense, sergeant. We boldly proceed ahead with nerve and panache. Aggression will win this night."

Cartwright tried to reach his tank commander again. "Tank 225, respond." Seconds of silence hung heavily in the air, underscored by the rumbling of the tank as it rolled down the boulevard. "Tank 225, this is Major Cartwright. I order you to respond."

Oh. Well. It's an ORDER now. Guess I'll have to favor the Major with a reply, thought Devaney, annoyed at the interruption. "Major Cartwright, Tank 225. The crowd is thinning now so our infantry can catch up if they hurry. I..."

Devaney interrupted himself when he caught sight of something unusual through the tank's light enhancing viewfinder. "Major, I see them. Black-suited figures, several stories up. Some inside the buildings, but I see some scaling the building exteriors towards the roofs! I'm ordering the tanks to open fire."

Devaney cut short the call and tuned to the unit's command channel. "This is Captain Devaney. Rebel troops are on the fifth and sixth floors of the buildings on this block. Lock in with the machine guns and fire when ready."

While the twin machine guns mounted atop Tank 225 opened fire to rake the buildings with heavy caliber bullets, the main turret barrel traversed upwards towards the enemy. Shattered glass, metal and other pieces of building began raining down to the street below.

Suddenly, Devaney could hear frightening shrieking sounds outside, punctuated by a rapid series of impact events that shook the ground so hard it could even be felt inside the tank. It most definitely wasn't the kind of shrieking panicked civilians make. It was much more ominous.

Still looking through his viewfinder, Devaney was temporarily blinded by streaks of painfully bright blue flame trails that shot down from all around from the interior of the same buildings he had ordered his tanks to fire upon. Tank 225 shuddered hard from an impact event right next to them.

Devaney spotted another dark figure that suddenly appeared in a darkened window with some sort of tube raised to his shoulder. *Has to be a weapon!* thought Devaney excitedly.

Devaney activated the remote control top mounted machine guns and began tracking to target the dark figure. He unleashed another volley to disrupt the dark figure's aim just as a blinding streak of blue light shot from the tube. The shadowy figure disappeared from sight in a hail of shattered glass and stone from Tank 225's as the bullets stitched up the side of the building.

Instead of smashing through Tank 225, the impact event was in the ground just beneath the front of the left tank tread. Pavement and the ground underneath erupted in a huge shower of debris and dust.

Devaney never knew if he lost consciousness from the shockwave of the impact, or when he hit his head on the inside armor as the tank tumbled sideways into the crater left behind by the weapon.

CHAPTER 64

RALLY POINT BLUE

Gustav wasn't sure whether he'd hit that lead tank due to the Firefly's tremendous recoil and having his concentration broken up when the tank's machine guns opened up on his position just as he fired. *Geez, these things have an awesome recoil!* he thought as he picked himself up off the floor several feet from where he had fired the Firefly.

Rather than expose himself to more gunfire, Gustav accessed a feed from one of Gamma 4s (Private Victor Berger) drones that was providing overhead tactical visual data.

Hrmmph. Missed. Lucky the impact knocked the tank out by taking out the ground underneath it instead, he noted to himself.

His commlink opened an incoming message from Blackwater. "LT, Gamma 1. Say status."

"Gamma 1, LT. I'm OK. I'm looking at the Tacnet data and visual surveillance from the drones. The vanguard and rear guard of the armored unit have been destroyed, trapping the armor in the middle of the formation. Get Gamma up to the rooftop of Rally Point Blue. It's time to disappear," Gustav ordered even as he moved toward the stairwell.

The Marines in or on the adjacent buildings wasted no time. They used their suits to leap across the dark about ten stories off the ground to eventually land on the exterior of the same building where Gustav was. Seconds after landing, they each scrambled inside.

Other Marines were likewise moving as they ran up the stairs two at a time from the ground floor, using the lighter gravity and their exosuit power to great advantage. Minutes later, they emerged on top of the building, ninety floors above the surface. Gustav was impressed with the amount of smoke that had drifted up this high from the ground level combat.

"LT, Gamma 1. Gamma team is all accounted for. Six WIA, mostly minor. No KIA," reported Blackwater when he spotted Gustav bounding out of the stairwell. Blackwater checked the chronometer displayed in his visor. "Fifteen tanks out of commission in a four-minute engagement, with the remaining armor corralled up for now on the wrong side of the river," he added.

Gustav smiled inside his visor. "Not bad for a bunch of crayon eaters. Alphonso's new Firefly launchers work pretty nifty."

"Yessir, but he's got to figure out how to reduce the recoil from the propellant. They're like trying to hang onto a kicking mule," Blackwater noted.

Gamma team took up positions around the rooftop. This high up, the winds were strong, making the building rooftop sway a few feet. Gustav had already sent the recall signal, but he couldn't tell where their ride was yet. "Angel Flight, LT. ETA?"

The reply was immediate. "LT, Angel Flight. Extraction in one mike. Dustoff in two. Over."

Gustav and Blackwater glanced at each other, each smiling inside their visors. "That's good copy, Angel Flight. We'll leave the porch light on," Gustav activated the retrieval beacon to guide them the rest of the way.

Bulldog 3 soon appeared out of the dark. Engines whining, it was lowering its ramp even as the shuttle dropped down onto the rooftop. Gustav looked at Tacnet as he moved towards their ride and confirmed Bravo team was likewise boarding *Bulldog 1* on the building at Rally Point Green which Bravo had occupied several blocks from Gamma's position.

Gustav was last on board after making sure none of his men had been left behind and he hit the ramp close button.

Jonsey looked over at Russo from his position in the cabin. "Gamma is aboard. Time to make like ghosts."

Russo nodded to the side to confirm he heard Jonsey without turning to look at his rearseater as he increased power to the still running engines. *Bulldog 3* responded instantly, leaping upwards into the dark sky.

"Chief Jonsey, all Marines have left the area. Detonate the charges," ordered Gustav. Down below, explosions wracked skyscraper after skyscraper, sending large fireballs rising into the atmosphere and showers of debris into the streets. A handful of smaller buildings collapsed into the streets, further trapping the remaining tanks between them.

"Take us home, Russo," said Gustav quietly.

CHAPTER 65

CERBERUS

Lieutenant Delgado reacted to the incoming message that appeared on her screen. "Captain, *Bulldog 3* just jumped into the return point. They say they have Gamma team aboard."

Ronin nodded. "Bring them home. Have Lieutenant Gustav meet us in the conference room."

Delgado replied, "Yes Captain," then passed along the order.

Minutes later, Gustav walked into the conference room where Ronin and Mueller were waiting. "Captain, Commander," he said with a nod as his way of greeting as he strode over to a chair.

"Good to see you again, Lieutenant. Report," Ronin ordered.

Gustav wasted no time summarizing the events of the engagement in downtown First City for Ronin and Mueller.

Ronin complimented Gustav. "Only six wounded is remarkable. That quick strike plan of yours worked well. We've intercepted Loyalist communications through the data tap. The military has been forced to consolidate its forces to break contact with the Cargo and protect the Officer Class. That consolidation will occur over the next few days, so we have some time to map out our next move. That separation from the Cargo Class will be very helpful because it opens up new strategic possibilities."

"Yessir. Panicking the Officers into overreacting and calling in the military so they lose their human shields is a great result. They still have half of that armor unit's tanks trapped downtown. Do we want to finish them off?" Gustav asked.

Mueller was ready for that question as they had been discussing it before Gustav's arrival. "No. Not yet at least. If we drop any ordnance on them from orbit, it might dawn on them that they're vulnerable if they consolidate. Besides, the Loyalists are busy trying to clear up the mess your Marines made downtown. Collapsing a few smaller buildings to entrap the tanks and seal off several blocks isn't something they're equipped to deal with easily."

Ronin smiled broadly. "Lieutenant. We thought you'd enjoy showing this news broadcast we recorded. For propaganda, it's quite entertaining." Dan tapped a button on the tablet in his hands and the large screen on the wall lit up.

CHANNEL 26 NEWS BRINGS YOU THIS SPECIAL REPORT: We received reports of a disturbance downtown this evening. Without provocation, rebels from the Borderlands attacked Officer neighborhoods in the center of our beautiful city. They rampaged like animals for a short time before the brave soldiers of the 7th Armored Cavalry arrived to stop them and capture hundreds of rebels. We go now to the reporter on the scene for more.

Ronin tapped his tablet again to stop the replay. Gustav had a strange expression on his face that was a combination of a humorless half-smile that didn't reach his eyes, and a furrowed brow of confusion. Ronin couldn't help but laugh softly to himself at the sight.

"But ... Captain. None of that happened. Who do they think they're fooling?" Gustav said.

"It's just propaganda, Lieutenant. No one believes it except maybe some government bureaucrats and gullible fools who don't want to face the truth," Ronin noted with a slight shaking of his head. "There's far too much evidence all around downtown that doesn't square with the fantasies of their propaganda broadcasts. Lying about it just weakens their own position with the people who know better."

Gustav shook his head with a disgusted look on his face. "Sure sounds a lot like the ridiculous propaganda the Collective used to put out there. I guess that's the kind of junk that unjust governments publish as a tool to help them stay in power." He paused for a moment before continuing. "Sirs. If that's all for now, I'd like to get my Marines squared away and get ready for the next action." Gustav said it as a question, but it really was more of a statement that he'd like to get back and see to his men.

Ronin smiled. "Of course. Don't let us keep you. When we acquire some new Intel as the situation evolves on the surface, we will assess our next steps then," he said to Gustav.

After the lieutenant left, Ronin and Mueller looked at one another for a few moments before Ronin broke the silence.

"Getting embroiled in a civil war with only a few teams of Marines aboard isn't playing to our strengths. Their performance down on the surface to cause the Loyalists to expose themselves sure helps re-balance the scales towards making the ship's weapons relevant again. What we need to do is eliminate their leadership," Ronin said thoughtfully.

Mueller lifted an eyebrow over Ronin's somewhat controversial conclusion. "I'm not sure naval command will approve of an assassination attempt. Foreign governments tend to take that kind of thing rather personally."

Ronin sighed. "No doubt. But if it occurs in the context of hitting a legitimate target instead of being a cloak-and-dagger kill, it's not really an assassination. It's more of a bonus then. And they made themselves legitimate targets by trying to initiate a sneak attack on Cerberus." Ronin's eyes unfocused as he leaned back in his seat and tilted his head towards the ceiling as if inspiration was lurking up there somewhere.

There were a few moments of silence. "Do you think Karl and the AI can cobble together a worm we can insert into the Loyalist's computer defense network?" Ronin suddenly asked.

The kind of worm Dan Ronin was referring to was like a computer virus on steroids. Part artificial intelligence, once a worm entered a system it constantly evolved to spread and remain undetectable while it fulfilled its purpose.

"I dunno. Let's ask," Mueller said as she tapped on her commlink. Her husband's voice came through in a moment. "This is Karl, what do you need?"

"Karl, the Captain and I are in the conference room and he had an interesting question for you. Can you and the AI design a worm we can insert into their military's defense net?"

There was a moment of silence while Karl considered the question. "It's ... possible? Maybe? Let me work on the question for a while and get back to you when I know more?"

"Sounds good. See you after shifts," Diane said as she ended the commlink. Her eyes refocused on Ronin after a moment. "What are you thinking?" she asked.

Ronin was still leaning back in his seat when he answered. "Could be many possibilities. Tentatively, assuming the Downtown Chaos and Mayhem campaign worked and the Loyalists pull back from the Cargo by consolidating their forces, I'd like to use that separation to our advantage using a worm to draw out the Officers Council into the open. The pre-arrival data we scooped up in our drone net probe suggests this secretive group controls the levers of power down there."

Mueller nodded. "That same data didn't contain any clues about how to find them, though. You think they'll be able to design a worm that can find them?"

Ronin smiled evilly. "Maybe we don't need to find them, so much as we can send them to a place of our time and choosing," he remarked cryptically.

* * *

"All right, on me, Marines!" Gustav shouted to be heard over the hubbub in the briefing room down in Marine Country. The noise died down.

"First of all, your performance during the battles at the bridge in the Borderlands, and downtown in First City showed me you are little more than barbarians who shouldn't be allowed to mingle with polite society," Gustav said loudly, drawing expectant looks from the gathered Marine teams. "I am very IMPRESSED because Marines do NOT belong in polite society anyway!" he added, drawing loud whoops, clapping and whistles from his men.

Gustav continued. "In fact, I'm pretty sure even our allies down there are kind of afraid of Marine savages who break things, and I like that too! We just put an entire planet on notice if they mess with the best, they'll die like the rest!" He was drowned out by more loud whoops and cheers.

"All right. Let's take care of our gear. The docs are already taking care of our wounded. And get cleaned up, especially you Bravo team. Whew. You guys are pretty ripe! Grab some chow, and we'll regroup here by teams at 2100 for a full debriefing that includes some amusing propaganda collected from broadcasts down on the surface. Dismissed!" Gustav finished, sending everyone off with a rousing cheer from the Marines.

CHAPTER 66

SEPARATION OF POWERS

"Secretary Ellis, after your failure to keep the rebellion out of their living spaces downtown, the Officers are demanding we reposition the military into a protective posture for their Class," said Speaker Hayward as he poured them both a glass of bourbon in the anteroom to Hayward's office. The speaker liked his caramel-colored liquor on the rocks.

Hayward handed Ellis a glass as they both sat in stuffed easy chairs arranged around a small coffee table. Nodding his thanks, Ellis took a small sip before responding.

"Mr. Speaker, we both know the Cargo Rebellion, as they've styled themselves, lack the resources and technology to create the firepower used against the armored unit downtown. That had to have come from Cerberus," Ellis concluded.

"Stanton," said Hayward, using the Secretary's first name, "I believe you but we have not been able to definitely prove it was Cerberus. We have some dark, grainy video captured during the battle of dark-suited men on the outside of the high rises downtown and shooting some remarkably powerful weapons. But otherwise, they're ghosts." Hayward paused for a sip before continuing. "But I'm pretty sure they're still out there somewhere."

Ellis' eyebrows shot up. "How do you figure?" he asked.

Hayward was somewhat surprised Ellis hadn't been informed yet. "That alert we received from one of the automated mining and ore processing operations in the asteroid belt. The command and control system there reported an unscheduled ship lacking authentication codes arrived and removed the metallic ore which had been mined and processed. Then the entire operation went offline."

"Have we eliminated any other possibilities?" Ellis asked.

"Yes. All ships and traffic accounted for. And our society doesn't have enough of a presence out in space to even entertain notions of piracy," Hayward answered.

"That leaves one possibility. Cerberus. How did they get so far out there that fast?" Ellis both concluded and wondered.

Hayward just shook his head, the expression on his face answering that he wished they knew. It was very worrisome.

"Speculation about why the ship is there is running rampant. Right now the Council's best guess is they are strangling our economy by depriving us of resources that can be used against the rebellion," Hayward noted.

Ellis nodded slightly. "Possibly. They might also have other purposes that go along with that. Hard to tell what to make of it, given our extremely limited information about Cerberus and what level of technology the ship has."

"The Officer Class residents in First City are pretty upset that so much of their prime living space was rendered uninhabitable during that downtown attack," Ellis said, getting back to the main topic. "And now they're crowding together into an even more confined footprint, bringing much of our military forces with them to make an inviting target for orbital bombardment. Doesn't the Officers Council see what's happening?" Ellis asked.

"Yes, but the political reality of it is the Officers are the powers behind the curtain on this planet. What they want, they get. And they want a blanket of protection right now. Nothing you or I can do about that," Hayward said, succinctly summarizing the political realities they now found themselves facing. "We would be swimming upstream against their wishes, and that's just not going to happen."

Ellis sat back into his seat, sipping the last of the bourbon. "Then we'll have to come up with a new strategy to defeat the rebellion. It seems our options are rapidly dwindling because of Cerberus. We're about to the point where we can only be reactive instead of proactive because the captain of that ship is a master of strategy and tactics."

Hayward drained the remaining bourbon from his glass. "You'd better hurry up on that new strategy. We're losing this rebellion."

Ellis looked at him for a moment, and then he said, "I have an idea."

CHAPTER 67

THE BORDERLANDS

"Commander, our spies are reporting all sorts of military assets repositioning in the center of First City and other cities around the planet," reported Loki three niner over the secure audio channel. He couldn't see his face, but Commander Hunt's resulting smile didn't reach his eyes.

"That's good news, Loki three niner. Keep us apprised of any new developments. Hunt out."

Hunt walked over to the map table in FOB Charlie. The base had moved several times since the rebellion began. Now, they were deep underground in long forgotten tunnels that crisscrossed beneath the Borderlands. The tunnels were originally bored by automated construction machinery carried between the stars by the Ark. The machines built First City's infrastructure during the planet's long terraforming. The finished cities were then populated after the colonists were birthed from the DNA which had also been carried aboard the Ark.

The rebels had installed strings of lights, powered by FOB Charlie's portable generators. The dim lights and shadows gave the rough cut stone walls of the tunnels an eerie appearance, which only became more unnerving in the larger chamber which the base now occupied.

Hunt's lieutenant, known only by the name Buckingham, joined Hunt at the map table. Hunt wasn't sure if Buckingham was the lieutenant's first or last name, or if that was even one of his real names at all. Buckingham wasn't telling.

"Well, chief? All our sources are confirming the Loyalists have concentrated their forces downtown. Assets and bases out on the perimeter and beyond are lightly guarded. Where do we strike next?" Buckingham said, using the term 'Loyalists' that had been coined by the Marines from Cerberus. That handy label had quickly been adopted by the Cargo Class rebels.

Hunt grunted, never taking his eyes from the map as he took it all in. His eyes looked at each Loyalist position marked on the map. "We can't hit a target just to hit something. We need to have a purpose behind it, and it needs to be a target we're capable of hitting."

Buckingham snorted as they studied the map. "Generating station?" he asked.

Hunt shook his head. "Making the Loyalists go dark is a nice idea, but we would have to hit multiple stations and power lines to turn out their lights. Not going to happen with our limited resources."

"Medical?" Hunt then wondered aloud.

Now it was Buckingham's turn to shake his head. "Hearts and minds, boss. That would just turn all of the Crew against us instead of just some of them. Same for water and food."

Hunt stabbed a finger down to the map. "What's this facility?" he asked.

Buckingham opened a file on his tablet and tapped in the coordinates for the facility from the map. "Says here it's a data processing center. No other information available. Our scouts bypassed it to check out more pressing targets."

Hunt's expression grew suspicious. "With modern computers, the Loyalist's need for a stand-alone data processing center are modest, to say the least. Put that position up on the big screen, Buckingham."

Buckingham cast the image onto the large screen behind the table.

"Now superimpose the water and sewer map over it," Hunt said without taking his eyes from the screen. The water and sewer map appeared, revealing that the place had unusually modest access to those services.

"Must be relatively automated to have such limited water and sewer service, Commander," Buckingham concluded.

"Yeah. Something isn't right though. It's a large building located well outside the city with not much around for miles. Why would the government have run water and sewer pipes all the way out there for an automated building that's all by itself and which isn't on the road to another place? Doesn't make sense." Hunt raised an eyebrow as he mulled the mystery over.

"Mind if I join you, Commander?" came the voice of Ambassador Gadre from behind, startling Hunt and Buckingham out of their concentration for a moment.

"Welcome, Ambassador. Please do. We're just trying to figure out a small mystery as we study the maps," Hunt said, motioning for Gadre to step up to the map table with them.

Gadre's eyes flicked to the map image on the screen. "What sort of mystery?" she asked.

Hunt tilted his head to the side briefly as he sort of shrugged. "Trying to figure out why the government went to the effort of running water and sewer lines out to a standalone data processing center way out in the middle of nowhere. And asking ourselves why they would site a data processing center so far away, too. We haven't scouted the facility, and it's unclear if we will bother with non-critical infrastructure anyway."

"That is a bit of a mystery, Commander. Would you mind if I put an orbital image of the place on your screen?" Gadre asked.

Hunt motioned for her to be his guest. Gadre pulled out her own tablet, and synched it with the screen. She cast the satellite image and they waited a few moments for the image to resolve with more clarity. Suddenly, they appeared to be a thousand feet above the structure.

"Ordinary looking warehouse, with several satellite dishes on the roof," Gadre muttered, before Hunt pointed to a corner of the roof.

"Wait! Can you zoom in on that?" Hunt asked.

Gadre nodded. "Yes, but it'll take a little bit. The surveillance drone optics can read the text on a book in someone's hands." She tapped the commands into her tablet.

The image zoomed in, taking a few more seconds to resolve into a clear picture. It showed camouflage netting, obscuring several men who were beneath it.

"That's an anti-aircraft battery hiding under that netting. Look, you can see their shoulder fired missiles. Zoom out a bit," Hunt asked, although it was really more of a command than a request. "See these positions here, here, and here?" he asked, pointing them out with a handheld laser pointer. "Those are machine guns nests to discourage anyone from nosing around on the ground."

Their interest in the facility had risen dramatically with the discovery. Gadre interrupted the silence as they studied the pictures. "Commander, I'm going to pull images from drone scans in different energy spectrums. Let's see what they can tell us."

Various looking scans appeared on the big screen, one at a time. They didn't look remarkable until the infrared image appeared and Buckingham motioned for Gadre to stop there for a moment.

"That building is producing a remarkable amount of heat, Commander," Buckingham said as he studied the image. "Far more than just some data processing would produce."

Hunt nodded. "Agreed. Some serious computing power would generate that kind of heat though. Ambassador, any more images?"

Gadre simply nodded. The next image confused Hunt and Buckingham. "What are we looking at?" Buckingham asked.

"It's a ground penetrating radar image," Gadre explained. "You're seeing up to ten yards underneath the surface."

They could see multiple power lines coming into the structure, the water and sewer lines, and multiple laser optic cable lines capable of moving massive amounts of data.

"That's no data processing center," Hunt concluded. "I'm guessing we've found where the military's artificial intelligence system is hidden. Data processing doesn't require anywhere near that high a level of laser optics, but an AI does."

CHAPTER 68

CERBERUS

Karl Mueller sat in the main conference room, joining Captain Ronin and Lieutenant Gustav, who were already seated at the table.

"Yes, Captain. We're confident we've developed a worm. But for it to work effectively, we'll need to bypass their network's encryption protocols and upload it directly into their defense grid. And merely transmitting it over the tap from the Ark won't work. There isn't sufficient bandwidth," Karl said, responding to the question in Dan's summons to meet them here.

"Ambassador Gadre has advised they believe they've located the Loyalist military's AI center. Will that be an adequate place to upload it directly into their grid?" Ronin asked.

Karl nodded. Definitely. As long as the AI doesn't prevent it's upload. And tell her we'll need the physical receiver specifications from Commander Hunt's people so we can make a hardwired connection to the system. I'm sure our plug-in configurations don't match theirs."

Ronin nodded. That made sense.

Karl then added, "Defeating the hostile AI's software coding protections will not be easy, Captain. I recommend we send a tech expert with the away team to increase the chance of success."

Ronin smiled evilly. "Lieutenant Gustav's Marines will do an excellent job of protecting you, doctor. It's time to start getting ready."

Karl's eyebrows shot up at that. Nobody sends the ship's mad scientists on a combat mission with the Marines. He covered his surprise by merely nodding, before he stood up to leave. "Will do, Captain," he said before departing.

After Karl left, Gustav spoke. "Hopefully our mad scientist there doesn't become a liability during a firefight. He hasn't spent much time with the knuckle-draggers who can't read without pictures."

Ronin smiled a half smile. "Fingers crossed. Karl sure hasn't spent much time around door kickers who break the nicer kids' toys and steal their lunch money. Make sure he doesn't get hurt, or Commander Mueller will cut us off at the knees, and that just won't be pretty."

"Yessir, that would be a terrifying prospect. I suspect it would be more pleasant to be tortured to death with electrodes attached to our nipples than to face her wrath," Gustav replied. He wasn't smiling as he said it.

Ronin nodded thoughtfully. "We would be praying for death. Get Karl down to the rifle range before you deploy. Make sure he knows which end goes 'bang' and won't hurt himself if he has to use it. "

"Will do, Captain."

DATA PROCESSING CENTER

"**H**ot up here," grumbled the Crew Class private who was attached to the machine gun. They were positioned underneath the camouflage netting strung across one of the corners of the roof of the data processing center they had been assigned to guard.

All he does is complain, thought Cpl. David Bradshaw, rolling his eyes in annoyance. "Not interested in your commentary and insights about the weather, Private," he replied. Hopefully that shuts him up, Bradshaw continued thinking, *or this is going to be a real long shift.*

To Bradshaw's way of thinking, guarding a seemingly low-priority target like the data processing center was a cushy assignment. It was surrounded by miles of quiet woodlands. Ponderosa pines, planted from seeds brought from Earth, gave the area a wonderful scent. It was quiet, and more importantly, far from the fighting that seemed to be occurring everywhere else on the planet.

As the sun continued setting, the reflected temperatures on the rooftop finally began to ease because the cooler night breezes began stealing away the heat rising from the stony materials used to make the roof. The darkening sky was still glowing various hues of orange and purple, marking the passing of the sun below the horizon.

Lying against the sandbags forming the machine gun nest, Corporal Bradshaw looked at his wristwatch. *Thirty minutes remaining until shift change*, he noted. As he raised his night vision glasses to scan the forest, there was a sudden clap of thunder off to his right.

"Thunder? But the skies are clear and nothing's in the forecast," said the private as they both looked toward the sounds.

Instead of an approaching thunderstorm, miles away they saw three streaks of fire that appeared a few thousand feet above the surface, and which rapidly shot down to the ground before suddenly winking out. No fireballs rose from the surface, which meant whatever caused the flame trails did not impact on the surface.

Bradshaw scrambled to grab his radio. He had to think for a moment to settle down and recall his position's call sign. "This is Overwatch 3, calling Mother Goose. Overwatch 3, calling Mother Goose. Come in, please."

The radio crackled to life. "This is Mother Goose, go ahead Overwatch 3."

"Overwatch 3, reporting the sounds of distant thunder and three vertical streaks of fire to the southwest. Distance estimated at ten miles. Over," Bradshaw reported.

"Roger, Overwatch 3. Nothing's on the radar, but that matches two other visual reports that just came in. We're sending out a patrol to investigate. Mother Goose, out."

Bradshaw set down his radio receiver, and raised his night vision glasses to visually scan the forest. Nothing, which set his senses to tingling. He turned his head to the left to speak to the private manning the machine gun.

"Something isn't right out there. Keep your head on a swivel," Bradshaw ordered.

"Yes, Corporal," was all the private said. His eyes were wide open as he nervously scanned the dark forest.

An angry sounding *Zzzziiippp!* sound flew past Bradshaw's ear, and something wet splattered on his left hand. Confused, Bradshaw looked at the private he had just spoken to so he could ask what that was.

Bradshaw gasped with horror when he saw the headless corpse of the private slumped against the machine gun.

* * *

"Keep us steady!" growled Bravo 2, Ed Wilson, who never took his eye from the targeting crosshairs displayed on his visor. Bravo 1, Brett Mackey, stood next to him as they picked out the next target their drone overflight had plotted onto Tacnet.

Wilson and Mackey were strapped in and standing on the lowered rear ramp of *Bulldog 1*, which was being piloted by Erin Johnson as it hovered low over the forest. Not visible with the naked eyes in the deepening night gloom at this distance, they had barely cleared the sight horizon to the gun emplacements on top of their objective with only a few feet to spare before they would drop down out of line of sight.

"I'm doing my best in these winds, Bravo 2!" said a distracted sounding Johnson over the commlink they had open so everyone on the shuttle could listen. The shuttle's engines were whining loudly with the effort to remain stationary and aloft.

Bravo 2 settled his Stinger sniper rifle onto the next target. It was a partially exposed face, peering over the waist-height retaining wall outlining the edge of the roof.

Letting a breath out halfway, Wilson coolly pulled back on the trigger in a smooth, practiced motion. The powerful weapon launched its projectile with a magnetic pulse. The face disappeared in a grotesque impact spray that was graphically displayed inside his visor.

"Tango down. Next tango to your ten o'clock, highlighting on Tacnet," murmured Mackey quietly.

The process repeated itself several times, with Wilson switching to airburst mode for the bullets to take down the tangos that stayed hunkered down behind the retaining wall. Airburst mode merely required the shooter to fire a round over the heads where it would burst and shred the hapless targets with deadly splinters from above. Tacnet showed the rooftop enemy being rapidly eliminated by the sniper teams operating from the ramps of all three Bulldogs.

"Like magic, Bravo 2," said Bravo 1.

Off in the distance towards the rooftop they just cleared, the forest lit up with a fireball. Seconds later, rapid flashes of light could be seen and *Bulldog 1* began accelerating towards the data processing center although their flight path would take them well away from the firefight that was now going on down on the ground.

Lieutenant Gustav opened a command commlink to the Bulldog crews and the Marine team Gunnery Sergeants. "This is the LT. Commander Hunt's folks have made contact with the patrol that was sent out to find us. They're engaging now. Enemy drones are in the air. Expect a hot LZ. ETA, sixty seconds."

Clicks of acknowledgment came in return from the Marines.

Bravo 1 had noticed the countdown timer displayed inside his visor about the same time Gustav mentioned it. With the ramp still down, the wind screamed past as the Bulldog broke past the sound barrier in seconds. Pilot Officer Johnson was driving her assault shuttle hard towards the insertion point because this was the phase of the mission where they would be most vulnerable to ground fire.

Bulldog 1 streaked across the remaining miles of forest. Mackey was jolted backwards toward the front of the shuttle when it suddenly decelerated hard and he was still facing the open ramp at the rear. Mackey's eyes flicked to the timer on his visor and he opened the team commlink. "Bravo team, ten seconds! Be ready!"

Their Bulldog settled lightly on the roof, engines still spun up and whining loudly for a quick dustoff. "Move, move, move!" Mackey yelled as Bravo team spilled out the still open rear ramp. Within seconds, they spread across the roof while *Bulldog 1* lifted off, its ramp closing as it rapidly accelerated away.

"Bravo 1, Bravo 7. The roof is secure. No survivors," reported Private Ty Jeffries. He and Private Cujo had bounded over to the machine gun nest and secured that position while the rest of the team did the same for the rest of the rooftop.

Crouched behind some sort of ventilation cover, Mackey opened a commlink to Karl Mueller, who was crouched next to him. "Some kinda fun, huh, doc?" he said, as they watched Bravo 4, Carlos Guthrey, quickly open the rooftop exit door ten yards in front of them and toss a couple of flashbang grenades down the stairwell from his position along the outside wall to the exit. They detonated with muffled thumps and bright flashes from the dark down below.

Bravo 4 then flew a tiny Butterfly drone down the stairs, when Karl looked at Mackey with a look of shock on his face that Mackey could plainly see since Karl didn't have an exosuit. He just had some body armor on with team commlink in his helmet. "You actually ENJOY this sort of thing, Gunnery Sergeant?" Karl said.

Mackey just laughed evilly inside his exosuit's helmet and responded with a thumbs up for Karl's benefit. Karl looked like he had just figured out he was stuck working with a madman.

"Bravo 1, Bravo 4. No contacts, Bravo 1. Moving down into the stairwell," Guthrey reported. The team leapfrogged forward to cover him.

"Message from *Bulldog 1* to all Marines. Bandits inbound to your position. ETA five minutes," came the voice of Gustav's exosuit AI over the common commlink that was active between all of the expeditionary force Marines on this mission. It was relaying the message from Chief Hal Patterson, the rearseater on *Bulldog 1*. Patterson's scans had picked up something headed their way.

Guthrey flew his drone into the top floor of the building while he stayed hidden behind the walls of the stairwell on the other side of the entrance at the lower floor's landing. The drone and its simple scanning for movement and heat signatures quickly confirmed there was no one there.

"Bravo 1, Bravo 4. The floor is unoccupied. It looks like building maintenance and utilities. Moving down another level," Guthrey observed.

Three floors from the top of the seven-story building, Guthrey's drone sensor sweep lit up. "Bravo 1, Bravo 4. Contact. Six tangos on the fourth floor. They're positioned to ambush us exiting the stairwell. Drone imagery indicates a large room containing what appears to be a server farm. It's dimly lit, and the ambient temperatures show strong temperature controls in there. It's twenty degrees colder on that level."

By now, Bravo team was lined up in the stairwell, and Mackey glanced over to Karl before he spoke over the commlink between them. "Doc, what do you think? A possible server farm sound like the kind of thing you wanted?"

Karl was looking at a replay of the Butterfly drone's video feed on his helmet's visor. "Yes, that should do nicely. It really does look like racks of computer servers. How do we get in there?" he asked.

CHAPTER 70

THE WOODS

Gunnery Sergeant Brett Blackwater looked at his Tacnet display inside his visor. "LT and Commander Hunt, Gamma 1. Enemy patrol still approaching your position at Wolf 1. Range now 300 yards, speed about twenty miles per hour. Four armored vehicles with an unknown number of tangos. Appears to include three light-armored tactical vehicles. The drones couldn't get us more than that," he reported.

"That's good copy, Gamma 1. Range 300. Contact imminent," Gustav responded, quickly passing along the information all of Gamma team.

Soon they saw the small patrol appear, rounding a curve in the road that wound through the forest. Large trees lined the road, making the deepening gloom even darker.

Gustav watched the patrol advance until it slowed to pass an obstruction of two fallen trees that appeared to have partially fallen in the road. In reality, they had been placed there by Gamma team minutes earlier. "LT to Gamma 3, they've reached Wolf 1. Light 'em up!"

Private Caron reacted immediately, and he triggered the detonators of the explosives Gamma team had pre-positioned several minutes before the patrol arrived. The results had been worth the effort.

A dozen small blasts erupted alongside the road, sending splinters everywhere as they blew through the bottom trunks of the large pine trees they had been attached to. The pines immediately toppled towards the road.

Simultaneously, a half-dozen explosive devices the team had implanted into the dirt road itself then covered up with loose dirt, detonated. Two of the three armored vehicles had rolled over mines, and the powerful blasts lifted the front end of the middle vehicle four feet off the ground and shredded its tires. When it crashed back to ground, it hit with a terrible crash as flames began spreading from the engine. Four stunned tangos stumbled from the vehicle into a hail of gunfire coming from the dark.

The lead vehicle didn't fare as well. The interior passenger area was ablaze, which could be seen through the reinforced windows. Several charred corpses still wearing their combat helmets could also be seen, with one memorably leaning in a ghastly tilt against the rear passenger window as it was back lit from flames.

The vanguard vehicle in the back came to a sudden stop as the road in front and behind was blocked by burning vehicles, and felled trees. One of the pines had also fallen on top of the trapped vehicle, partially obscuring it from view.

With bullets ricocheting off the still exposed parts of the armored vehicle, a tango popped up through the hatch in the roof into the armored gunners' turret. The Loyalist kept low as he grabbed a hold of the mounted heavy caliber machine gun and charged the chamber by racking the first round into it. Within seconds, he opened fire at the bright flashes in the dark behind the rear of the vehicle.

Amid the sounds of impacting rounds off to his right, Blackwater reported to Gustav over the commlink. "LT, Gamma 1. We're taking heavy fire directed at Commander Hunt's men. Their weapons make a visible flash when fired. I'm ordering them to cease fire, and we'll pick up the slack using the Marines."

Hunt shook his head. "LT, Gamma 1, this is Hunt. The patrol vehicle is trapped and out of the fight. Another armored force is inbound. I think we should withdraw."

Gustav glanced at the Tacnet plot, which the drones had updated with the incoming bandits in the air and a new ground force that was approaching from the opposite direct of the data processing center. The drones had tagged the new force as possible armored cavalry. "This is LT. Negative on the withdrawal for now. I don't want to leave any tangos behind to report what happened to the new force that's approaching. Our short-range jammers prevented word from getting out, so they don't know what they're headed for. Gamma 2," Gustav said, bringing Cpl. Jefferson Langley into the commlink conversation, "Gamma 2, can you use your Stinger rifle on that shooter?"

Langley had already moved closer to a closer position to the side of the armored vehicle. He had chosen a position somewhat ahead of the ambush so he could get a line of sight to the unprotected rear of the gunner who was still firing to the rear.

"LT, Gamma 2, in position. Can Commander Hunt's men who are behind the vehicle continue firing for now? I want them to keep the guy's attention on them with the flash of their weapons so he doesn't swing around this way."

Hunt responded quickly. "This is Hunt. Can do. Giving the orders now."

The gunner on the trapped vehicle was pouring lead into the forest. Brass casings continued to waterfall around him, which Langley noted as he looked through his night vision image on the inside of his visor display. Langley settled the cross hairs on the back of the shooter's skull, and gently pulled the trigger. The powerful rifle created a gruesome corpse that slid back down into the vehicle.

Once the gunfire ceased, no one else tried to man the mounted gun, and the LT barked over Gamma's common channel that was also being shared by Hunt's men at the moment, "Cease fire, cease fire. Gamma 5 and 6, advance and check for survivors. Gamma team, remain in position and provide covering fire if needed."

Privates Addington and Diaz leapt up and bounded over to the remains of the patrol. It only took them a few seconds. Crouching low beneath the windows, Diaz edged along the side before reaching up to yank open the driver's side door. Waiting for the opening, Addington quickly stuck his weapon into the face of the frightened driver.

"I surrender!" yelled the driver, as Addington roughly pulled him from the vehicle while Diaz swept the rest of the interior. There were obviously no other survivors inside.

Meanwhile, Hunt's men had now been ordered forward to the other two vehicles. Between the crispy corpses in the burning vehicle, and the now-dead guys who had tried to exit the other, there wasn't much to find. "Commander Hunt and LT, Gamma 6. No other survivors," reported Diaz.

Addington and Diaz tied the prisoner's hands behind his back using a strong plastic zip tie, and then they walked him to where Gustav, Blackwater and Hunt had gathered. The prisoner was shaking slightly from the adrenalin overload.

Gustav walked over and stood in front of the prisoner. "How many are guarding the building you came from?" he demanded to know. The prisoner just shook his head and looked at him.

"How many are guarding the building?" Gustav said, emphasizing he word.

"Who are you? Where did you get those suits and weapons?" said the prisoner, raising his chin slightly and giving Gustav an imperious look.

Gustav wasn't terribly surprised at their prisoner's haughtiness, and he didn't have time to waste on him. "Answer our questions or we'll have no further use for you," he replied.

"You can't make me answer anything!" the prisoner snarled, managing to sound like an elite snob despite his predicament.

"You're right, I can't," Gustav said, just before raising his rifle and shooting the prisoner in the head.

"Lieutenant! You can't just shoot prisoners of war! The Geneva Conventions forbid it," yelled a startled Commander Hunt.

Gustav and Blackwater looked at each other with confused looks that were hidden behind their visors. "Who's Geneva, and why did she have a convention?" Blackwater asked aloud for both of them, speaking for the first time since the prisoner was brought to them.

Hunt shook his head slightly as he sputtered "Your governments signed documents granting rights to prisoners of war in the nineteenth and twentieth centuries in Geneva, Switzerland. Its murder to kill a prisoner!" he raged.

Gustav just looked at him for a moment. "Those governments ceased to exist on Earth during The Fall many centuries ago. And Geneva, Switzerland is ... a place? Where is it?"

Blackwater nodded his head and chimed in. "I've never heard of Geneva or Switzerland, either."

Hunt was stunned. "What do you mean? Switzerland is a peaceful nation in central Europe. Don't they teach geography on Earth anymore?"

Hidden behind his visor, Gustav's eyebrows shot up. "I'm from a place in Europe that we believe was once called Deutschland, or Germany as it's pronounced in American. I have never heard of this Switzerland place you're speaking of, but I won't claim to be an expert regarding all those ancient nations that are lost to history. Commander, due to The Fall we have less information about Earth's ancient history than you do, while you have none of the information about Earth's recent past that we have."

Hunt shook his head slightly in the dying light of the flames of the burning vehicles. "But how can you just kill a prisoner? Surely that doesn't happen on Earth?"

Gustav checked the Tacnet to assess their position before responding. "We need to be gone from here before those bandits arrive. I'll tell you along the way, but send your people to the next ambush point."

Gustav clicked on the common commlink being used by the assault expeditionary force. "Gamma team, LT. Displace to Wolf 2." Gustav switched back to the commlink with Blackwater and Hunt as they disappeared into the darkness under the trees to get under cover.

"Commander, the protocols for dealing with prisoners that became the norm during our war with the Collective was that prisoners on both sides who refused to help when ordered were simply killed. All the warfighters on both sides were aware of that, because in space combat there aren't any extra resources to waste on uncooperative prisoners. We assumed the same practice existed here because it hadn't occurred to us to wonder otherwise. So you can see why we were unaware you believed the ideals enshrined in some ancient treaty between long dead nations has anything to do with our combat operations."

Hunt shook his head, although he was now too far away in the dark for either Blackwater or Gustav to see it. "It's difficult to grasp that the Earth civilization we were taught about in school ceased to exist centuries before our ancestors even arrived at this colony, and no one here knew anything had happened."

CHAPTER 71

FOURTH FLOOR

"**B**ravo 4, I don't like the math," Mackey said to Guthrey over the Bravo team commlink. "That still leaves four of them unmolested."

"It's the best I got, Bravo 1. We only have two Wasp drones. What do you figure we can do about the others?" Guthrey replied.

"If we send Cujo in, that's just suicide for our war dog and isn't a viable solution. We can't just toss in grenades — those are too powerful this close to the server farm. There's gotta be something we can do other than charge straight into their killbox. Any of you apes got an idea?" Mackey said over the team's commlink.

"Bravo 1, Bravo 2. Last I heard, both our drone types can carry one pound of weight for a short distance. Why not rig all four of our drones to carry Stinger rounds set to detonate into splinter mode, then use the two Wasps to zap the last two guys?" said Wilson.

There was silence for a moment while Mackey and Karl looked at each other in surprise. "Bravo 2, Bravo 1. What, you go to college this week or something?" Mackey asked.

"Bravo 1, Bravo 2. We can use the existing data link that the Stinger rounds are keyed to. All we really need to do is strap a round to the drone, and let fly."

"Bravo 4 and Bravo 2, Bravo 1. Job opportunity. Rig up the drones with Stinger rounds ASAP," Mackey ordered. He turned to look at Karl, who was still standing next to him like he had been ordered to.

"Wow! I guess Bravo 2 isn't as dumb as he looks," quipped Bravo 6 over the commlink, Private Steve Cupper.

"Maybe so, but he still has a face made for radio. Whoo wee! I bet the docs slapped his mother when he was born," Bravo 5 added, drawling it out in his Southern accent.

Bravo 2's Midwestern accent and deep voice suddenly filled the team commlink. "I really hate you guys!" he said, drawing guffaws and a few derisive whoops from his teammates.

While Wilson and Guthrey worked quickly, they suddenly heard the sound of jet engines screeching low over the building before disappearing as quickly as they had appeared. The commlink for the assault force came alive. "Bravo 1, LT. Be advised, enemy fighters rule our skies. Gamma team is going dark until our next engagement. Estimated time till contact with next ground force, ten mikes."

Mackey replied immediately. "LT, Bravo 1. Good copy. We're almost ready to begin our assault to take the server farm."

Gustav clicked an acknowledgment.

Mackey turned his attention back to his current situation. There wasn't anything he could do about the enemy fighters overhead.

"Bravo 1, Bravo 2. We're ready," reported Wilson, as he and Guthrey set up a linked data stream. Guthrey was handling the drone flight ops, while Wilson was handling the shooting using his exosuit's fire control systems.

"Bravo 2, Bravo 1. Make it happen," Mackey ordered. He was stacked up behind Bravo 5 along the wall outside of the stairwell exit. Mackey could hear Cujo straining at his leash behind him.

Bravo 5 suddenly pulled the door open, prompting the ambushers inside to open fire. The far wall began to heat up from the X-rays fired through the doorway into the stairwell. All four tiny drones quickly zipped around the now open doorway into the room beyond, moving far too fast for the troops inside the room to follow with their weapons.

Seconds later, there were four sharp cracks, followed by the sounds of ricochets. The sound of enemy fire dropped to almost nothing immediately. Three seconds after that, there was nothing but silence from the server farm room.

"Bravo 1, Bravo 4. Five tangos down," reported Guthrey.

"Secure this level!" Mackey roared. Cujo immediately bounded past them looking for someone to maul, quickly followed by his partner Bravo 7. As the rest of Bravo team rushed through the doorway, there was the sound of several X-ray shots being fired from further inside. The X-ray weapon quickly stopped in conjunction with the mixed sounds of a bloodcurdling scream and those of a large, angry dog growling and biting.

The sound of a Marine mag-rail carbine being fired cut the scream short.

"Bravo 7, are you hit?" yelled Mackey as they moved to secure the room first.

"Yeah, but not bad. My exosuit registered the hit, but it says they aren't packing a lethal dose for someone in an exosuit," responded Jeffries, sounding confused about not only still being alive, but unhurt as well. "My suit sure got a lot warmer when the beam hit me, though."

Bravo team quickly cleared the floor and all its rooms. Cujo seemed somewhat disappointed at the lack of more unwilling enemy combatants for him to chew on.

"It's OK, boy, there's still plenty of 'em to go around out there," said Bravo 7 soothingly as he patted his partner's furry flank for a moment. Cujo looked up and panted with his tongue out.

"OK, doc. Come in and do your thing," Mackey said over the team commlink.

Karl gingerly stepped around the corner, stopping for a moment in shock at the sight of the dead corpses. Four of them were shredded, one had a smoking hole burnt into the side of its skull, and the sixth and most recent corpse had both a smoking hole in its shoulder and mag-rail rounds stitched across its chewed up torso. The gruesome sight was the closest Karl had ever come to combat.

"Doc, shake a leg! There's an armored ground force coming this way that Gamma won't be able to hold off forever," Mackey said insistently.

Mackey's reminder spurred Karl into action and he quickly jogged into the midst of the server farm, scanning for an access node as he moved.

"Here! This is the access node!" Karl said as Mackey moved over to stand next to him while he kept looking around for threats. Karl set his bag on the ground and opened it to start removing its contents.

"You sure about that, doc?" Mackey asked, while also looking around to assess where to place Bravo team for defensive coverage.

Karl, feeling somewhat part of the team, replied with a smile as he continued pulling wires and a computer from his bag. "Yep. I figured that out from the little sign on this unit that says 'System Access,' Bravo 1."

Impressed with the snarkiness, Mackey looked down at Karl and grinned. "C'mon doc, I'm just a Marine. Everybody knows we can't read without pictures."

Karl stopped and looked up at Mackey, before they both burst out laughing while Karl shook his head and finished assembling his gear. He booted up the computer he had brought with, and said, "Here goes nothing," as he plugged into the AI.

Seconds crawled by while Karl tried to outsmart the Loyalist's AI and its defense network. Mackey put the time to good use. "Bravo team, there's only one entrance to this floor. Bravo 5 and 6, keep covering the stairs. Bravo 4 and 7, scout the floors below us, but stay out of contact if possible. We don't have much time before we have to leave, and we can't afford to get trapped here," Mackey ordered.

The four Marines clicked their acknowledgments and rushed back to the stairwell. Cujo's nose told them the stairs were still clear as Privates Allison and Cupper took up defensive positions just inside the door. They pointed their weapons towards the stairs as Privates Guthrey and Jeffries slipped past with their weapons at the high ready position. Cujo was already waiting for them on the landing.

Using hand signals, Guthrey and Jeffries signaled to softly continue on down the stairs. They reached the next floor down, and both stacked up against the wall next to the door for the exit. When they were ready, Guthrey slowly opened the gray metal door, and peeked inside. It was dark, but Guthrey's visor automatically switched to starlight mode so he could see inside.

Guthrey crouched down, and opened the door wider as he pointed his rifle towards the direction he was facing. He surged forward across the threshold to the other side, with Jeffries close behind him. Moving in a low crouch and pointing their weapons towards any possible threats, they made their way further into the room and details began to emerge in the dark.

Jeffries opened his commlink with Guthrey. "Looks like all the comforts of home for garrison troops," he said.

Guthrey nodded. "Agreed. Cafeteria to our right, restroom and separated changing facilities to our left. Let's clear the rest of the floor."

They moved through a doorway on the far side of the large room to discover a long hall with many doorways. Their progress slowed as they checked each doorway for threats.

"Cujo's quiet. He doesn't smell anyone," Jeffries noted as they continued their sweep of the hallway. They came to the end, which had a white sign with red print on it that said, "Armory."

Guthrey looked at Jeffries. "It's Santa's toy shop. Shall we go inside and see who's on the Naughty List?" he said.

Jeffries grinned. "Oh yeah. I've been very, very naughty!"

CHAPTER 72

FLY THE FRIENDLY SKIES

"Take cover!" roared Gustav as the fighters made another pass overhead. Their guns ripped matching trails of destruction through the woods where the ground assault force had been spotted when the enemy warbirds appeared.

The heavy caliber shells tore through trees and men alike. Gustav checked Tacnet. Four Marines from Gamma team were dead on that first pass, and several others were badly wounded.

"Here they come!" yelled Gamma 2.

"Which ones?" yelled Gustav, trying to wish the enemy fighters away. "I count twenty-two fast movers!" Gustav continued.

"LT, Gamma 1. Armored cavalry is closing fast on this position," said Gunnery Sergeant Blackwater in a remarkably calm voice, considering they were under heavy fire.

"Gamma 1, LT. Wolf 2 is compromised and the armored force obviously knows we're here. Fall back 500 yards towards the data processing center then set up another ambush at Wolf 3. Over," Gustav ordered as he crawled over to a wounded man to check on him.

"LT, Gamma 1. That's good copy, LT. I'm not sure we can lose those fast movers up there in these woods."

"Gamma 1, LT. Archangel is inbound. Move your butts!" Gustav replied.

Through the trees, Gustav could see the fires of the fighter's jet engines against the dark, starry sky as the next pair lined up for a high speed attack run. He stood up and wrapped the arm of the injured rebel around his neck, and they stumbled and moved out of the way as fast as they could go. Even in the lighter gravity and the power of the exosuit, Gustav found it tough to maneuver.

Just then, high above their heads, a massive fireball suddenly appeared in the sky. It was screaming down towards the surface like some sweet meteor of death about to cause an extinction level event on the planet.

* * *

"Jump complete, Captain!" yelled Lieutenant Perez from his station at the helm as soon as Cerberus appeared in the planetary atmosphere. The ship was rumbling and shaking from jumping into the air halfway to the planet's surface.

"Launch fighter wing!" ordered Ronin without hesitation.

"This is the bridge. Launch Taurus squadron!" said Lieutenant LeCroy into the commlink he already had open to the ship's launch bays. "The clock is running. Counting down from sixty seconds!" continued LeCroy loudly over the noise, fighting to sound in control despite the strain. He shared that countdown clock on the individual station screens all around the bridge so he wouldn't have to say more about their rapidly diminishing altitude and time until impact.

Lieutenant Delacroix was glued to his scanners. "Hull temperatures rising rapidly!" he reported. The fire caused by Cerberus' rapid plunge through the atmosphere was making it difficult for his scanners to collect information, and Delacroix was hanging on for dear life despite being strapped into his seat for what they knew would be a rough arrival.

Down in the launch bay, Archangel and Bouncer heard the launch order over the commlink in the cockpits of their Tomcat fighters. "This is the bridge. Launch Taurus squadron."

Archangel had no hesitation. He pressed the launch button, and the two were slammed back into their seats as the fighters shot through the launch tubes towards the flames and dark sky beyond that seemed to be streaking upwards past the portal of the tubes.

This is the craziest launch I've ever heard of, thought Lt. Kelvin Sunderland as his Tomcat punched through the flames into the night sky.

After a few seconds, the high Gs of their acceleration eased off enough to breathe, and he heard a while whoop from Bouncer in the next Tomcat.

"Wahoo! We ride again! Tacnet finally updated when we cleared the atmospheric interference. Twenty two bandits. Heading 184 degrees. Range ... almost nil. Angels between 5,000 and just 500 feet. They're breaking off their strafing runs and turning to intercept," Bouncer said loudly on the commlink.

The Loyalist's fighters were below them and slightly to the north, stacked between 5,000 and 500 feet in altitude as they were making strafing runs on the ground forces until Cerberus crashed the party.

Seconds later, Sunderland could see an unusually bright jump flare at the bottom of the long flame trail that now extended far below them. It had continued reaching towards the planet's surface after the Tomcats launched. The trail suddenly ended when Cerberus jumped back to space before she impacted into the ground. *I wonder why the jump flare seemed so bright?* wondered Bouncer, who had been looking at the ship while he oriented himself.

Sunderland confirmed his current position relative to everyone else's. As first out of the launch tubes, his Tomcat was also highest in relative altitude compared to the last of his birds to leave the nest. "Taurus Squadron, this is Archangel. Form up on me as we pass. Let's break 'em up!" Sunderland ordered as he pushed his Tomcat into a steep dive and hit the thrusters as forty of his fighters pulled into tight turns and formed up on his wing as he passed by. His wingman, Bouncer, was trailing slightly behind and above his right wing.

Unlike the long periods of flight involved in space combat due to vast distances, tonight they didn't have long to wait before contact because of Cerberus' flashy entrance practically on top of the battlespace. The warbling tones emitted by the Tomcat's threat detectors had started the moment they left Cerberus.

"Launch detection! Multiple inbounds," said Bouncer. Sunderland was already juking while Bouncer tried to break the enemy radar locks.

"I can't break their radar lock! They're still being guided by the Loyalist's AI down on the surface!" Bouncer concluded as Tacnet showed four birds turning red and disappearing.

Sunderland didn't respond as he held his breath and threw his Tomcat into a wild corkscrewing maneuver that ended behind a Loyalist fighter who didn't realize they had come into Sunderland's sights. The Loyalist was occupied by chasing another Tomcat and failed to stay alert. Sunderland pressed his firing buttons. The mag-rail rounds fired from the cannon, invisible to the naked eyes. Their devastating effect wasn't, as the Loyalist fighter exploded into a flaming shower of fragments. Another Loyalist fighter that had been streaking to intercept suddenly peeled away in a turn too tight for a Tomcat to follow as it chased easier prey.

Too bad we can't use our missiles in atmosphere, Sunderland thought for the tenth time since they had planned this op. Their missiles hadn't been designed to operate anywhere but in space, and there hadn't been time to retrofit them to handle the vastly different environment before it was Go Time. Being unable to use missiles would put the Tomcats at a severe disadvantage, so Captain Ronin tried to shift the odds back into their favor by a surprise jump into the atmosphere. They literally jumped right on top of the enemy, who only had time to loose a few missiles before Taurus squadron engaged them in a good, old fashioned dogfight.

Despite having four birds blown away at the beginning of the engagement, Taurus still had the superior numbers. The opposing formations broke up into individual engagements with every pair of wingmen on both sides, creating a huge furball of individual air combat maneuvering.

"Remember, use dives and climbs, Taurus squadron. Those atmospheric fighters are more maneuverable than we are down here in the soup, but we're much faster. We can't turn with them, but they can't catch up," Sunderland reminded everybody over the squadron's common commlink. He eyed his Tacnet display as they searched for another target.

CHAPTER 73

THE WOODS

It sounded like the thunderclap to end all thunderclaps. An explosive boom that went on for about a minute, growing louder overhead all the while.

Hunt couldn't help but look up in horror to see the booming fireball descending from the heavens. It looked like the power of God had been thrown down to smite the impudent mortals fighting on the surface. It was such a fiery show, all the combatants on the surface paused to gaze upward at the approach of what certainly appeared to be their collective doom. Seconds before impact, he could see the dark image of a massive ship had begun to resolve through the flames before it suddenly disappeared from the center of the storm.

The superheated air and firestorm, now deprived of the energy provided by a falling warship to push the kinetic energy in front of its direction of travel, quickly dissipated and expended its remaining force upon the surface. Everyone but the Marines in their exosuits had to duck and shield their eyes from the dust stirred up by the powerful downdraft and brief blast of furnace like heat. When Hunt raised his head again after the moment passed, he immediately noticed a few of the tree tops had caught fire.

"Commander Hunt, LT. Archangel is here. His Tomcats will be keeping the Loyalist's warbirds busy for now," Gustav said over the commlink.

"Acknowledged, LT. We're in position at Wolf 3. We took a beating from those fighters, so there's less of us than I'd hoped," Hunt responded.

Lieutenant Buckingham had done a quick head count already. "Forty percent of our force is spent already," he added.

Gustav wasn't happy about those numbers. "Copy that," Gustav switched to a commlink just between him and Blackwater. "Gamma 1, LT. Archangel bought us some time, but Hunt's people took it on the chin. Forty percent is combat ineffective now."

Now it was Blackwater's turn to sound unhappy. "Copy that, LT. We've got the trees rigged to blow along the roads at Wolf 3, and mines in the ground. That should slow them down a bit."

"Gamma 1, LT. Acknowledged. We're about to shoot and scoot. We'll be displacing towards your position at Wolf 3 as we go," Gustav noted. He had detached several Gamma team Marines to accompany him as the forward command element. The four of them were about to do something very dangerous. *Dangerous ... and stupid. Just the sort of thing we'd love*, Gustav thought to himself.

Gustav and Gamma 5 had hidden themselves as far from the road as they could, while retaining a clear enough line of sight between the trees to actually see the road using their exosuit's night vision. They were ducked down in a small draw, with a small creek behind them as they lay against the earthen bank on the side closest to the road.

There were at least forty armored vehicles of several different types in a long column rumbling up the road. "Looks like a dozen tanks following behind their version of an armored personnel carrier, LT. Several smaller types of fighting vehicles too. No cannon, but heavy machine guns on those," Gamma 5, David Addington, said as he and Gustav waited for the column to pull even with their position. Addington was tracking the column using a drone flying overhead. The ground began shaking from the weight of the heavy vehicles approaching.

Gustav nodded. He was watching Tacnet closely as he kept his attention focused on their ambush point over the launch tube he had laid on the ground. The leading vehicles passed by them. At least four armored personnel carriers and one tank rumbled by before Gustav marked two targets for them on Tacnet and simply said, "Now!"

They both fired their Firefly's. Instantly, streaks of blue propellant leaped out of the launch tubes and searing brief afterimages of blue streaks of fire into their optic images on their visors. Gustav's shot punched through the sixth vehicle in the column. It was a troop transport with armored sides. The Firefly blew through the armor on both sides and threw the vehicle into a rolling tumble away from Gustav. The sheer force of the impact and the raging inferno inside the vehicle left little of the soldiers inside.

The second target designated by Gustav was the heavy tank that was seventh in the column. Addington's shot likewise blew through the armor on both sides and created an inferno of death inside. Instead of getting swept aside like a child's toy, the heavier tank remained where it was although its own momentum ended up turning it sideways in the road before the tracks gave out.

The column reacted quickly. The heavily armed vehicles began spraying the woods where the deadly blue streaks came from.

Gustav found himself lying face down in the loam of the opposite bank. He gave thanks he hadn't tumbled up out of the creek bed from the Firefly's awesome recoil. Gustav tilted his head up slightly to get his bearings while tracer rounds flew overhead. Several explosions from the tank's main gun shredded tree trunks in their vicinity.

Addington wasn't so lucky, and quickly crawled back down into the creek bed to escape the return fire before the incoming fire found him. Addington had ended up on the surface behind them, and knew he really didn't want to be there.

"Gamma 5, displace!" yelled Gustav to be heard over the noise. The two of them crouched low and did their best to move further along the creek bed while staying out of sight.

"I don't think they liked your party favors, LT," said Addington as they moved.

Gustav snorted, keeping his attention on the uneven ground. "They're an acquired taste, Gamma 5."

"My girlfriends are an acquired taste too, LT. And yet, they can still hurt me," Addington quipped.

"Yeah, but your taste in woman is just awful, Gamma 5. That last one, what was her name? Becky something. She was a piece of work, hoo wee!" Gustav retorted, coming to a stop. "We're about a hundred and fifty yards away now, and they've stopped firing. Team 2, they're headed your way," he announced over the commlink.

"LT, Gamma 12. That's good copy. In position," came the terse response from Pvt. George Tyburn.

"Betty," said Addington.

Gustav turned to look at him. "Betty? She the brunette with the eye patch, yes?" he asked.

"No, sir. That was Rhoda. Betty was the brunette with the bad cigar habit."

Gustav roared with laughter. "Oh, THAT one was Betty? She smelled like a tobacco fire and..."

A loud KABOOM about a hundred yards behind them interrupted Gustav mid-sentence. Flames splashed forward in a pattern that matched the direction of the crash impact. Fortunately it was the opposite direction from where they crouched. Gustav and Addington could hear the sound of metal tearing, and trees being felled with the impact.

"What was that?" said a surprised Addington.

"Fighter plane. Can't tell if it's theirs or ours. Let's move out to our next spot. Tacnet shows the column started moving forward again." The two of them began moving much more quickly despite the dark as their exosuit visors lit the way.

Their commlinks chimed with the next message. "Team 2 in contact. Firing now." Gustav and Addington couldn't see the shots as they were running through the forest out of view of the road trying to get ahead of the column. Tacnet showed which two vehicles were hit, again several spots back from the leading edge of the column.

"Sir, this would be easier if we didn't have to close within a hundred yards to take the shot due to the trees," Addington remarked as the scrambled over a hill overlooking the road. It was a good vantage point, and they could see the forest on the opposite side of the road get lit up from gunfire about two hundred yards back down the road. The burning wrecks of two tanks blocked the road, and several more tanks moved forward to push them out of the way.

"Here they come!" Gustav said as the column began surging forward again. On Tacnet, Gustav followed Team 2's progress in their deadly game of leapfrog while the vehicles closed to within a hundred yards of the hill. When they cleared the last of the trees in their way, Gustav gave the order. "Fire!"

Like before, the twin blue streaks of spent propellant were almost too fast for the eye to follow as they seemed to appear from thin air. The next two targets Gustav had selected were both heavy machine gun carriers in the front. The Fireflies reduced them to flaming wrecks, one of which was literally blown into two halves.

Gustav and Addington found themselves in a mixed up heap at the bottom of the hill on the opposite side from the column which was now sending bullets their way.

"Alphonso really needs to work on that recoil! It's like he thought Godzilla was going to be using it or something," Gustav grumbled as they untangled themselves.

"That's an affirmative, sir. We're going to feel this in the morning."

"Morning? I'm already aching," Gustav retorted.

"Time to move, sir!" Addington said as he helped pick Gustav off the ground. The two crouched down and sprinted back into the forest for cover as they moved to their next stop.

CHAPTER 74

WOLF 3

"**G**amma 1, LT. Inbound to your position. ETA two minutes," Gustav advised, his voice sounding strained from the effort of moving that quickly.

"LT, Gamma 1. Acknowledged. Two minutes. Any word on Gamma 12 and 13?" Blackwater asked. He'd seen their symbols go red on Tacnet, but he was clinging to the hope it was just their transponders that were down.

"Gamma 1 ... They're not coming," Gustav responded glumly.

Blackwater shook his head slightly. More Marines dead or wounded. Since they discovered this colony a few weeks ago, the Marines were becoming rapidly depleted. It wouldn't be much longer before they became a spent force.

Even though he was monitoring their progress on Tacnet, Blackwater still seemed surprised when Gustav and Addington bounded into view. His exosuit's thermal imaging showed several hot spots on their exosuits, visible even though the mud and debris they were coated in.

"Have fun playing in the dirt?" Blackwater quipped when Gustav slid into the trench a few yards away.

"Yes, Mom. Miss us?" Gustav retorted, puffing hard.

"It was nice and quiet while you kids were gone. Don't forget to wash up for dinner," Blackwater said, sounding somewhat distracted as he was looking at the column's progress on his Tacnet display.

"Looks like the column is down to 28 operational vehicles. And they're being cautious, speed is down to 10 miles per hour." They'll be here in a few minutes," Gustav said.

"Has the doc got the worm into the AI yet?" Blackwater asked. "We could skip this whole party if he's done."

Gustav shook his head. "We aren't that lucky. Bravo 1 says they're still working on it."

They fell silent as they waited, each man lost in his own thoughts. The Marines and rebels were about to engage a bloodied, but superior force. The odds weren't in their favor.

They could hear the armored column approaching before they could feel it. Engines and clanking treads combining to make a loud rumble.

Blackwater broke their reverie. "Tacnet scans show they still don't have surveillance drones overhead. Hunt's people are really good at knocking those down."

Gustav just grunted in acknowledgment. The column was getting close now, with tanks leading the way.

Suddenly the first five tanks exploded. Fires splashed every direction.

"Who's doing the shooting? Who's doing the shooting?" Blackwater yelled over the team's commlink. His voice had an angry edge to it as he hadn't given the order to fire yet.

Seconds later their answer screamed past overhead. It was a Tomcat, the pilot using up the last of his ammunition on the armored column as a target of opportunity before returning to the ship.

"Not bad for a flyboy. Now there's only 23 of them," Gustav muttered.

The burning tanks were quickly pushed out of the way, and the column lurched forward again. They only traveled about a hundred yards when Blackwater designated individual targets for the Marines, and gave the order over the commlink.

"Open fire!" Blackwater shouted.

Eight Fireflies streaked into and through the vehicles at the head of the column. Bright flashes winked in rapid fire from the woods next to the road as Hunt's rebels unleashed a barrage of bullets.

The heavy machine guns and beam weapons of the column answered back. They raked the woods, targeting the rebels with thermal imaging guided weapons. Screams of pain could be heard over the battle as men died in agony.

Relying upon the distraction being provided by the rebels, the Marines picked themselves off the floor of the trenches they had fired from.

"Ungh," Blackwater managed to grunt as the picked his Firefly up. He was woozy from being slammed into the back wall of the trench from his weapon's recoil.

"It's not the recoil, it's the abrupt stop," muttered Gamma 2, who was likewise resettling into a firing position.

"Ooof," Gustav exclaimed in agreement. He'd been "kicked" repeatedly tonight thanks to his shoot and scoot strategy.

Blackwater shouted into the commlink. "The column is moving again! Prepare to fire the second salvo."

Eight more vehicles were designated on Tacnet and assigned to the shooters. Each Marine clicked to confirm when they were ready.

"Fire two!" Blackwater ordered. The next eight vehicles died a flaming death.

This time the column refused to slow down or stop. They just continued ahead, pushing the flaming wrecks out of their way and shredding the woods with firepower as they went.

Blackwater stayed low in the trench after he regained his senses from the beat down inflicted by the Firefly's recoil, and the abrupt stop by the trench wall. He had one last play.

His hand reached down to where the detonator was attached to his utility belt, and he unclipped it. Raising it in front of his face, Blackwater opened the team's commlink and said, "Gamma team, Gamma 1. Initiating roadbed bombs in five seconds. Four. Three. Two. One. Detonation!"

Blackwater pressed the trigger three times to bypass the safety and send the activation signal. Dozens of blasts erupted from underneath the road, beneath the lead vehicles. About fifty yards of road was turned into a smoking ruin, leading up to a bridge over a wide, deep creek that was likewise reduced to rubble.

Gustav gave the order. "Gamma team, fall back to the data processing center!" It was time to become scarce while the remains of the column were distracted by the sudden need to ford a sizeable creek.

As Gustav and the rest of Gamma team scrambled away from the Wolf 3 ambush site, he opened a commlink to Mackey. "Bravo 1, LT. We're bingo on Fireflies and heading to your position. Enemy column has reached the river."

Mackey responded instantly. "That's good copy, LT. Still no joy here."

CHAPTER 75

DATA PROCESSING CENTER

"'mon doc. We're running outta time here," Mackey said as he paced.

"I know, I know. I'm trying everything I can think of here," Karl replied, not looking up from his screen. "The AI has thwarted everything so far."

"Bravo 1, Bravo 2. The charges are rigged up and ready to blow," reported Corporal Wilson. He was busy double checking the explosives they had attached to the AI and around the building.

"Acknowledged, Bravo 2," responded Mackey. "Bravo 4, Bravo 1. Status?"

"Bravo 1, Bravo 4. We're placing the explosives we found in the armory," Guthrey said over the commlink.

Outside the building, Guthrey and Jeffries had dug several small holes in the paved footpath leading directly from the parking lot to the entrance of the building. Cujo alertly stood guard as the war dog's attention was directed towards all the noise emanating from the forest. It was coming closer.

The ground began to shake slightly as the remains of the armored column approached.

Must go faster. Must go faster, thought Jeffries as he began wiring the bombs as fast as he could.

Guthrey didn't bother thinking it, as he muttered aloud to himself while he also wired bombs. "Slow is smooth. Smooth is fast. Slow is smooth. Smooth is fast."

The rumbling grew loud, but neither Marine looked up as they worked.

Cujo crouched down and began growling loudly as the lead vehicle pulled into the parking lot.

"Done! Run!" shouted Jeffries as he grabbed Cujo's harness grip before springing up and darting away in an exosuit powered sprint with Cujo in his arms. Guthrey was right behind them. There was no way Cujo could match the flat-out sprint speed of a powered exosuit.

Speed saved them. The armored personnel carrier that had survived opened up on them with its top turret machine gun, but the rounds merely tore up the landscape and building behind them as it couldn't track fast enough to catch up to the Marines.

"We've got company!" shouted Guthrey over the common commlink as they ran into the building. The Gamma team Marines were already inside taking up their defensive fire positions.

"This is the LT. That's good copy, Bravo 4. Hostiles are on the perimeter," Gustav confirmed for everyone.

The Loyalist troops quickly spilled out of the carrier. There were at least thirty of them, and the carrier opened up with its guns to provide covering fire.

The windows of the first floor quickly shattered as the bullets punched into the building.

* * *

"Doc! Anytime!" said Mackey, trying to sound calm. The sounds of gunfire could be heard coming from outside through the broken windows, only to be drowned out by the impact of a shell hitting the building.

"I'm trying. Only thing left to try is to spoof the signal from The Ark and see if that works!" Karl shouted.

"Do it!" shouted Mackey as he headed for the stairwell.

Karl's fingers flew over the keyboard as he triggered the last application he had brought with him. The wire tethering his machine to the AI swung freely as he tapped the keys rapidly.

* * *

"Gamma team, Gamma 2. Here they come!" yelled Langley as he chanced a quick peek over the retaining wall on the rooftop. He was hidden in the position where the machine gun was posted and his thermal imaging showed Loyalist troops approaching from the parking lot.

"Gamma team, LT. Hold fire until they walk over the IEDs," Gustav said over the team commlink. He wanted the Improvised Explosive Devices that Guthrey and Jeffries had buried between the parking lot and the main entrance to serve as the signal to begin. Gustav then added, "Gamma 2, trigger the IED's on your discretion."

Langley replied, "Copy that, LT."

The Loyalists advanced smoothly, taking advantage of all the cover they could, and leapfrogging ahead.

Langley kept watch from his perch on top of the building, barely noticing that the sky was beginning to lighten with the coming of dawn. "Gamma team, Gamma 2. Make ready. Thirty yards. Fifteen. Five." Langley didn't bother to announce when he triggered the IEDs.

WHOOMP! WHOOMP! The detonations echoed through the shattered window front of the data processing center, which juddered from the powerful concussions. It was quickly followed by screams of pain and moans of the wounded.

* * *

"What was that?" asked Karl on their commlink, as he looked up at Mackey and Corporal Cupper who were standing near him. Dust sprinkled down from the ceiling, punctuated by the sound of shattered glass falling to the floor.

Mackey and Cupper looked at each other, unseen grins inside their exosuits. "Sounds like Gamma team just used the "P" for Plenty formula," Mackey noted for him.

Cupper nodded. "Hopefully it put a bunch of them out of our misery," he quipped as he glanced over to completed percentage bar on Karl's computer. "Only fifteen percent firewall penetration so far. C'mon!" he muttered in frustration.

"My system is still searching for a backdoor through their AI's firewall, but this is farther than we've penetrated before. It's still climbing, too," Karl responded.

* * *

On the roof, Langley shook his head to clear it as he lifted his head from where he had been lying face down. Dust and oily smoke angrily swirled around as bits of debris rained down from above. His suit communicated the sounds of shattered glass falling all around the building's exterior to his ears.

"Bravo 4, LT. How much of that Boom did you guys use?" Gustav said over the common commlink, his voice rising in pitch slightly at the end in emphasis. Langley smiled when he heard that over the commlink.

"LT, Bravo 4. Yes," came the pithy reply from Guthrey. Guffaws from the other Marines broke out over the open commlink. Just then, several Bravo team Marines exited the stairwell on the roof to Langley's left. Crouching low, they ran to several different corners of the roof and motioned to each other to signal when they were in position. Langley also thumbed up in response when they looked at him.

"LT, Gamma 2. Bravo is in position on the rooftop with me," Langley reported.

"Gamma 2, LT. That's good copy. Loyalists are moving in again. Hold fire until I give the order," Gustav said.

Langley peeked over the retaining wall again. More Loyalist troops had arrived. The Loyalists arrival was uncoordinated and discombobulated as a result of the delaying action by Gamma and the rebels that killed and wounded quite a lot of them, and destroyed the road to the facility as well.

"Tacnet counts about a hundred and fifty ground troops," Gustav said on commlink. Gamma and Bravo were heavily outnumbered and surrounded by thick forest on three sides.

"Here they come again!" Langley warned.

"This is LT. Rooftop Marines, fire at your discretion!" Gustav ordered a few seconds later.

Langley moved into a crouching position behind the sandbagged machine gun nest, and he pointed the captured machine gun at the oncoming troops. They were advancing in a wide, staggered formation. Obviously the Loyalists didn't want to bunch up into another clump that could be taken out by any other hidden IEDs that might be buried in their path.

Almost simultaneously, Langley and the Bravo team Marines on the rooftop opened fire and unleashed a hail of bullets down on the advancing Loyalists.

Langley swept a stream of heavy caliber bullets across the bodies diving for cover down below. More screams of wounded could be heard.

I love this gun! thought Langley as he felled Loyalists, and the trees some of them tried to hide behind. Dozens fell, as Langley yelled, "Get some! Get some!"

Suddenly a Tacnet targeting warning began flashing inside his visor screen. Langley immediately dropped the smoking machine gun dived to the side over the sandbags. Behind him, the retaining wall abutting the sandbagged nest exploded inwards. The force of the blast pushed Langley into a tumble across the rooftop that was further than he might have imagined before he lost consciousness. Tacnet turned Langley's symbol to yellow, indicating a badly wounded Marine.

"Man down, man down! Corpsman!" yelled Bravo 3, who was still shooting his mag-rail carbine over the retaining wall even as debris from the impact near Langley rained down around him.

The shot had been fired from a tank that had driven to the edge of the woods across the far parking lot. Only the end of the gun on the turret could be seen sticking through the trees. The Corpsman, Gamma 7 (Private Aldo Pena), burst through the stairwell exit onto the roof. Running at a crouch, he quickly reached Langley.

Rolling Langley gently over, Pena was checking Langley's exosuit medical readings even before he arrived, and he began administering additional drugs and aid that the exosuit wasn't normally equipped with.

"LT to Gamma team, fire at will!" barked Gustav. Gunfire poured from all floors of the building into the advancing wave of Loyalists. The screeching blue streak of a Firefly suddenly ripped through the air, crashing through the tank that had nearly ended Langley.

Loyalists again advanced towards the data processing center, this time using heavy covering fire.

CHAPTER 76

CERBERUS

"Chief. Damage report!" said Ronin loudly over the commlink. There was smoke drifting about on the bridge, and some of Lieutenant Delacroix's sensor screens were shattered although Delacroix himself seemed unhurt.

"Sub-light drives are down. We don't have an estimate of the extent of the damage to them yet. Jump drives are still online. Life support is down on decks twelve and fourteen, with explosive decompression and vacuum in the passageways trapping crewmembers in their airtight compartments on those levels. Auxiliary fire control is gone. Port landing bay is down. Hull breach extends from decks twelve through fourteen on the port side of the ship, but the bulkheads on level 13 are holding for now. External hull temperatures have risen a thousand degrees. Internal temperatures are up over fifty degrees. We can't take another hit like that, Captain!" replied Chief Engineer Elvis Lazarus over the commlink, who coughed slightly during his quick report from the drifting haze and smoke in Engineering.

"Thank you, Chief. Update us later when you can," Ronin ordered before he cut the commlink.

"Lieutenant Perez, where are we?" Ronin asked.

At his helm station, Perez had already been trying to find the answer to that question. "Captain, I think we're right where we're supposed to be at Dixie Station. Most of my instruments are offline, so I'm still trying to confirm," Perez responded without looking up so he tilted his head slightly to talk over his shoulder. His hands were rapidly pressing various buttons on his station to check to see what was still operational.

"What hit us?" Commander Mueller wondered. She was holding her wrist, which was hurting as she walked to stand next to Ronin. Like everyone else on the bridge, they were sweating from the combination of heat and stress.

Ronin just looked at her and shook his head slightly. "I don't know, but it sure packed a lot of energy. Caught us just as we were jumping back."

"Captain, Doctor Taketa sent in a casualty update from sickbay and triage. Wounded count over 160, dead count over 30. Injuries ranging from minor bumps to critical burn cases and serious hypoxia," said Lieutenant Delgado as she turned to look at Ronin from her communications station.

"Thank you, Lieutenant," Dan responded. He looked back at Mueller. "Commander, check in with Lieutenant Alphonso in Fabrication and coordinate between Fabrication and Engineering to make what we need for immediate repairs of the most critical systems. We're fortunate Alphonso's area is undamaged."

Mueller nodded. "Right away, Captain." She turned to leave the bridge to talk to Alphonso face to face.

Ronin walked over to the tactical station and leaned slightly over the station so he and Lieutenant LeCroy could confer privately. "Matt, what do you think hit us? Some sort of large scale energy weapon?" Ronin said, using LeCroy's first name.

"That's my guess too, Captain. We've got heightened radiation readings near the hull breach, and residual heat dissipation bleeding from there out into space."

Ronin cocked an eyebrow. "X-rays?" he asked.

"Based on the captured weapons we have, that'd be my guess as well, sir," LeCroy noted. He pulled up the tactical sensor logs and checked their readings from just before the jump. "Captain! Look at this log entry. We were hit with six pairs of X-rays, all concentrated at the same point on the ship."

Ronin leaned in and squinted to read the information. "OK. Now we know what it was. Work up what you can find in a report and we'll have a status and strategy meeting in the conference room in two hours. Pass the word."

Two hours flew by for the crew on the wounded ship, and the department heads or their representatives had gathered in the main conference room, which now felt noticeably colder than normal. Their muted conversations among themselves died away when Captain Ronin and Commander Mueller entered.

Ronin was as exhausted as the rest of them, and saw little point in wasting anyone's time with unnecessary pleasantries. "Right, then. Let's get to it. Chief Lazarus, let's have you go first as we know you're a bit busy at the moment."

Lazarus nodded his head in thanks, his grease smudged face looking quite tired. His normally clean uniform tunic was torn and frayed over the right shoulder, and there were unidentifiable stains and smears of grease and fluids spattered about.

"Thank you, Captain. I anticipate my crews will restore the sub-light drives to 50 percent operability within the hour. Jump drives are undamaged. Damage control crews have rescued the crew who were trapped in the airtight compartments on decks twelve and fourteen, which still don't have life support.

"Repairs to patch the hull breaches on twelve through fourteen won't be completed for two days, maybe three. Other than heat scoring and the hull breaches near the sub-light engines on decks twelve through fourteen, the hull and the black diamond hull coating is undamaged other than heat scoring. The black diamond hull coating deflected approximately two-thirds of the energy and radiation from the weapons that hit us.

"We've dialed down the life support thermostat for the ship a good ten degrees, which has us all feeling a bit chilly. That's necessary for now to reduce the stress on our Life Support Systems, which was working overtime because of the heat from the energy weapons, our blazing fall through the atmosphere, and battle damage to the systems. Repairs should be completed on Life Support within the next two hours at the outside. Hopefully sooner."

Ronin nodded, and Mueller spoke for the two of them. "Thank you, Chief. Good work. Keep us informed of any updates," she said.

Lazarus nodded, and rose from his seat to leave.

Ronin looked over to the medical nurse, who was there to report for sickbay. "Nurse Abara, how bad is it?" he asked.

Nurse Chrizanne "Anne" Abara pursed her lips for a moment, dark eyes reflecting the horrors she had seen the past few hours. Her voice normally carried the accent common to West Africa, where she had been born and raised, but now it was somewhat more noticeable due to her sheer exhaustion. Considering the nature of her medical duties when the ship is in combat, Ronin did not fail to notice Abara must have donned a fresh uniform tunic for this meeting.

"Captain, Commander. Doctor Taketa sends his regards and apologizes for not coming. Sickbay's casualty update is up to 34 killed in action, 178 wounded. 105 minor and non-critical injuries have returned to their duties for now with medical follow up when available or as needed if they worsen. The remainder are either in surgery, are awaiting surgery, or are in recovery," Abara reported.

As was common aboard the shipboard medical personnel, they customarily refer to each other as doctors and nurses like Abara just did instead of by official naval ranks. That custom had long ago spread to the rest of the fleet.

Ronin's face showed how devastating the casualty report was, and the officers and crew in the conference room could easily see his compassion for his people despite Ronin trying to hide it behind his iron clad composure. Ronin's reputation for caring about the welfare of his crew was legendary in the fleet.

Ronin sighed very softly, almost unnoticeably. "Thank you Nurse Abara. When you have a spare moment, please express our sincerest appreciation for the good work being done by our medical staff to Doctor Taketa and the others. We'll let you go now as obviously you have much better places to be than stuck here in this conference room."

As Abara left to return to sickbay, Ronin had a faraway look for a moment as he collected his thoughts and emotions before proceeding. The faces expectantly looking back at him were both concerned and tired.

"Lieutenant LeCroy, any update on the weapon system that hit us?" Mueller said, filling up the moments of silence to keep things moving along. Ronin glanced over at Mueller and silently nodded his thanks for stepping in as they traded a quick look.

"Yes, ma'am," LeCroy responded, tapping the screen on his handheld tablet as he did so to activate the holo in the center of the table.

"Our sensor and Tacnet logs revealed Cerberus was hit with six pairs of X-rays just as we were jumping away back to space, all concentrated at the same point on the ship. We were able to identify they came from mobile weapons platforms instead of fixed emplacements. The mobile platforms are these vehicles you see here on the holo," LeCroy said, as a clear picture of a large truck attached to a long trailer appeared. They were both painted in a camouflage pattern.

"The trailer is quite long. Approximately 75 feet, thus the half dozen of paired wheel axles below it to support the length and weight that you see here. Due to the power required to create X-rays of this magnitude, they are single shot weapon systems using what our AI suggests is a controlled nuclear bomb burst to provide the necessary energy."

LeCroy's announcement that they were hit by a nuclear powered energy beam weapon system raised eyebrows all around the table.

"Lieutenant, do you think the AI in the data processing center was meant to be a trap for Cerberus? My thoughts are these weapons were prepositioned near an extremely high value target that had unobtrusively been hidden in plain sight prior to our arrival, and their targeting was no coincidence," Ronin said, but more as a conclusion than a question.

LeCroy nodded as he responded. "Yessir. I agree. And they clearly didn't expect Cerberus to show up the way we did. Our AI analysis says their positioning was to maximize their effectiveness against a target in orbit. They clearly were caught by surprise when Cerberus instead jumped into the atmosphere and fell like a meteor towards the planet surface while she launched Tomcats left and right to engage their fighter cover."

LeCroy changed the holo to a tactical schematic of the battlespace down on the surface. "The fighters have been cleared away by Taurus Squadron, and Lieutenant Sunderland is leading them to the retrieval point. They should arrive in approximately ten hours, during which time we will continue making repairs to Cerberus before we go pick up our warbirds unless they encounter trouble earlier. If that happens, the Bulldog monitoring their progress will jump away and call in Cerberus for help."

The tactical schematic zoomed in further, and now Lieutenant Kanagawa leaned forward slightly to handle this part of the report, wincing because his serious injuries were still quite painful. "The fighting retreat by Gamma team has delayed the Loyalist's ground element throughout the night to buy more time for Dr. Mueller. Gamma has now joined Bravo team at the data processing center, and the Loyalists are only now just beginning to assault the data processing center while Dr. Mueller continues to try to bypass the AI's firewalls and insert the worm into their defense network. He's been trying to pass the firewalls all night. Bravo rigged the building with the decoy explosives, including some they found in an armory inside the building.

"Lieutenant Gustav reports their time is nearly up, so if Dr. Mueller is successful, some of the staged decoy bombs won't be detonated. The Loyalists will hopefully believe they disarmed them in time instead of concluding we planted them as a ruse to hide our true objective of inserting a worm into their AI and defense network."

"And if Dr. Mueller is unsuccessful?" asked Commander Mueller, trying to sound detached about her noncombatant husband's presence in the center of a major firefight. She didn't succeed, but no one present would have lacked the grace to react unprofessionally to the concerned tone of her voice.

"Regardless of the success of Dr. Mueller, the extraction plan is the same. They will follow the underground utility tunnel from beneath the building to this point a little over five miles away where the tunnel intersects with the main powerlines here," Kanagawa said, pointing to the map with the designated coordinates now blinking in red.

"Surveillance shows a maintenance access point there, and the Bulldogs will jump in to bring our guys home. The Marine ground commander will trigger both sets of bombs and destroy the entire facility after they depart only if Dr. Mueller is unsuccessful.

"If Dr. Mueller is successful, then only the second stage of bombs will be triggered to collapse the entrance to the tunnels and prevent the Loyalists from following them. The second stage bombs are designed to appear as if they accidentally severed the connection for the first stage bombs, so the seeming mistake should help sell the ruse that the Loyalists took the facility back from us as we wouldn't leave the facility still standing if we had been unsuccessful in penetrating their computer systems."

Mueller looked relieved that the assault plan hadn't had to change much since the engagement began. "Thank you, Lieutenant. You can return to your post," Mueller said. Due to the extent of his injuries, Kanagawa had to be helped to his feet by Ronin, who was seated next to him.

"You sure you're up to carrying on right now, Lieutenant?" Ronin asked. His concerned expression as he looked at Kanagawa spoke volumes.

"Oh, yessir. The only thing more dangerous than a heavily armed combat Marine is that same Marine without anything else to do. I'd just get into trouble. Again," Kanagawa said with a straight face and a mischievous glint in his eyes.

Ronin snorted with a soft laugh and smile. "Well I certainly can't disagree with that, Lieutenant!"

The meeting continued for another half hour. Ronin finally returned to his quarters after what felt like ages. His dirty uniform was rumpled, and he smelled like smoke and grease just like everyone else who had been rushing to repair Cerberus.

"Daddy!" yelled his son, Edward Ronin, as he ran over and collided with Dan in a bear hug as he stood in the living room. "Ew, Dad. You stink!" Edward suddenly noted as he caught a whiff.

"Well. Love you, too, tiger," Dan said with an amused tone as he hugged the boy. "Old Dad needs to hit the showers. There are a lot of stinky, smelly folks wandering around the ship right now," he noted.

Sarah wandered into the living room just then. "Wow. Dad. Rough day at the office I hear?"

"Unnhh," and some head nods was the only reply she got from Dan.

"Dad, it was pretty bad, wasn't it?" Sarah continued.

"Yeah. It was. Cerberus took a hard shot from some energy weapons of all things. We don't have anything like those, although we do have some captured handheld units to study when all this is over. I'm just glad you two are safe. It'll be a few days before the repairs to Cerberus are completed, so access to parts of the ship will be restricted until then for safety."

After he said this, Dan looked at the time and realized what seemed off. "Hey, it's the middle of the night for you two. What are you doing up?"

Edward laughed as he pulled a sandwich and drink out of the small fridge and set them on the table next to Dan. "You look starved, Dad. And who can sleep during a battle when the ship was shaking and got all hot and stuff from that bad hit?"

Picking up the sandwich, Dan's eyes unfocused for a few moments as he nodded at the truth of Edward's observation. *No one, that's who.* Taking a bite, Dan suddenly realized he was famished. *When did I last eat?* he wondered.

* * *

Showered and in a clean uniform, Ronin strode onto the bridge. "Lieutenant Perez, status?"

"Cerberus is ready to jump, Captain. We have full sub-light engine power and life support again. Port landing bay is partially operational, starboard landing bay is undamaged," Perez responded, turning slightly in his seat to look at Ronin.

"Very well. Let's go get our Tomcats. Jump the ship," Ronin said as he took his seat in the center of the bridge.

"Yessir. Coordinates laid in. Jumping in five. Four. Three. Two. One," Perez drawled before he pushed the screen button to jump the ship.

Cerberus reappeared at the retrieval point. Within seconds, Tacnet lit up from plotting the positions of their Tomcats that were hanging around. Terra Station lit up part of the sky behind the Tomcats waiting to thumb a ride with Cerberus.

LeCroy opened the commlink for Taurus Squadron. "Archangel, this is Cerberus. Time to come home. Use the starboard landing bay only."

Lieutenant Sunderland was more than ready to land his fighter. They were flying on fumes, and getting pretty cramped after sitting for so long in their cockpits. "Cerberus, Archangel. That's good copy Cerberus. Starboard side landing bay. It's good to see you again," he replied.

Sunderland could see Taurus Squadron lining up behind his Tomcat on Tacnet, and his commlink activated with a traffic control message from the starboard landing bay flight controller. "Archangel, this is Cerberus flight control. Approach starboard landing bay. Hands on approach. Speed one-nine-zero. Checker's green. Call the ball."

Before responding, Sunderland quickly confirmed he had correctly aligned with the instructions before responding. "Copy that flight control. Starboard landing bay. Hands on approach. Speed one-nine-zero. Checker's green. I have the ball."

As he approached closer, Sunderland suddenly noticed the damage to Cerberus. *WHAT happened while we were gone?* he wondered in alarm for a few seconds before the demands of landing his Tomcat on a fast moving spaceship consumed his attention.

Half an hour later, LeCroy turned to face Ronin on the bridge. "Captain, Taurus Squadron is aboard."

Ronin nodded. "Now all we do is wait for the recall signal from our ground force."

CHAPTER 77

DATA PROCESSING CENTER

"Bravo 6, LT. Shift fire to your ten o'clock. They're pushing through the woods!" yelled Gustav over the commlink when he spotted a several larger groups of soldiers suddenly sprint out of the woods under heavy covering fire. *They're more organized this time*, Gustav noted to himself.

The building shook from another shell impact, knocking dust from the roof. Gustav's eyes flicked up to check the rafters above him. When he first noticed them, he thought they were decorative wood rafters. He finally realized their true purpose after enough shell impacts — they were flex steel reinforcement beams disguised as wood to hide the building's function as a defensible military facility.

The building suddenly shook from repeated shellfire, punctuated by a storm of bullets flying through the now missing windows that gouged small marks in the interior walls. Gustav checked Tacnet and was dismayed to see hundreds of enemy icons approaching. The end was near.

Gustav opened the common commlink being used by all the Marines on the operation. "Bravo 1, LT. We won't be able to keep them out any longer. Prepare for withdrawal."

"LT, Bravo 1. That's good copy. We'll move out on your order," Mackey replied from the fourth floor where he was shooting out the windows. Mackey had been watching the situation deteriorate too.

"Doc, pack your bags. It's time for our road trip!" yelled Mackey on a separate commlink over the pandemonium as he continued putting rounds downrange at what had become a sea of targets.

Karl didn't look up from his screen. He was too stunned at what he was finally seeing to even respond.

ACCESS GRANTED

"Doc! Doc?" Mackey yelled, suddenly realizing that Karl wasn't responding. Mackey checked Tacnet to confirm Karl was still alive and was relieved to discover he was, and hadn't moved. "Might as well not come back from this operation if I don't being Doc back to the Commander in one piece," Mackey muttered to himself as he crawled away from his position near the windows to check on his charge.

Gustav's voice was suddenly loud in Mackey's ears. "This is LT. Bravo team break contact and head to the basement. It's time to leave."

"LT, Bravo 1. That's good copy. Break contact and get to the basement," Mackey responded. He switched to a private commlink with Karl and moved into a crouch to move faster.

"Doc! It's Go Time! Ready or not, we have other places to be," he roared as he rounded the corner in the server farm and skidded to a stop. Karl was intently watching his screen and not moving a muscle.

"Doc!" roared Mackey.

"Ten seconds! I just need ten seconds!" Karl replied as he held a hand up, not taking his eyes from the completion percentage on his screen.

"What! Are you in?" Mackey said, yelling to be heard over the battle as he came closer to the Doc's position.

"Yes! It's finished! We did it!" Karl said triumphantly. He yanked his connection cable out of the server rack he had plugged his laptop into.

Karl was suddenly on his feet, helped by a power assist from Mackey as the building shook from another impact. Mackey spoke over the commlink "Lt, Bravo. Primary objective complete. Repeat, primary objective complete! Bravo team and the Doc are en route to the basement."

Gustav's eye brows shot up inside his exosuit at Mackey's report. "Hustle it up, Bravo 1. The natives are restless down here. Gamma team, break contact in one minute and get to the basement." Gustav could already hear the thundering of steps in the stairwell as Bravo team ran past on their way to the basement.

Seconds later, Mackey and Karl joined Bravo team in the basement. There was a large room with tables and chairs, and a hallway down towards the end in a corner of the room with a sign next to the hallway that said "Utilities" with an arrow towards the hall. That's where they needed to go.

"You guys stop for coffee and doughnuts up there or what?" Bravo 2 quipped as Bravo 3 strapped Gamma 2 to the back of his suit. Langley had been injured too badly to move on his own, and Marines wouldn't leave a wounded man behind if at all possible. Exosuits were able to transport wounded Marines or exosuits that lost their powered mobility.

"Yeah. Sorry we didn't bring you any. My bad, buddy," Mackey quipped as he turned and crouched down a bit so Karl could climb on his back and grab the small hand held grips on the back of his exosuit.

Mackey stood and looked at his team. They all nodded or motioned that they were ready with thumbs up signs. Mackey spoke over the common commlink again. "LT, Bravo 1. Bravo is history." He spoke over the Bravo team only commlink right after messaging Gustav. "Bravo team, let's move out."

Bravo team swiftly moved to the hallway, where there were multiple doors. Mackey stopped at the door marked, "Underground Utilities Entrance" and he tried to open the door by turning the handle. It was locked, so he stepped back and kicked the door open with a power assisted kick. The heavy, metal door ripped off its hinges and fell into the room as Mackey stomped in.

Karl noticed there was a deep boot print indented in the door next to the handle where Mackey kicked it. "You know, Bravo 1. For spaceship-based Marines, you seem to spend a lot of time battling on a planet's surface and escaping underground," Karl quipped.

Mackey stopped and straightened slightly, turning his head to look at Karl in surprise. Mackey snorted and was about to reply when Bravo 2 spoke up. "You know, he has a point Bravo 1."

Mackey tilted his head to the side slightly as he thought about the composite Force Omega team's dramatic underground escape from the Kremlin during the Battle of Earth. "Yeah, seems like it. But at least we get to travel to exotic new locations to meet interesting people," he said as he turned back to walk to the stairs he spotted that went down. Mackey added over the commlink, "And kill them, in a loud, grotesque military manner. Much more interesting than watching spaceships shoot at each other from a zillion miles away."

They climbed down several flights of cement stairs until they reached the bottom where it ended on a platform adjoining a large utility tunnel. Gustav's voice was now loud over the commlink. "Bravo 1, LT. We're moving down to the basement now."

Mackey responded quickly. "Copy that LT. We're in the tunnel now," he said as he stepped down into the tunnel. It was a tall tunnel, about ten feet high and wide. The tunnel was dimly lit with sparse lighting that stretched off into the distance.

"Alright doc, hang on," Mackey said as he started a power assisted jog in his exosuit. It was only a few miles. Five minutes into his easy run, the sound of a large explosion came from behind, far down the tunnel. In the gloom of the tunnel, Gustav's voice seemed disembodied on the commlink.

"This is LT. Second stage detonation. First stage remains intact."

There wasn't much to say as the Gamma and Bravo Marines jogged on.

CHAPTER 78

CERBERUS

ollowing the medical orderlies who were carrying out the wounded, Lieutenant Gustav walked down the lowered rear ramp of *Bulldog 1* into the starboard landing bay as dirty, smelly Marines filed out behind him. Carrying his inky black exosuit helmet in his hand, he reached the bottom and stepped out of the way. Gustav's ears suddenly perked up at the noise level. It was high enough to penetrate the fog of Gustav's exhaustion. It was exceptionally crowded in the landing bay. As Gustav quickly turned his head from side to side to take it all in, Gunnery Sergeant Blackwater sidled up next to him.

Gustav and Blackwater shared confused glances at the ruckus, and Blackwater motioned for a tired looking deckhand to stop as he was walking past. "Ensign. What's the situation here? Why is the landing bay so crowded?" Blackwater asked.

The deckhand looked momentarily surprised at the question until his eyes registered that the Marines were just returning from an away mission. "Gunny. Lieutenant. The port landing bay is still being repaired from the hit we took right before we jumped away during the raid down on the planet's surface. Some sort of massive energy beam hit us and caused a lot of damage and casualties, and this landing bay is receiving most of the flight traffic for the time being," he said with nod of his head towards the rest of the landing bay.

Karl Mueller overheard the deckhand's impromptu report, which was highly alarming and he opened a commlink to his wife. "Diane? Are you and the kids alright?"

"Karl! We're fine. We're all fine. Our quarters are on the opposite side of the ship from where the damage is. Are you unhurt? The initial mission summary forwarded by Lieutenant Gustav didn't mention anything about you being injured," Commander Mueller replied from the bridge. She didn't bother to conceal her mixed relief and concern that Karl was back aboard.

Gustav and Blackwater likewise overheard Karl and Diane's conversation, and they each shared a knowing look. "You know, we would have had a fate worse than death if we brought the good doctor back dead or injured, wouldn't we?" Blackwater muttered, but he said it as a statement and not a question.

Gustav shuddered a moment. Blackwater couldn't tell if it was fake or real. "She would have cut us off at the knees if we were lucky. Best we just be happy that he came home a hero with a great story to tell those kids of theirs, and count ourselves fortunate," he replied to Blackwater.

Gustav's commlink node chimed and Ronin's voice greeted them when Gustav opened the commlink. "Lieutenant, report for debriefing in two hours in the main conference room."

Both Blackwater's and Gustav's eyebrows rose. It was a bit unusual to have a debrief so quickly after returning from a fiercely fought, extended ground engagement. "Yes, Captain," he said. With that, Ronin closed the link.

"Something must be up. And don't forget to hit the showers, BEFORE you show up this time," Blackwater said, this time with clear humor at the jab.

Gustav snorted. "Should be plenty of hot water left for me. You lot still haven't figured out how to work the shower fixtures yet."

Blackwater laughed. "I asked Chief Lazarus to install some simple pictures to show us how to use all that shower handle and stuff, but he must have forgotten. Very complicated. I hear we might even learn to control the water temperature one day."

Not quite two hours later, a freshly scrubbed Gustav left Marine country and walked towards the main conference room. He munched on an energy bar as he walked through the ship's passageways, thoughts wandering as he occasionally stepped aside repair crews and machinery that were moving about. Due to the occasional scorch patterns on the deck and walls, parts of the ship's interior clearly had sustained multiple equipment fires. The slight tinge of smoke still wafted through the air as he walked.

Soon enough, Gustav arrived at the main conference room and he walked in to a debriefing that was already underway so he settled into an open seat. Ronin glanced over as Gustav walked in an nodded in greeting while Karl was talking.

"The worm was finally embedded into the Loyalist's AI and defense network through a spoofing of the computer protocols we obtained from the Marine raid on The Ark. Apparently they never thought of blocking access from the ancient ship that had orbited the planet all their lives, because it had always been that way. Thanks to the worm, we can access anything and we took the liberty of confirming whether their military believes we failed in our attempt to breach their AI. They fell for it, but I would have to caution how we use this access. I suggest we use a low profile to avoid raising suspicions," Karl concluded. Like Gustav, Karl had just enough time to shower and change into a fresh uniform before he arrived.

Ronin nodded. "Agreed. It's nice to know we can bring it all down if need be, but for now we need to proceed with caution and a light touch."

Ronin looked to Gustav. "Lieutenant, your Marines did outstanding work down there. They paid a heavy price, but I'm very hopeful their sacrifice will bring about a swift end to this conflict. What's your tentative assessment of the Marine's readiness status?"

Gustav nodded. "Thank you sir. I'll pass that along to the men. Right now, we have about one full Marine team available if needed and if we use them as a consolidated unit. About half of my guys are recovering from lesser injuries, but they can still pull a trigger. Beyond a consolidated team of questionable fitness for duty, the Marines are a spent force between the casualties from more serious injuries and our KIAs." Gustav saw no reason to sugar coat the situation and he just said it like it is.

Ronin nodded thoughtfully before speaking again. "Ambassador Gadre reports the Cargo Rebels are being fairly successful in pushing the Officers out of the downtown metropolitan areas, but she confirmed what we've been thinking. The Officers in control of the Loyalist military haven't been defeated."

"Captain, I must again protest against using my protocol officer to take sides in a rebellion. It sets a bad example," Dr. Wright suddenly said. Although Wright was seething now, he'd been relatively quiet for two weeks since he last clashed with Captain Ronin. The death of one of the other protocol officers when the ship was hit over the data processing center was close to pushing Wright to the brink.

Just before Ronin could respond, Commander Mueller did it for him. The dangerous tone of annoyance in her voice did little to hide her anger and contempt at Wright's continuing ignorance at the implications of the attempt to ambush Cerberus when the ship first entered orbit. "Doctor. That isn't nearly as bad an example as allowing a corrupt and hostile government to destroy this ship and everyone aboard it. If you don't like it, I'd be happy to ship you off to join the Loyalists and even things out to your satisfaction."

Impressed by Mueller's response, Ronin merely leaned forward and interlaced his fingers while placing his elbows on the table. His face was humorless as he interrupted Wright's attempt to rebut Mueller before it got started.

"Doctor! Once the Loyalists declared war by attempting to ambush Cerberus, your mission changed along with ours. I have an assignment for you and your people, but only if I trust you to come through with it," Ronin retorted, raising his eyebrows slight to emphasize his words.

Still somewhat surprised at being included in this debriefing because he had never attended one before, Dr. Wright asked, "Yes, Captain. How can we be of assistance?" For once, Wright was wise enough to keep snarky words out of his message.

Ronin nodded slightly. "Doctor, please work up a postwar governance structure for Terra Station that factors in the abuses of power by the Officers and some of the Crew Class in the population. The people there need to believe they will have a fair and just system of government, equality of opportunity and rights, and they must be heavily invested in seeing the new government become successful."

Flushing slightly, Dr. Wright nodded slightly as he said, "Yes, Captain, we've had some preliminary discussions about that very topic. I'll get with my people and we'll firm up our ideas by tonight. You want I should circulate our draft plan to the senior staff officers?"

Pleased at Wright's amenability to his request, Ronin simply responded, "Yes, that would be excellent."

Ronin shifted his gaze. "Senior officers, I want your thoughts and notes about Dr. Wright's draft on my inbox by 0900 hours."

Looking back at Lieutenant Gustav, Ronin added, "Lieutenant, what's your sense of using Cargo Rebels to help capture the Officer's Council if we bring the Council to a place of our choosing? I'm presuming, and excuse me if I'm stepping on your people's shoes here a little bit, doctor, that the people would want the Council and their key staff brought to justice for crimes against humanity? Or should we simply stand off and eliminate the Council using an orbital strike?"

Now it was Gustav's turn to be somewhat surprised. That was a weighty strategic question with long-term implications. Face pensive, Gustav measured his words. "Captain, while typically I prefer the simple solutions because those are more likely to achieve success as there's fewer things to go wrong, like erasing the Council in an orbital strike for instance ... in this situation my gut tells me we have to do it the hard way and try to capture the Council to put them on trial. The Cargo Class and much of the Crew Class have been greatly wronged by their Officers for centuries. They will want a spectacle where the wrongdoers face justice instead of merely being ended and turned into dust without being required to answer for their crimes."

Doctor Wright nodded thoughtfully at Gustav's words, and he spoke before Ronin or Mueller could comment. "Just so, Lieutenant. We've been thinking the same thing in our area. The word we're applying to that is catharsis. A spectacle of justice, as the Lieutenant puts it, is a form of catharsis for a population that puts it on the path to healing and forgiveness."

Ronin and Mueller shared a short glance. Neither of them expected agreement between Dr. Wright, Lieutenant Gustav, and themselves on whether to capture or kill the Council.

Ronin decided to include capture and trial in his orders. "All right. Commander Mueller and I discussed that point earlier and we agree with Lieutenant Gustav and Dr. Wright. Doctor, include your team's thoughts on a structure of holding trials in your report please. Lieutenant, work up a proposed plan for how we plan to capture the Officers Council and let's discuss later tomorrow. All right, let's return to our posts and we'll regroup later with the stakeholders who are needed."

Sensing they were dismissed, everyone stood and left except Mueller and Ronin, who stayed behind after the hatch closed. Mueller spoke first. "Repairs are coming along ahead of schedule, and frankly Dan, you need to go grab some rack time. You look pretty rough."

Ronin snorted softly. He felt pretty rough, too. "Look in the mirror! We BOTH need to be rested before the next operation. This ship has had a frenetic pace of operations ever since we arrived in orbit. When was that? Two weeks ago? We're worn down already."

"When was the last time you got some sleep?" Mueller asked. She wasn't going to back down on this.

Ronin's face screwed into an expression of concentration as he tried to recall when that was. "Uh. I dunno. I take it you're about to throw a mutiny if I don't go get some sleep? You need some too."

"Age before beauty, Dan. You've been awake longer than I have, I think. I'll take my turn right after you."

Ronin smiled tiredly. She knew him too well by now. "All right, Diane. You win. I can't say I feel much like putting up a fight about being ordered into my rack." Dan and Diane both stood and headed for the exit.

* * *

"Commander Hunt sends word that his people have a sufficiently armed strike force in the required numbers to participate in the raid on the Officers Council, Lieutenant," Ronin said to Gustav as the senior officers sat around the table in the main conference room. His eyes flicked over to Karl, who was also present. "Doctor Mueller, all is ready on your end?" he asked.

Karl nodded. "That's right, Captain. Thanks to the worm, we now have the necessary level of control over their communications system to make it appear a message slipped through that directs the Council and others to appear at a time and day of our choosing. That message would carry all the proper code and authority authentications needed to seem genuine."

Turning his head to look directly at Lieutenant Sunderland, Ronin merely needed to raise his eyebrows to ask the question Kelvin was waiting to answer. "Yessir. Bulldog crews are ready to go. They've had their few days of rest, and they're going to start getting into trouble if we don't give them something to do."

Ronin snorted slightly with a smile at Sunderland's articulation of his Bulldog pilots' readiness status, and he looked next to Chief Lazarus.

Lazarus was the most tired looking of all of them because he was still overseeing the feverish pace of repairs to Cerberus while everyone else had gotten more opportunity to rest in the past few days. "Captain, we'll complete the large majority of our field repairs within the next three hours. Anything beyond that will take a shipyard."

Ronin smiled slightly and nodded to Lazarus, acknowledging Engineering's remarkable feats the past few days. "OK. Gustav and Dr. Mueller. Use our AI to find a meeting location meeting these parameters ... Distant enough from urban areas that we can vaporize it with our railguns if needed, but would severely limit civilian exposure to the impact. At the same time, it should not be so distant as to make them feel exposed and unsafe, like they're being led into a trap, yet the heavy majority of the Officers Council should also be able to travel to the site. Most of them are located in or near First City, which will help in finding a suitable spot. Questions?"

Karl raised his hand, which was awkward since they weren't school-children. "Captain, our worm has been feeding us significant amounts of information from the planet's databanks. While it's been directed mainly at information of a strategic or tactical nature for combat purposes, now that we've scooped all that up we have a chance to access the records of Earth's history that were carried over on The Ark. I'd like permission to grab that information for posterity's sake."

Ronin looked startled. "How much history are we talking here? Enough to fill in the gaps that we have because of The Fall?" he asked intently.

"Yessir, but only up until the point of The Ark's departure from Earth for the most part. The records appear to contain a highly detailed history of our peoples from prior to The Fall," Karl said, using 'peoples' to refer to all of humanity in his response. "Most of that historical information has been locked away by the Officers Council and inaccessible to rest of the population of Terra Station except for what the Officers Council selectively has distributed to help them control the population."

"Of all the places I would have looked to find our missing historical information, eighty-one light years from Earth isn't where I would have thought to start. Yes, please do. We are doomed to repeat the mistakes in our history if we don't know what our history actually was to help guide our thinking as we move forward," Ronin said. Seeing no other questions, it was time to get ready for the next big push.

CHAPTER 79

SECRETARY ELLIS

"Secretary Ellis, why didn't Cerberus just destroy the data processing center from orbit?" asked Speaker Hayward as he sipped his coffee. They were seated together with Wallace Seaver at the small conference table in Hayward's office.

"The data processing center was chosen as our ambush site because it was near enough to a small village to discourage orbital bombardment if they wished to avoid civilian casualties, but still be a valuable target they couldn't afford to ignore and not investigate. We leaked the location intel to the rebellion through one of our spies and placed our mobile X-ray units to maximize their effectiveness against an orbital target in anticipation Cerberus would act as the mission platform for a raid by ground units attempting to capture our defense network AI down on the surface."

"So ... what happened then?" Seaver asked as he leaned forward in his seat with interest. He hadn't heard about the attack.

Ellis took a breath as he shook his head slightly. Lips pursed, he replied after a moment. "Cerberus took the bait, but the ship wasn't where it was supposed to be when it arrived two days ago." As he said this, Ellis pressed a button and the screen on the wall next to the table lit up. There was a light enhanced picture of the data processing center taken from a distance, and several glowing areas in the forest away from the building.

"Instead of jumping into orbit, this happened," Ellis said, as he started the video.

Seaver leaned forward as the video began playing. "I see glowing areas in the forest flickering with multiple fires…?" he began to say when a small flash suddenly lit up the sky, immediately followed by a massive flame trail rapidly fell to the surface. "What IS that?" he asked, eyes locked onto the video playback.

Ellis froze the video and explained, "Those flickering, glowing areas on the ground represent several different ambushes and surface firefights that have already occurred. Overhead, our fighters were in control of the airspace, and that falling meteor flame trail is actually Cerberus. The ship suddenly appeared in our atmosphere, launched small combat fighters as they plummeted to the surface, and disappeared again. We have no records of the ship approaching or leaving before this and our scientists have come to the obvious conclusion that the ship has some sort of faster than light drive. Anyone could have figured THAT out just from the ship's arrival here without taking generations to do so."

"So the ship escaped again?" Hayward asked, sounding somewhat disgusted.

"Yes, but we believe our mobile X-ray units still managed to damage the ship before it disappeared. Watch here," Ellis said as he started the video again. Just as there was a flash at the bottom of the flame trail, he stopped the playback so it froze on the flash. There was a large ship visible in the light.

"This is what Cerberus actually looks like, although we don't have a clear image of the ship due to the light and interference. As you can see, she's quite different that what we originally believed arrived in orbit a few weeks ago. Notice the port side of the ship…"

Ellis trailed off as he zoomed in on the image. "There appears to be a strike on the ship here from all six mobile X-ray units. Targeting was provided by our AI, which had little time to calculate a new firing solution due to the flaming, low atmospheric arrival of the ship instead of the expected high orbital target. And then the AI had even less time to point the weapons at that new aiming point based on its firing solution."

Seaver had to ask: "Any damage estimates?"

Ellis shook his head. "None. We don't know the layout of the ship. We don't know the hull composition. We don't know how much of the beam energy was deflected, because it appears a significant portion of the energy WAS deflected away from the ship. We literally don't know what we don't know."

Hayward nodded thoughtfully. "We'll need to come up with another plan to draw Cerberus out and destroy her before we run out of time and resources down here. Time is not on our side." As he said this, Hayward's intercom beeped softly.

"Mr. Speaker? We're receiving an encrypted, text only message from the some of the higher ranks on the Officer's Council. They want to reconvene at the earliest opportunity and they command Secretary Ellis to attend."

Hayward's glanced up to meet Ellis' eyes. "It seems we have some limited portion of our communications network restored," Ellis commented.

Hayward nodded. "So it seems," he replied, as he leaned forward and opened his mic. "Please advise the Council we would be pleased to attend."

CHAPTER 80

THE VALLEY

Hunt looked up into the night sky expectantly. It was clear and starry, and he could see The Ark beginning to make it orbital transit across the vast expanse. It looked like a bright star in the sky that happened to be moving.

It was very quiet, and his rebels were silently waiting along with him. Glancing around, Hunt could see shadows both in, and beyond, the broken walls of the ruined buildings they currently occupied on the edge of the Borderlands. Like him, those shadows remained quiet as they waited. *Could this be the last fight for our freedom?* Hunt found himself wondering.

As he checked his watch for the tenth time, the sound of three thunderous peals suddenly appeared high above their heads and Hunt quickly looked up. Three falling flame tails rapidly streaking towards the surface while the thunder sound clarified into the sound of powerful engines pushing against the planet's gravity in their efforts to slow their descent before they cratered into the surface. Thirty seconds after suddenly appearing in the night sky, the Bulldogs deftly landed on the surface and began lowering their ramps as a few flight ops loadmasters were waiting to exit and help expedite the loading of each assault shuttle.

Impressed with the piloting of the Bulldogs, Hunt and Buckingham exchanged glances and Buckingham shook his head slightly. "I just don't know how the Officers thought they could fight the kind of tech we're seeing, Commander. Appearing from nowhere, disappearing off enemy radar before they can be targeted, if they ever appeared on radar to begin with. Those fabulous Marine combat suits. The firepower carried by Cerberus. I just don't get what they were thinking."

Hunt nodded as they all stood up and began jogging towards the Bulldogs. "Yeah, I guess they didn't realize what they would be up against for some reason. The Officers were desperate to hold onto power, and desperate people often do stupid things instead of adjusting to a changed reality."

As they reached the ramps, the loadmasters were already counting the numbers loading into each Bulldog. In less than three minutes, they were fully loaded and the ramps began to close again. The loadmasters quickly checked on their new occupants to ensure they were strapped in. Hunt realized the whine of the engines had never stopped the scant few minutes they were on the ground, they were just running in neutral so the shuttles could quickly leave again.

The commlinks Hunt and Buckingham had on loan from the Marines crackled to life.

"Commander Hunt? Lieutenant Buckingham? This is Chief Jonsey. Welcome aboard *Bulldog 3*. We'll be micro-jumping in thirty seconds. Be ready for a few moments of discomfort." Jonsey unknowingly reverted to using his regular rank instead of his fake rank of Flight Officer that Ronin had assigned for the initial contact mission.

Hunt and Buckingham exchanged alarmed glances as Hunt asked, "Micro jumping?" for both of them. Suddenly they felt slightly disoriented.

Jonsey's voice again came through their commlinks. "Micro-jump complete. We are coming in hot over the landing zone now. The Bulldogs will make combat landings with the engines still spun up, followed by immediate dustoff. As soon as your men are off the shuttle, form up on Lieutenant Gustav. Landing in 30 seconds."

Even more confused, Buckingham shook his head. "How could this shuttle have flown 400 miles in just a few seconds?" Hunt just shook his head to indicate he had no answers to that.

Although three Bulldogs departed with the rebels from their pickup location, four now jumped low into the airspace near the mountainous resort located about a hundred miles from First City in a coordinated assault. They had appeared with small jump flares hidden by the foothills separating a valley adjacent to the edge of the mountains and another valley deeper into the mountains where the resort was located.

The resort, named the Officers Club, was the exclusive playground of Terra Station's elite. It existed solely for the benefit of the Officers Council, government leaders, and their families. The Officers Club was only accessible by air or the dedicated underground maglev subway from First City. This controlled access served to keep the Cargo and Crew Classes far away so they couldn't spoil the resort's pampering of the Officer Class elite.

Bulldog 3 suddenly decelerated hard, engine thrusters creating an audible roar inside the shuttle. As they settled into a surprisingly gentle landing, the engine whine could still be heard over the sound of the rear ramp dropping. The loadmaster along for the ride suddenly stood up and yelled loudly for everyone's attention while the ramp lowered: "Everybody, just follow my instructions."

The loadmaster then touched a glowing red button on the side of the hull next to where he had been sitting. The red turned to green and the all the seatbelts suddenly released their hold on each of the rebels. The loadmaster gestured with both palms facing up for all to rise.

"Rise up! Face the rear of the shuttle. Ramp cycle is done in three seconds. Two seconds. One second. Clear the shuttle! Out! Out! Out!" As he urged everyone to exit quickly, the loadmaster's sweeping hand motions pointed towards the lowered ramps.

Exiting in two long lines, the rebels surged forward to clear the Bulldog. One minute later, they were on the ground and four Bulldogs pushed into the sky before jumping away again. Hunt and Buckingham had no problem spotting Lieutenant Gustav and the Marines as they had come directly from Cerberus in *Bulldog 1.*

Hunt and Buckingham's commlinks chirped with an incoming message from Gustav. "This is Gustav. We're ten miles from the resort. I'm detaching a Marine demolition team to sever the subway line. Have your men follow me, we are humping over those low hills into the next valley for the assault on the resort. From here on we are radio silent."

Hunt responded quickly. "Affirmative, Lieutenant." He then turned and repeated Gustav's orders to the rebels while the Marines passed out flashlights to the rebels so they could see where they were walking. Their exosuits visors automatically adjusted light levels for their wearers, so the Marines didn't need flashlights.

They walked two abreast for several miles in strict radio silence. The tension was thick. They looked for ambushes around every tree.

Gustav was monitoring their progress on Tacnet. Using his external speaker, he said quietly to his Marines, "Demo team, heads up. We're almost to the fork in your road. Call out when you split off the main group."

The Demo team nodded to silently acknowledge Gustav.

Minutes later they found a game trail leading towards the valley where the Officers Club was nestled. Gustav checked his Tacnet plot. They were right on time, and right where they were supposed to be. Gustav's thoughts were interrupted by the departure of the Demo team.

"Splitting off now," reported Pvt. Rhee Lee, the young Echo team heavy weapons specialist. His young voice betrayed no emotion about the tension they were experiencing during the long, all-night hike. Rhee and Privates Han Pak and David Danfries quickly vanished in the dark as they moved deeper into the shadowy groves of trees in the valley.

Hunt and Buckingham had their hands full keeping their people together while they hiked through the uneven terrain in the dark. *To their credit, they've made little sound and voiced no complaints about how hard this hike is,* Hunt thought to himself. He was proud of them.

The sky ahead slowly lightened with the coming dawn as they reached the edge of the valley and crossed into the valley where the Officers Club was. They stuck to the shadows provided by groves of trees that were thicker than were in the previous valley, and forded the few small mountain streams that flowed downhill to the lake and were hidden by the trees. The sun began to rise in the sky ahead, and would soon be glimmering off the surface of the placid lake occupying the floor of the valley.

Eventually, Gustav held up his hand, signaling the group to halt. He could see the resort through the trees. It was perched on a low promontory of a mountain that rose behind it like a monolith of stone and forest.

Gustav motioned for Hunt and Buckingham to come over. He used his external speakers, talking low so his voice wouldn't carry far.

"All right. There it is. Satellite optics indicated we are most likely to remain unseen by scaling up the lower base of Mount Icefell over there. That way we approach the Officers Club from above, where the trees are thicker and it's not as steep and rocky as down below," Gustav said softly.

Hunt and Buckingham nodded. From their vantage point, they could see the tree coverage on Mount Icefell extended for quite a ways above the resort. "Lieutenant, don't you think they would have sensor coverage in those woods like they would everywhere else?" Buckingham asked. He'd been wondering how they would get close to the objective the entire hike and had no answers.

Gustav smiled slightly under his visor so neither of them could see it. "Our ship's AI has quietly taken control of the club's security systems in preparation for our arrival. They won't know we're coming unless someone actually spots us with the naked eye."

THAT was news to the rebels. Like the Marines, the rebels had also paid a heavy price for the deception and assault at the data processing center. They were about to experience one of the benefits of that down payment.

Gustav motioned for everyone to sit down and take a rest. They still had a long day of hiking ahead.

CHAPTER 81

THE OFFICERS CLUB

"Welcome to the Officers Club, Mr. Speaker. I'm Captain Phillipe Oretell and will be your host for the day," said the maître d'. His "rank" was just an honorific that had been adopted for working at the resort. Oretell wore a dark navy suit, with shiny brass buttons and gold braid at the wrists. The faux gaudy outfit was clearly something that looked like it belonged on a cruise ship.

Speaker Hayward stepped from the plush maglev car into the ornate, underground subway station. It was the end of a very private subway line that had no other stops between the station and its counterpart below the most exclusive Officer Class tower in the heart of First City.

"Thank you, Captain Oretell. It's always nice to spend time at the Officers Club. Is my standard suite ready?" Hayward asked.

Oretell nodded, tilting his head slightly to the side as he did so. "Yes it is, Mr. Speaker. I had the staff prepare it the moment we received word you would be arriving for a Council meeting here."

Hayward nodded, pleased. "Excellent. Secretary Ellis will be arriving on the next train. See to it that his accommodations are ready as well. The Officers Council will be in session early this afternoon. Have the Cargo Class servants ready to meet their needs after the Council concludes its business."

It wasn't Oretell's first rodeo. He had already made the necessary, typical arrangements to bring the pretty, young, unwilling Cargo Class "servants" in for tonight's festivities. Hayward and Oretell continued chatting as they walked to the escalator that lead up to the lobby of the Officers Club. They had to settle on a suitable menu for tonight's feast to help put the Council into the mood for their late night activities.

CHAPTER 82

MOUNT ICEFELL

Gustav glanced up as they hiked through the pines on the slope of Mount Icefell. The sun had crossed its zenith, and was now starting its downward path to the horizon. *The Council will be meeting soon, he thought to himself.* He looked closer at the rebels, measuring how much gas they would have left in their tanks. *Enough. Just barely,* Gustav concluded.

The endless hike was tiring, even to Marines in exosuits operating in a lower G environment than they were used to. His commlink suddenly clicked twice, and Gustav held up a hand to call a halt. Using hand signals, he motioned for Hunt to join him.

They moved on ahead, following the direction indicated on Tacnet to where the scouts were located. Crouching down, they ended up climbing downhill to where they were. "What have you got?" Gustav said quietly using his external speaker.

"Right there, LT. Through the trees? See that?" pointed the Pirate, Echo 2. Corporal Longman was half lying on his Stinger rifle as he quietly indicated to Gustav where in the forest they were supposed to look. It was downhill and to their right. Bravo 2, Corporal Wilson, was lying on the ground a few feet away, as he scanned the area with his own Stinger rifle, searching for targets while the Pirate handled passing word along. The 2s were serving as the forward scouts with their long range rifles.

"I see it!" Gustav replied. Neither of them was using the commlinks as they spoke softly. Hunt could barely hear the exchange. "You and

Bravo 2 find an overwatch position and set up in a sniper hide. When you're ready, the assault force will move on the objective."

Both the Pirate and Wilson looked at Gustav as they nodded and began moving away at a crouch. The two were remarkably quiet as they moved through the woods towards a rocky outcropping they had spotted that offered a clear view of the resort down below.

Motioning for Hunt to follow him, Gustav scrambled back up the slope to where the rest of the force was holding position. Still using hand signals, he waved Gamma 4 over. Private Victor Berger quickly walked over in response to Gustav's motion.

"Boss?" Berger asked quietly over the speaker.

Gustav wasted no time. "Echo 2 and Bravo 2 are setting up an overwatch position. I want you to cover their six while they're covering us."

Berger checked Tacnet briefly to confirm their location. "On it, boss," he said quickly as he bounded away.

Gustav then motioned for his team leaders to lean in closer. Bravo 1 and Gamma 1 were standing next to him. "1s, take your teams to the right flank of the resort. The site maps our AI loaded onto Tacnet have the council chamber over there. Wait for my command, and then move in by team. Once the 2s on overwatch give the word, we'll move in. Questions?"

There were none.

"OK. Make it happen."

Both Mackey and Blackwater nodded and they quickly gathered their teams to pass the plan along.

Gustav and Hunt shared a glance, while Buckingham joined them. "Where do you want my men, Lieutenant?" Hunt asked.

Gustav had been thinking about it and believed he had a perfect setup for the rebels and their gear. "Split into two groups. The first group will engage and clear any Loyalists they encounter in the facility outside the council chambers. The second group will go around the left flank and take control of the grassy field on the far side. The grassy field is our extraction point, and we need to hold it."

Buckingham and Hunt nodded. "The extraction point is a big area to control, but I think we can do it," Hunt noted.

"It's a difficult job, but one I think your people can pull off. Once the Bulldogs are away, a team of your rebels will need to fade away into the woods and move to the alternate extraction point because the ride they came in will be full of captured Officers for the initial return trip like we discussed earlier."

Hunt nodded, knowing it was never hurt to hear parts of the plan again. Soon the assault force took up their positions, still hidden in woods above the resort.

As Gustav was lying on the ground next to some brush and a pine tree, he noticed there were several heavily armed guards patrolling the perimeter, while several pairs of guards patrolled inside and could be seen through large glass windows. The resort consisted of several large, attractive buildings with exteriors of natural stone and wood. They had plentiful numbers of large windows to allow in natural light that filtered down through several floors that circled a beautiful atrium inside. The guards were armed with side arms and automatic weapons. They wore matching dark gray uniforms, with a red stripe down the outer side of the legs.

Lying flat in their positions on the stone outcropping about two hundred feet higher than the resort, the 2s exchanged glances. They were still maintaining radio silence and wouldn't use commlinks until the shooting started.

The Pirate could see Gustav from his vantage point, and Gustav had made sure they could see him while he stayed hidden from the resort below. Gustav made a 'thumbs up' gesture to Longman, which was their signal to engage when they thought the time was right. He turned his head slightly without taking his eyes from the resort down below and whispered loudly, "Wilson! It's Go Time. Let's take those two on the outside walking a circuit when they get beyond the interior windows so the guards inside can't see what happened to them."

Wilson nodded his head. "I got right. You take left." He'd been thinking the same thing. A few seconds passed as the two on the outside slowly walked. Two steps beyond the windows where large stone walls blocked the views, and Wilson softly said, "Take 'em!" Their Stinger rifles recoiled powerfully as they magnetically propelled a pair of heavy caliber, hypervelocity bullets towards the unsuspecting guards.

The guards dropped out of sight, and the 2s continued on to their next targets. "Rooftop, main building. Opposite corners," Wilson murmured.

Longman nodded and replied, "Right. On three." Their individual targets were pre-designated for each shooter on Tacnet so they wouldn't waste a round shooting at the same guard.

"One. Two. Three!" Longman whispered loudly, and the rooftop tangos likewise dropped from sight behind the retaining wall lining the rooftop. "Do we take the guards we can see inside?"

Wilson shook his head and whispered, "Not yet. Let our guys get into position, and we'll start shooting just before breaching to avoid giving them any advance warning." Wilson clicked on his commlink for the first time in quite a while. "LT, Bravo 2. Exterior tangos down. Advise when in position and we can hit a few of the tangos inside for you."

Two clicks from Gustav confirmed the report was received.

Down below them, Longman and Wilson could see the Marine team swiftly move forward. They were deadly silent. Even the two squads of rebels moved quietly, if somewhat more slowly. Gustav led the depleted team of Marines over to the right flank of the main building where the council chambers were. Right behind them was a larger team of Cargo Rebels. Another team of Cargo Rebels circled around the other direction to go secure the grassy field.

Two minutes after reporting to Gustav, the Marine Lieutenant's voice filled Wilson's and the Pirate's ears over the commlink, this time he was using the team commlink instead of a private channel as they were now in position for the main assault. "Echo 2 and Bravo 2, LT. In position. What do you see?"

Longman had a slightly better angle to peer inside the building, so he replied. "Six known tangos, we have eyes on three of them near your entry point. Be advised the remaining three are roamers, current disposition unknown."

Gustav checked Tacnet to see where the Pirate had the three known hostiles positioned. Suddenly, the plot updated and ten more tangos were plotted on the map projection and the voice of his exosuit's AI spoke on the team commlink for the first time in a long time.

"Current position of all armed hostiles are now on Tacnet." The Cerberus AI had decided it was time to tap into the resort's internal sensors and update our tactical information as the secret of the Marine presence at the Officers Club was about to vanish anyway.

Gustav nodded to himself and clicked acknowledgment while he studied Tacnet for a moment. "Overwatch 2s, wait for my command to fire. Bravo 1, your men take the six tangos on the floor below where the council chamber is. Gamma 1, take the four near the front door. Remaining Marines on cleanup for any other shooters we encounter. Got it?"

Clicks acknowledged his orders.

Gustav waited a moment for all the acknowledgments and he designated each group's targets for them on Tacnet before ordering the go ahead. "Overwatch, execute plan."

The large picture windows immediately shattered when hypervelocity Stinger rounds blew through them. Wilson and The Pirate then dialed their weapons to Airburst Mode, and pulled the triggers several more times. As the hail of deadly splinters shredded the three guards behind the desks near the entrance, Gustav shouted "Go, go, go!" into the unit's commlink. Marines burst through the glass doors in the main entrance. They just didn't bother opening the glass doors first.

Mackey took four Bravo team Marines plus Echo 6 as they rapidly vaulted the interior guardrail of the atrium and jumped down onto the floor below. Other Marines simultaneously acted as a form of overwatch as they rapidly scanned the visible parts of the floor below for targets from along the inner edge to the atrium. They couldn't see the entrance to the Council chambers as it was recessed back under the overhang of the upper floor, but they nonetheless had good coverage of the area.

Using the advantage of lower gravity and the power of their exosuits, Mackey and his men didn't bother rolling when they landed. They just simply landed with slight bounce steps and their rifles up. It happened so fast, the guards below were clearly surprised as four were still standing next to the door to the council chambers while two froze midway to the edge of the atrium to check and see what the above commotion was.

Mackey had activated his external speaker while they were jumping, and he wasted no time putting it to use. "Drop your weapons, or die."

The six guards shared frightened glances. "I'm not going to take one for the Council," the guard nearest Mackey quickly declared as he slowly bent to lower his weapon to the ground.

The other guard next to him wasn't so bright and he tried to swing his weapon to bear. Too bad it was on a strap and hanging over his rear shoulder when the Marines decided to crash the party. Private Gonzales (Echo 6) simply said, "Barqhest!" and Echo team's war dog shot ahead at the command from his handler.

Barqhest was very smart, and well trained. The big dog knew to bite the weapons hands of an enemy to keep them from hurting his Marine teammates, and Barqhest could bite very, very hard.

The unwise guard screamed in agony as the war dog put on a spectacularly vicious display of violence, taking monster bites of flesh and crunching bones. The remaining guards were shocked into lowering their weapons to the floor and raising their hands in surrender by the hideous sight.

Mackey then loudly ordered, "Bravo 4, Cuff 'em." Mackey then nodded towards Gonzales. "Echo 6?"

Gonzales responded with a thumbs up towards Mackey to acknowledge the combination question and command as he simultaneously said, "Barqhest! Cease!"

The large war dog complied instantly and backed off a few steps, growling menacingly all the while, as the Rottweiler never took his eyes off his bloodied prey.

Other Marines joined them moments later, having taken the stairs and Gustav glanced down at the savaged guard who was moaning on the floor. Looking up at Gonzales, Gustav said, with a shake of his head, "There's always some idiot who wants to roll the dice."

Gonzales's half-smile was hidden inside his suit, but his amused response spoke for everyone. "Yessir. Some people just can't help but overestimate their chances."

The heavy, large double doors of the council chambers suddenly opened and an angry looking Speaker Hayward imperiously walked out shouting "What is the meaning of th…" Hayward cut himself off mid-sentence when he realized he was facing an awful lot of firepower, most of it already pointed right at him.

Gustav strode forward to meet Hayward, who was speechless for once in his life. Hayward hadn't noticed the other members of the Officers Council had begun to follow him out to see what was going on.

Over the commlink Gamma 1s voice suddenly declared, "Gamma 1, LT. Remaining tangos down or in custody. Building is cleared."

Hearing that, Gustav wasn't in any mood to waste time as he recognized who he was looking at both from the Intel provided by Commander Hunt and the Cerberus' AI infiltration of the planetary defense network. "Mr. Speaker. You're all under arrest."

Gustav nodded at several of his Marines who had switched their weapons for a bag of zip ties, and they quickly moved in to finish the cuffing job on the Officers.

Hayward was surprised, but unwilling to simply give in. "You can't do this! You can't do this! We're Officers, not common criminals!" he raged, his voice climbing as he sputtered his indignant protestations.

Gustav didn't bother responding to Hayward as his Marines overpowered the man and cuffed him anyway.

CHAPTER 83

CERBERUS

"**C**aptain, I implore you as an Officer and…" Hayward began saying in what he thought was a reasonable sounding tone.

"You have no idea what it means to earn the right to be called an officer," Ronin stated, cutting off Hayward curtly. Ronin was angry, and spoke in a loud, commanding voice that carried over the entire hanger bay.

Ronin's sharp retort caused the Marines who were herding their prisoners out of the Bulldogs to turn their heads and see what the commotion was.

Ronin continued, his voice nearly growling due to his seething anger. "Your selfish arrogance in attempting to kill thousands of my crew on this warship is unforgivable. You've committed crimes against humanity through murder, enslavement of most of your population, and a host of other offenses. It's time you and your ilk faced justice."

Hayward tried to portray a brave condescension, which seemed far less believable in the full 1G on Cerberus as he wasn't used to that much gravity. "What do you think you're going to do? Line us all up and just shoot us? We have rights, you know."

Ronin smiled, but there was no warmth to it at all. "Your people are going to get a fair trial, followed by a first class firing squad, courtesy of the Cargo Rebels. But you, and Secretary Ellis, gave the orders to fire on this ship and declare war. That makes the two of you all mine."

As one of the Marines put a hand on Hayward's shoulder to guide him to the brig, Hayward shouted at Ronin, "You can't do this! I demand a trial by jury a jury of my peers according to the Geneva Convention!"

Commander Mueller, who had joined them during the short exchange, interjected angrily, "The Captain is the sole authority over captured enemy combatants on this ship during wartime," she snarled without taking her eyes off Hayward. "Put him in the brig with the others!" she ordered to the Marine.

As the exosuited Marine forced Hayward's cooperation with an encouraging but irresistible shove roughly towards the direction of the brig, Ronin looked towards Mueller with raised eyebrows. "Geneva Convention? Who or what is that?" he asked calmly.

Lieutenant Gustav, who was now walking past them as he carried his exosuit helmet in his hands, answered Ronin's question. "It's a long story, Captain. Something from another time and another place. I'll fill you in during our debriefing." Gustav saluted and continued onwards to see to his men.

"Going to be an action-packed debriefing session again," Mueller observed quietly.

Ronin glanced at her with a half-smile forming on his face. "We do seem to have a lot of interesting debriefings on this ship," he responded.

"I suspect we'll be graced by Dr. Wright's presence in this debriefing. Again," Mueller said with a grin.

Ronin tried not to roll his eyes. He wasn't entirely successful, and snorted softly as he shook his head. "That man has been insufferable almost this entire mission. It was quite surprising when we all agreed on the need for holding trials. I was beginning to think we couldn't even agree on what time of day it was, much less anything else."

They began walking in the direction of the bridge, and their quiet conversation continued when they were alone. "He's pompous, arrogant, conceited, and unable to see that his needs don't take top priority on this ship. And his people skills are atrocious," Mueller noted, shaking her head slightly.

* * *

The ship's main conference was buzzing with conversation and anticipation when Ronin and Mueller entered. As they walked to their seats, Commander Hunt, Lieutenant Buckingham and Louise Abernathy were seated to Ronin's immediate left. The three of them were engrossed in a discussion with Dr. Wright and Ambassador Gadre, who were seated to their left. Lieutenant Gustav was seated across the table from Ronin and Mueller.

The conversations quickly died away as Ronin began speaking. "All right, everyone. It's been quite a ride the past few weeks. I'd like to welcome Commander James Hunt, the leader of the Cargo Rebellion, Louise Abernathy formerly of the planetary Space Control Center, and Lieutenant ... Buckingham, aboard Cerberus. I'm sorry, Lieutenant Buckingham, I don't believe I ever caught your first name."

As Buckingham simply smiled, Hunt responded for him. "That's okay, Captain. I don't know Buckingham's first name either. Our people have wagered quite a pool of money on what it might be, if he ever tells."

Gustav broke into a huge grin at Hunt's reply. A mysterious identity and name is just the sort of thing he liked.

Ronin's face broke into a funny expression too. "Okay, then! Commander, what's the situation on the ground?"

Hunt cleared his throat slightly before proceeding. "Thank you, Captain. After the capture of the Officers Council a few days ago and the removal of all its top decision makers, Loyalist forces effectively collapsed and ultimately surrendered to the Cargo Rebellion.

"This process was sped along when Cerberus' AI took complete control of the entire planetary defense network. For now, we are consolidating our government and preparing to hold the first free and fair elections in this planet's history. I was just discussing the situation with your Dr. Wright and comparing ideas for how we will go forward." Hunt nodded his head to the side towards Dr. Wright as he mentioned him.

"That's right," Wright confirmed. "Commander Hunt's people have followed Ambassador Gadre's suggestions for holding unbiased elections, and they have a solid plan in place. Ambassador?"

Gadre, happy to be aboard Cerberus again, nodded. "Yes, that's correct. The election will feature the following that will require a 70 percent super majority of voters to make any change. All government budgets and taxation laws are subject to majority votes of the citizens who actually pay the taxes. No elected officials or non-taxpaying citizens may have a vote in those two matters. Budgets will be required to balance.

"There will be in place a citizen referendum process on any other matters that qualify for the process based on specified population percentage petitioning for the process. Elected officeholders may only serve two, four-year terms of office, and they will be disqualified for all other elected offices thereafter. No government employee may work for any level of government for longer than ten years in total, and then they will be disqualified for government service thereafter to strongly discourage the problems unaccountable bureaucrats always seem to create.

"Civil service protections are limited to ensuring they are nonpartisan employees, and nothing more, because we don't want bureaucrats to grow too complacent like they always get if they enjoy unfair levels of job security. No one who was an elected officeholder may later serve as a government employee, or vice versa.

"Taxation is set at 10 percent of income and may not vary based on a person's net worth or level of income. Everyone pays the same percent, unless they had no income. The current Officer Class is disqualified for government service or running for elective office for life. Class distinctions are otherwise eliminated, and the next generation's children will all equally be eligible," she said at length.

Heads nodded in agreement around the table at the structure because it encourages justice, accountability, and responsibility. Ronin's eyes flicked over to Dr. Wright again. "Doctor? What's the preliminary plan for trials for the Officers Council?"

Wright nodded towards Ronin, his face looking gravely serious. "Captain, we are recommending a bifurcated imposition of justice. For the Council, we are recommending full Due Process protections borrowed from our Uniform Code of Justice for the accused. They will be aided by legal counsel. The accused have the right to confront and question all witnesses. They will have the right to review the evidence against them to aid in the preparation of their defense. They will be tried to a court, and face potential conviction by a jury of citizen peers, excluding those from the Officer Class of course. Things of that nature. Only two persons will face a different court ... Speaker Hayward and Secretary Ellis."

Wright's culling of Hayward and Ellis from the herd surprised Ronin, who clearly expected Wright to argue they be treated the same way. "Why do you think Hayward and Ellis should face a different form of justice, Doctor? Don't you want everyone treated the same way?"

Wright shook his head, slowly and sadly. "No, not this time, Captain. They were the primary cause of hostilities directed at Cerberus when we came in peace. They precipitated many deaths, mostly down on the surface but also the deaths of some of our crew and too many of our Marines. They also are responsible for the death of one of my people. Captain, in my mind, all of that clearly gives you the right to mete out justice to those two as you see fit."

Mueller and Ronin shared a glance. Wright's change of heart was refreshing. Before either could say anything, Hunt interrupted their thoughts.

"Captain, if I may? We agree you have full discretionary authority over Hayward and Ellis, but I would request that Ambassador Gadre's idea of bifurcating Ellis' sentencing and carrying out of the sentence be put into place. You would sentence Ellis to whatever form of justice you deem appropriate, while we would carry out the sentence on your behalf. Publicly, if possible. It would be a sign that all of us are working together to bring about justice."

Ronin looked at Hunt for a few moments while he considered the proposal. "Agreed, but be prepared to carry out my sentencing immediately. Justice will be swift."

Hunt and Buckingham nodded, with Buckingham responding for the both of them. "With pleasure, Captain."

"What are our next steps, Captain? How do we move forward from here?" Hunt asked.

"We will stay in orbit while your people stabilize the situation on the surface, and help repair some of the priority facilities. Once the trials start, it will be months until they all conclude. During that time, Cerberus will return to Earth. No doubt another ship will arrive at Terra Station soon thereafter.

"Ambassador Gadre ... I presume you wish to remain on Terra Station as the ambassador from the Confederacy?"

Gadre nodded quickly. "Definitely Captain."

Hunt and Buckingham echoed her sentiments. "That would be our wish as well, Captain," Hunt noted. Wright simply nodded his agreement.

Ronin simply said, "Agreed. Miss Abernathy, I hear you and your fiancé Ryan will be running the Space Control Center now? You'll have a lot of contact with Cerberus and other ships in the future."

Louise nodded her head. "Yes Captain. We're looking forward to it. We're going to be very busy in the near future."

Ronin nodded in response. Then his face turned serious as he looked at the assembled group. "I'll impose my judgment regarding Hayward and Ellis today, and Commander Hunt can take Ellis when you return to the surface. Questions?" He looked around the table after asking. There were none.

"Dismissed. I'd like Dr. Wright, Commanders Mueller and Hunt, and Lieutenant Buckingham to remain behind please."

The room quickly emptied except for the five of them.

Ronin looked at them. "I have had plenty of time to decide their fate. I'd like for you four to accompany me to the brig for the sentencing."

"With pleasure, Captain. When do you want us to meet you there?" Hunt said.

"Right now. I see no need to delay and we have many other things to attend to which are more important, so let's just get this done," Ronin stated. His voice was deadly serious, and he rose as he finished his statement.

The five of them walked to the brig. They were somber, not saying anything as they traveled. Two armed Marines in exosuits stood guard outside the entrance to the brig, and they saluted as the party approached.

Ronin and Mueller returned the salutes, and Ronin said in surprise, "Gunny Kanagawa, YOU are guarding the brig?"

Toshi replied over his external speaker since he was suited up. "Yessir. My guys paid a high price for those clowns in there. I wanted to be present and be a witness for my men when you passed judgment." His posture and voice had strengthened considerably as his body healed from the terrible injuries he had suffered a few weeks ago, and now he sounded more like his old self even though he was still recovering.

"You have certainly earned that right, Toshi. Lead the way, Gunnery Sergeant," Ronin said, his face reflecting his profound respect for Kanagawa's initiative, and his use of Kanagawa's first name reflecting their respect for one another.

"Yessir. One moment." Kanagawa nodded as he opened a commlink. "Echo 4, Echo 1. The Captain and party have arrived. Open the security door."

Private Han Pak clicked acknowledgment and immediately entered the commands for the heavy security door to the passageway outside to unlock and open.

"If you would all follow me?" Kanagawa courteously asked, although it was really more of a command than a question. He led the way into the brig's outer chamber where the guards monitored the prisoners. Pak was there, heavily armed and standing at attention while rendering a salute which Kanagawa, Mueller and Ronin quickly returned.

Kanagawa led them to the cell at the end. Then he turned to face the party that had followed.

"Hayward and Ellis were separated from the others and placed in isolation in this cell. Ready for me to open the port?"

Ronin nodded, his eyes turning to the port and focusing while Kanagawa reached over to slide the small metal viewport to the side. The noise drew the attention of Ellis and Hayward, who each had been quietly lying on their bunks with their hands behind their heads as they awaited their fate.

"Captain, I demand that ... Hayward angrily began to say when Ronin cut him off.

"On this ship, you demand nothing!" Ronin said, calmly but forcefully, his eyes landing on Secretary Ellis. "As Captain of Cerberus during a time of war, I hereby pass the following judgments upon you. Secretary Ellis, your crimes in aiding and abetting the attempted destruction of this ship and her crew merit the death penalty. So be it. I sentence you to death by hanging. Sentence to be carried out immediately upon your return to Terra Station by Commander Hunt and his people. Your execution will be broadcast, to the public, along with a recitation of your crimes."

Ronin's eyes then focused on Hayward. "Speaker Hayward, your crimes are even more heinous. You have participated in enslaving a large portion of your population. My only regret is that you will not be held to answer again for a crime of that magnitude. What IS in my power is to hold you responsible for engineering the sneak attack on this ship. You are sentenced to death, said sentence to be carried out aboard this vessel immediately. Gunny Kanagawa?" As he said this last, Ronin stepped aside.

Kanagawa immediately raised his sidearm pistol and unceremoniously fired through the viewport at Hayward. The bullet passed through Hayward's skull, forever ending the stain of his existence. Everyone in their party jumped at the suddenness of the execution. They hadn't imagined quite how immediate Ronin had meant.

Ronin glanced at the others in the party, taking note of their shocked expressions. Only Kanagawa didn't seem surprised at all. "Let this lesson sink in. Defending Cerberus takes top priority, and justice must be imposed on those who try to destroy her."

Nodding slightly, Kanagawa murmured, "And sometimes justice is swifter than they expect."

Everyone's eyebrows raised at Kanagawa's comment.

Ronin glanced at the Marine and nodded slightly. "Get a crew in here to dispose of the body out an airlock. There won't be any ceremony for the corpse." Looking towards the rest of them, he ordered. "All right, everyone back on task. We have a planet to repair."

CHAPTER 84

DEPARTURE

"Captain, we'll be looking forward to the next visit. In the interim, we're going to get Dr. Wright's restructuring plans fully in place," said Commander Hunt over the commlink node in Ronin's ready room.

Ronin and Mueller were both seated at his small desk. They had been reviewing their final departure preparations for the past hour when Hunt's commlink call was patched through.

"No guarantees the next ship will be Cerberus, Commander, but if it is, we'd love to come back. And next time there won't be anyone shooting at us!" Ronin said with a grin.

Hunt laughed. "Whoa, whoa, whoa, there, Captain! I didn't make any promises no one would be taking potshots at you!"

Mueller and Ronin laughed loudly.

"Until next time, Cerberus," Hunt said with smile. It was time to go.

"Take care of yourself down there, James. Cerberus Actual, Out," Ronin replied and closed the commlink.

Ronin leaned back in his seat slightly, clasping his hands behind his head. Mueller snorted slightly, a small smile still on her face.

"I can't decide whether the Admiralty will have a bigger conniption over Cerberus finding an unknown colony from before The Fall, or over Cerberus bombarding that same colony from orbit," Ronin said thoughtfully, his head tilted slightly to the side as his unfocused eyes looked up towards the corner of the room.

Now it was Mueller's turn to look thoughtful. "You're one for three."

Ronin's eyes flicked down to look at her and his face looked confused. "One for three?"

Mueller's face took on a teasing look. "Of the three planets that we know of where humanity has an established presence, the only one you haven't bombed from orbit is Mars."

"Yet..." Ronin said, his mouth turning up into a half smile.

Ronin's commlink node chimed. "Captain, Lieutenant Sunderland is requesting to see you and Commander Mueller in your ready room," announced Lieutenant. Delgado.

Mueller and Ronin looked at each other in surprise. "Send him in, Lieutenant," Mueller said for both of them.

The door swished open and Sunderland marched in carrying a plain black box. When the doors closed behind him, Ronin asked, "What can we do for you, Kelvin?"

Sunderland grinned evilly. "Well, sirs, we've been so blasted busy since Cerberus arrived here two months ago that I haven't issued the final rations to you both."

"Rations?" Ronin asked, with a suspicious yet simultaneously hopeful tone of voice.

Sunderland stepped forward to set the box down on the desk as he responded. "Yessir. I believe it's time to toast those who aren't with us any longer, and the survival of another mission for those who are," he said as he reached inside and passed out several icy cold bottles of his home-brewed beers.

"Now that's the best thing on today's whole agenda!" Mueller replied as Ronin quickly reached into his desk to retrieve a bottle opener. He was grinning as he did so.

Ronin raised the dark beer bottle to head height as he said, "The mysterious Colonel Hobson proposed such a toast while we were in Admiral Rodding's office on Wayside Station after we won the war. I think it's very appropriate here, too. To our fallen. May our people never suffer from war again."

Both Mueller and Sunderland raised their bottles and said "Here, here!" before taking a gulp of the cold contents.

Mueller looked at her bottle appreciatively. "Keith, I think you've outdone yourself on this batch. These are spectacular!"

Ronin nodded in agreement as he took another swig.

"Thank you, ma'am. Practice makes perfect," said Sunderland, taking another drink.

They soon finished their beverages.

"Is it time?" Mueller asked, looking at Ronin.

Ronin nodded. "Yep. Lets go home. We've got a long road ahead of us."

As they stood to return to the bridge, Ronin couldn't help but wonder to himself, *Will we be returning to Terra Station?*

SOLARA

After rediscovering the unknown Lost Colony of Terra Station and helping win the Cargo Rebellion, Cerberus is quickly readied and sent back to deep space to look for more Lost Colonies. This time, they found one of the legendary Lost Colonies, Solara, which the Confederation had expected to host an advanced civilization.

Instead, they found Solara just wasn't the civilized, peaceful colony that they had hoped to find. It was wild, untamed, and home to dangerous subcultures who competed with each other for dominance. Competition was deadly business on Solara.

The story continues in the next installment of the Cerberus series.

About the Author

John Filcher is an amateur author who lives in Ashwaubenon, Wisconsin, not far from Lambeau Field. He has a somewhat unhealthy obsession with local craft beers, and dreams of someday living somewhere warm.